wild SURRENDER

WILD SURRENDER

WILD SAVAGE HEARTS
BOOK 1

KIMBERLY QUINN

WILD SURRENDER

3rd Edition

Previously titled: ***Complex Kisses***

Editing by: Kim Wilson

Cover design by: KiWi Cover Design Co.

Alternate cover design by: Covers by Marika Veil

Photography by: Wander Aguiar Photography

Cover model: Travis S.

Mature audience only. 18+

BOOKS BY KIMBERLY QUINN

Wild Savage Hearts
Wild Surrender
Wild Obsession
Wild Devotion
Wild Promise

Savage Hearts Syndicate
Sweet Chaos
Lovely Torment
Pretty Ruin

Savage Hearts Empire
Tempt the Devil
Tame the Devil
Break the Beast
Steal the Bride
Claim the Killer
Betray the King

Canyon Spring (Co-Written with S.M. West)
The Cowboy Bargain
The Cowboy Hitch

For updated book lists and the latest news, join Kimberly's newsletter, Letters from the Edge: https://kimberlyquinn.myflodesk.com/vipnl

CONTENT NOTE

Wild Surrender was originally published in 2016 as Complex Kisses.

This book contains themes of illness (specifically cancer) and death which may be triggering for some readers.

It also contains graphic language, explicit sexual encounters, limited violence, alcohol abuse, and physical assault.

Your mental health is important.
Please take carc.

WILD SURRENDER

Coming home wasn't a choice. It was an obligation I couldn't avoid.
Fake dating Eric Alexander just…happened.

He's the town's most eligible bachelor. Dominant. Controlled. Far too convincing as my boyfriend. The arrangement is a harmless lie to keep my past quiet and the life I've built for my son intact.

No feelings. No future. No risk.

Until every touch starts to feel real, my past slams into us, and pretending turns dangerous. Eric becomes the only protection standing between me and everything I swore I'd never face again.

Because lies have consequences.
And if this one unravels, it will cost me everything.

For my younger self, my broken self,
and all who've felt lost along life's journey.
You can be found.

10 YEARS AGO

JAMIE

THE SLAP RANG IN MY EARS, AND THE PAIN THAT FLARED ACROSS my cheek was hot and stinging. So sharp, it stole the air from my lungs.

Or maybe it was shock that had me sucking in a ragged gasp.

He'd hit me.

My father fucking hit me.

He stared at me with glassy eyes like he was looking through me. Like he didn't recognize what he'd done. Or worse, like he didn't care.

No apology. No regret. Not even an angry curse.

Nothing.

He stood with his fists clenched at his sides, jaw locked tight, and rage humming off him.

His silence cut deeper than the smack he'd just delivered, and something inside me cracked under the weight of it. I'd known things were bad, but this felt final. Like whatever we'd been—father and daughter, a team once upon a time—was already gone.

I pressed my palm to my burning cheek, trying to make sense of how we'd gotten here.

How had we fallen so far apart?

I'd come to him for help. For reassurance. For any sign that the man I used to rely on still existed underneath the anger and alcohol.

My dad. *Daddy* if I reached back far enough.

I wanted to believe he could pull himself together, even a little, for me. For the future.

Except he was too deep in his own grief and self-pity to be the father I needed. Too drowned by booze to see the truth. And there was nothing I could do to change it.

Still, I wouldn't let him pull me down with him.

A small, steady spark lit somewhere inside me. Not strong or confident. It was only enough to keep me standing.

I lowered my hand and let him see the swelling on my cheek. Let him see what he'd done. I wanted it to register, even if only for a second.

His anger only tightened, rolling through him until it finally cracked open.

"I'm glad your mother's not alive to see you now. To know what you've done." His words slurred, spit flying from his lips. "She'd be disgusted. I'm disgusted. You're nothing but a whore."

Tears welled, finally overflowing as I choked on his distorted truth. I swallowed back the urge to scream, to throw every hurt part of me right back at him.

Instead, I gave him exactly what he'd given me. Nothing.

In silence, I turned and walked away.

His shouting followed me, along with the smashing of innocent objects, but I didn't slow. Each step felt like prying myself loose. Not just from him, but from this house full of broken promises. From this whole goddamn town that had watched and whispered while I tried to hold together what was left of my family.

I was done trying to fix something I hadn't broken. Something that couldn't be fixed.

It was time to build something better. Something mine.
Fueled by his rage, I chose a brighter future.
I ran.
And I didn't look back.

DAY MINUS 8

CHAPTER ONE

JAMIE

Depression is more than just feeling blue.

- Feelings of sadness, guilt, helplessness, or hopelessness

- Changes to sleep patterns and/or eating habits

- Impacts to physical health, including joint pain and muscle ache

- Anger or irritability

Check. Check. Check. And double-check. My entire existence had been summed up in four bullet points. Although, depressed wasn't exactly right. It was more like wallowing.

Deep, committed wallowing.

For two long days and two sleepless nights, Copper Ridge Regional Hospital had been my home.

Halfway through day three, I was desperate enough to dig through discarded medical pamphlets, hoping one might tell me why I felt like I was unraveling.

I folded the little booklet in half, then in half again, until it was small enough to disappear into my pocket. Like that would make anything better.

How could it? My real problem didn't have a neat and tidy diagnosis.

My father was dying, and it was slow, painful, and ugly. The worst part—the part I didn't want to admit out loud—was that the strongest thing I felt wasn't sadness. It was resentment. Sharp and bitter, it curled in my gut every time I thought about what I'd left behind in Toronto.

Who I'd left behind.

I'd built a life there from nothing. Scraped and fought and planned until every piece fit just right. And now I was back here, in the place I'd promised never to return, disconnected from the things that mattered most. All while I sat at the bedside of a man who hadn't wanted me for years.

Guilt followed close behind the resentment, heavy and obligatory. What kind of daughter resents her dying father? What kind of person feels trapped by someone else's death?

Me, apparently.

My chest ached again, the now-familiar tightness pulling at my ribs. I pressed my palm to my diaphragm, breathing carefully, counting down the way my father's nurse, Judy, had shown me.

Stress, she'd said. *Your body's just reacting.*

I believed her. Sort of.

Still, my mind drifted where it always did when things felt too big, too heavy to deal with. To my son, Hunter.

He was more than two hours away, safe with people I trusted. People I had no reason not to trust, anyway. But the distance gnawed at me, a low hum of worry I couldn't shut off.

My phone sat face-down on the table.

I flipped it over. No new messages.

He's fine. It's the middle of the school day. Silence doesn't mean anything's wrong.

At least, that's what I told myself. But I'd told myself so many things over the years. A lot of them lies.

"Here, I think you need this more than I do." An open container of chocolate pudding appeared in front of me without warning.

Startled, I looked up to find a boy grinning down at me from across the table.

He was about fourteen, fifteen at most. Bald and pale, his illness impossible to miss. And yet he was beautiful.

His blue eyes flashed with mischief, bright enough to steal my breath.

He dropped into the chair across from me. "I had a bite already. Hope you don't mind. It's really good pudding. Lots of sugar. I was enjoying it, but then I saw your face and figured you needed it more than me."

"I look that bad, do I?" Not that I needed the confirmation. I hadn't showered in two days, my hair was a tangled mess, and I was wearing a sweatshirt with a spot of yesterday's dinner on the sleeve.

A total disaster.

But next to him—a sick kid who was smiling at me like I was the sun—I was the perfect picture of health. It was disgusting that I'd spent even a moment worrying over my imagined symptoms.

First chance I got, I needed to toss the pamphlet.

"Hell no. You're the hottest woman I've ever laid eyes on," he said with a straight face. "But you looked sad, so I figured I'd make you smile. I bet you'd look even hotter with a smile."

A loud, ridiculous snort of laughter escaped before I could stop it. My hand flew to my mouth like that would somehow hide it.

Maybe he was working overtime to flirt. Maybe he was genuinely trying to make me feel better. Either way, it was working.

I dropped my hand and gave him the biggest, brightest smile I could manage.

"There it is. Yeah, that's stunning." His face shone with sincerity.

"Is this a prank? I'm not going to end up looking like a fool in your next social media video, am I?"

His smile vanished. "What? You think I hand out chocolate pudding to every woman I see just for likes?"

My chest tightened again at the hurt in his voice. "No, of course not. I'm sorry. I didn't mean it like that."

His expression cracked wide open as he burst into laughter.

"I'm kidding." He wiped imaginary tears from his eyes. "But hey, you smiled. Did I mention how pretty you are when you do that? Keep it up."

For the first time since I'd arrived in Copper Ridge, the ache in my chest eased. It wasn't much, but enough that I could finally breathe without effort.

Until a low, commanding voice cut through the moment. "Caleb. Are you hitting on unsuspecting women again?"

Tingles shot down my spine, and all the wonderful breathing I'd been doing stopped.

Who was this magnificent man?

He was tall and broad, with the kind of presence that demanded attention. Everything about his stance said he was used to being in control.

My gaze dragged over his strong, shadowed jaw to the cleft in his chin. Like a beacon, it seemed designed to draw my attention to his wide, perfect lips. His expression was amused but assessing, highlighted by incredibly expressive blue eyes. Even his slightly untamed eyebrows somehow worked.

Everything about him worked.

"…don't you think?"

I blinked, dragging in a gasping breath before managing to stutter, "W-what?"

He huffed a quiet laugh, stepping closer. "Caleb can be a bit in your face. If he's bothering you…?" His sapphire eyes danced over my face, his lips tipping into a slow, knowing smile.

That smile said, *I see exactly what I'm doing to you. And I like it.*

"I was being a gentleman," Caleb argued. "She's having a rough day, so I offered her some of my chocolate. I wanted to see her smile." He turned to me again. "You really do have a fantastic smile."

"I thought you were giving me all of your chocolate." I couldn't help but grin. "Except that one bite you stole."

A deep, gruff laugh rumbled from the gorgeous man. He was already impossibly handsome, but when he smiled…damn. Dimples and everything.

My insides reacted in ways I did not approve of.

"Ah, jeez. Eric, you've done it again." Caleb groaned. "You're stealing the show. How am I supposed to compete when you've got a full head of hair?"

My cheeks flamed.

Eric only smiled more, resting a steady hand on Caleb's shoulder. "Caleb, no one can compete with you. All the ladies love you."

He threw a sly wink my way, and the world tilted.

My emotions were a messy tangle—lusting after a stranger, joking with a sick kid, while my father lay alone in another room dying. No wonder I felt like I was splitting down the middle.

"Yeah," I said. "Definitely a charmer."

"So…" Caleb leaned in. "What's got you so bummed? Tell me who stole your puppy so I can kick their butt."

Both he and Eric gave me that same protective frown, ready to fight whatever monster I named. And for a second, it hit me how surreal this was. These two wore their hearts openly, while I was hiding behind made-up medical diagnoses.

Sad? Must be depression.

Chest pain? Could be a heart condition.

Never mind my dying father or the fact that I'd left the most important person in my life behind. Easier to pretend my body was falling apart than admit my life was.

"I'm just missing someone." They were honest words. Too honest, maybe.

"Someone male or someone female?" Caleb asked with a grin.

"Someone almost as charming as you. And I'm worried he's probably sitting at home missing me. Or worse, he's not missing me at all. Maybe he's busy having the time of his life while I'm away."

Eric's jaw tightened, something dark flashing in his eyes. "If he's not missing you, he's a fool."

The sharp edge in his voice caught me off guard, and the sting of his words hit fast. Criticism of Hunter always lit my fuse. Nobody got to judge him. Not without going through me. Except Eric didn't understand Hunter wasn't just some random guy. He was my son.

"No—" I tried to correct him.

"Eric. Not cool," Caleb cut in. "The lady needs cheering up. We can be nice, right?"

I tried again. "It's okay, but—"

"Sorry. Caleb's right. That was out of line." Eric's voice softened, but his intense gaze held mine, pinning me in place. "And it's not my business."

My pulse spiked as I broke eye contact, my face flaming brighter.

"Hey! I didn't even ask your name." Caleb exclaimed before I could try to speak again.

"Jamie." I cleared my throat. "Well…Jamison, technically. But everyone just calls me Jamie. Verdict's still out on whether I like it."

Perfect, now I was rambling.

"Well, Jamie," Caleb said warmly, "it's a lovely name. Suits you. I'm Caleb. That big idiot is my brother, Eric. I make no apologies for him. He's acting a bit douchey, but usually he's a great guy." He smirked, clearly pleased with himself.

"Okay, hotshot." Eric rested his hand on Caleb's shoulder again. "We need to get going. Mom and Dad will worry if you're gone too long."

The protectiveness in his voice was unmistakable. This was a man who took care of what was his.

"Yeah." Caleb sighed dramatically, then brightened. "It was really nice meeting you, beautiful Jamie. You can keep my chocolate pudding. And if you stop missing that other guy, come visit me. I'm in room 1202A."

Eric let out a warning groan, but he was smiling. "Really?"

"Too much?" Caleb asked.

I smirked. "No, it's perfect. Just what I needed." Scooping a huge spoonful of pudding, I shoved it in my mouth. "Chocolate's my favorite," I mumbled around the sugary goo.

Both guys laughed. Caleb's smile was bright and proud. Eric's smile was something else. Big, yes, but threaded with a deeper hint of recognition. Like something between us had clicked into place, and he had every intention of exploring it.

Too bad I'd probably never see them again. As charming as the invite was, I had zero plans of wandering into Caleb's hospital room for a casual visit.

"It was nice meeting you boys," I said around another bite, hoping Caleb would remember me as a bright spot in his day, the way he'd been in mine.

I waved my chocolate-covered spoon as they walked away, something tight and unfamiliar scratching at my heart.

At the doorway, Eric turned, gave me one last smile, and called over his shoulder, "See you around, beautiful Jamie."

I was in a town filled with one too many bad memories, stuck in a hospital miles away from my son, watching the father I'd avoided for ten years die…

But there was a smile on my face.

And this one was real.

DAY MINUS 7

CHAPTER TWO

JAMIE

ANOTHER SLEEPLESS NIGHT HAD COME AND GONE. THAT WAS three in a row of zero rest.

At least I'd managed to shower and throw on clean clothes this morning. That alone felt like an accomplishment.

Not to mention, I was still here.

It had taken a solid ten minutes of bargaining with my reflection, but I was back at my father's bedside, wondering if the walls were actually closing in or if it was all in my head.

How long could someone go without sleep before they lost their grip on reality?

The urge to look it up was like a reflex. Before I was even aware of the decision, my phone was in my hands, *insomnia* already typed into the browser search bar.

"Goddammit," my father growled. "Why do I have all these machines hooked up to me?"

My head snapped up. Mouth open, I froze.

He looked…alert. Not just awake, but aware. More present than he'd been since I'd arrived.

"Mr. Hartley," the nurse greeted, already reaching for the line he was fumbling with as she rushed into the room. “Please don’t do that. You’ll hurt yourself.”

“Don’t *Mr. Hartley* me.” His voice rose, sharp and slurred. “I don’t give a shit about this stupid thing or your stupid ideas of what’s good for me.”

There he was. This was the version of him I remembered.

All asshole, all the time. No filter.

As much as I hated it, part of me felt relief. This was familiar territory. I’d had plenty of practice dealing with him like this. It was the confused, quiet, broken version of him that kept knocking the air out of my lungs.

Still, watching him struggle made something ache in my chest. There was no dignity in this. Even with good care, even with the morphine drip, being trapped in a failing body had to be unbearable. I wouldn’t wish it on anyone.

Not even him.

“Dad, stop,” I said. “She’s just doing her job.”

“Ah, fuck you too, James.”

The name hit harder than his cursing.

James. Only he ever called me that.

It used to be our thing. Something he’d say while tugging my hair or poking my ribs, his eyes twinkling with mischief. *You find my daughter yet, James?* Mom and Trina would laugh, playing along with the old joke. I’d roll my eyes and act annoyed, but inside I’d be glowing.

It had mattered more than I’d ever let on.

Still did.

He hadn’t used the name in so long I’d almost forgotten it belonged to me. Not since Mom and Trina died. Not since the house went quiet and the laughter all stopped.

Hearing it now felt like being handed a piece of who we used to be—a father and daughter who had inside jokes and gentle teasing. Before everything went wrong.

A cracked and fragile souvenir from a childhood I didn't get to keep.

"You're useless here," he went on. "Useless, just like me. You might as well leave like you did before. Eleven years…and now you come back? For what?"

His voice faded toward the end, the anger draining out of him as his body gave up the fight. He'd never cared who heard him rage before. Never softened his words for an audience. But now even his cruelty lacked conviction.

"It's only been about ten years," I said, my voice steadier than I felt. "But ten years or ten days doesn't really matter. I'm here now. And I'm the only one." I nodded toward the nurse. "Other than her. And she's trying to help, whether you like it or not."

Telling him to calm down was pointless, so I didn't bother. He didn't have the strength to keep going. His hair, once dark and thick, had thinned to wisps of white. His skin had taken on a grayish hue that made him look more like a ghost than a man. He'd lost so much weight his face looked hollow, sharp in places it had never been before.

It was nothing like the last time I saw him. Back then, he'd been round and red-faced, screaming at me like he had all the energy in the world.

"Just leave me alone," he rasped. "Just let me die."

He meant it.

The truth was there in his eyes. There was no fight left in him. No stubborn refusal to quit. Only exhaustion. Like life had stopped offering him anything worth holding on to.

And that made something ugly twist inside me.

You selfish bastard.

All that time. All of it wasted. Every chance he'd blown, every door he'd slammed shut, every moment he'd chosen pride and anger over love. Ten years of birthdays and Christmas mornings and milestones he'd never asked about.

And still I was here, counting heartbeats instead of packing lunches or helping with homework, for a man who made it clear he didn't want me.

He resented my presence here almost as much as I did.

"Mr. Hartley." The nurse shook her head. "Please. Your daughter's here for you. We all are."

His glare didn't soften. If anything, it sharpened.

"I don't want a thing from any of you," he growled. "And she's the worst excuse for a daughter that ever existed. So don't pretend I should care that she's here."

Worst excuse for a daughter.

The knot in my stomach spread, taking hold of my chest.

"You hear me, Jamie girl?" His eyes locked on mine, flat and cold. "I don't want you here. You might as well leave."

The room was suddenly too small. Too tight.

I'd spent ten years convincing myself I was immune to him. That time and distance had created an impenetrable barrier not even Frank Hartley could break through.

Fuck, was I wrong.

"Fine." I shot to my feet and stormed out of the room, my messy hair flying around me.

Did it make me look childish? Maybe.

Did I care? Not one bit.

Let him think I was throwing a tantrum. It didn't matter. His opinion of me couldn't get any lower.

But the second I hit the hallway, my bravado faded.

Tears blurred my vision, and my chest felt like it was cracking in two. I pressed my lips together, but it didn't stop the sob that tore out of me, raw and humiliating.

I hated crying. Always had. It made me feel exposed and weak. Proof I wasn't as strong as I pretended to be.

This was more than simple tears, though. My entire body was shaking, and I couldn't stop it.

I took the stairs at the end of the hall two at a time, head down, breath ragged, hoping no one would look too closely. I didn't care where I ended up. I just needed out.

Away from the room. Away from him. Away from the power he still had to tear me apart with a single sentence.

At the bottom, I turned the last corner too fast and slammed straight into someone solid. Strong hands closed around my arms, stopping me before I could get away.

"Easy now," a low, calm voice said. "I've got you."

I looked up to find bold, blue eyes staring down at me. And they were filled with the exact same concern as the last time I saw them.

"Jamie." Eric's brows drew together, his grip tightening protectively. "What's wrong?"

The sound that came out of me wasn't dignified. It definitely wasn't pretty. Hell, I didn't know I was even capable of making such a horrid noise.

All because this man—this stranger—looked at me like I mattered, like he actually fucking cared, when my own father couldn't stand the sight of me.

Something inside me gave way. My knees followed.

Eric was there before I could hit the floor, arms firm around my back, holding me upright like gravity was just an inconvenience. He didn't ask any more questions. Didn't offer to fix anything. He just held me, his body a solid wall between me and the rest of the world.

"I've got you," he repeated, his voice rough with certainty. "You're safe."

Wrapped in his steadiness, I folded into him, pressing my forehead to his chest. The soft fabric of his shirt caught the sounds I'd stopped pretending I could hold back.

He stayed exactly where he was, bearing my weight without complaint, like protecting me was the most natural thing in the world.

And maybe it was. Because after ten years of running, I felt tethered. Safe enough to let myself fall apart.

CHAPTER THREE

ERIC

ONE SECOND THE STAIRWELL WAS EMPTY. THE NEXT, SHE WAS there, plowing into me with the force of someone twice her size.

I caught her on instinct, hands closing around her upper arms before she could bounce off me and keep running. The contact sent something primitive surging through me.

"Easy now. I've got you."

She looked up, her watery gaze catching mine, her face a mess of tears and torment. And still, she was the most breathtaking creature I'd ever fucking seen.

"Jamie." My chest tightened. "What happened?"

Whatever was holding her together snapped.

The sound she made gutted me. Raw and unfiltered, like something torn loose that had been under pressure for too long. She folded in on herself, knees buckling, and I moved without thinking.

My arms came around her, pulling her against me, but Christ, watching her fall apart was destroying what little control I had left.

Normally, my shit was buried deep—the anger, the fear, and

the hollow ache that grew with every bad test result and each brave look my brother gave me. But today had left me exposed. The hard truths about what Caleb and my family were facing had landed all at once.

Still, she was falling apart in my arms, and somehow that steadied something in me. Gave me something to focus on that wasn't the slow-motion disaster of watching my little brother fight for his life.

I didn't get to break. That wasn't my job. My job was to be the rock everyone else could lean on.

So I held her tighter, letting her forehead press against my chest, her breath hitching, and shoved everything else down where it belonged.

A dark, possessive urge took hold. Someone had pushed her to this point, and my body reacted before my brain caught up. The need to find whoever had done this and make them pay burned hot and immediate.

The man she'd mentioned flashed through my head. The one who might not be missing her. If he was the cause of her breakdown, so fucking help me…

I wouldn't go looking for him. But if he came around to hurt her again, I wouldn't hesitate to put him on the ground.

Right or wrong wasn't part of the equation. It felt *necessary*.

Which was insane, considering I'd only met her yesterday. I didn't even know her. Hell, I could count the facts on one hand.

Her name was Jamison. Jamie for short.

She had a sharp sense of humor that cut through the bullshit.

Chocolate was her favorite.

And she was wasting time on some asshole who didn't deserve her.

There were too many things I didn't know, and a hell of a lot more I wanted to find out.

Finally, her sobs eased into smaller, broken sounds. Half-swallowed sniffles that made my jaw ache. The moment she came back to herself, her body went rigid, like she'd suddenly remembered where she was. Who was holding her.

"I'm sorry." Her voice was muffled against my chest. "I didn't mean to…"

She tried to pull away.

I gave her room to breathe but kept her close enough that retreat wasn't an option.

Eyes down, she dragged a sleeve across her face, staring at my soaked shirt like it held all her secrets. "I'm sorry, I'm not normally a crier."

She was retreating now. Folding everything back up, shoving the emotions somewhere she could pretend they didn't exist. I recognized the move. Hell, I'd done it more times than I could count.

A dry, embarrassed laugh followed. It was thin, defensive, and not fooling anyone. "I don't even know what that was about."

"Bullshit."

Her head snapped up. "Excuse me?"

"You heard me. I call bullshit." I studied her red-rimmed eyes and blotchy cheeks, memorizing every detail. "I'm sure you don't cry much. You seem like a tough girl. But tough girls don't cry without knowing the reason. Something upset you, and I bet you know exactly what—or who—it was."

She crossed her arms, bristling. "Is it a family trait, then?"

I frowned. "What?"

"Your brother yesterday, and now you. You're both so direct." Her mouth twisted. "But at least he was nice about it."

"I'm not nice?" A short laugh escaped me as I glanced down at my tear-stained chest. "Jamie, you just cried all over my favorite shirt. How am I the bad guy here?"

Her expression cracked despite herself. Flustered, her bottom lip disappeared between her teeth, and my brain chose that exact moment to betray me.

I forced my gaze away. Focused on the exit sign. On anything but the delectable curve of her mouth and what I wanted to do with it.

"Look." I reset, voice steadier. "I don't need the details of your life. But you don't have to lie to me about it either. It's okay that you cried. And it's okay if you don't want to tell me why."

She hesitated, blinking like she might lose it again.

Fuck, I couldn't handle round two. Not when every instinct in me wanted to hunt down whoever had hurt her.

I took another step back. "We're not doing this again."

She frowned. "Doing what?"

I gestured at my shirt. "You crying. Me wearing it."

A startled laugh escaped her, sharp and unplanned. It bounced off the stairwell walls, cracking something open between us.

"That's better." I couldn't help but smile.

She laughed again, breathless this time, like something in her chest had finally loosened.

And somehow, the hospital didn't feel like it was crushing me alive anymore.

Her laughter faded slowly, reluctant to leave us alone. When it did, the silence that followed wasn't heavy. It was charged.

She swayed slightly, still catching her breath, and reached out without thinking.

Her palm landed flat against my chest.

Right over my heart.

The contact was innocent. The effect was fucking devastating.

I froze, every muscle locking as heat sparked beneath her hand. Every instinct in me snapped to full attention, demanding I hold her there, claim this moment and make it mine.

She didn't pull away. Didn't seem to realize what she'd done. Her fingers stayed splayed, grounding herself while I fought to stay in control.

It was simple contact. It was also the most intoxicating thing I'd felt in months.

Before I could talk myself out of it, I covered her hand with mine, fingers closing over hers and holding her exactly where she was. Not rough, but firm enough to make my intentions clear.

Stay. Right here. With me.

Her eyes lifted to mine, wide and searching, her breath catching as she held my gaze.

Something electric shot between us. A live thing, humming with possibility.

She leaned in. It was just a fraction, but it was enough to bring every memory of her pressed against me roaring back to life. Enough that my pulse kicked hard and fast, like it was trying to outrun my better judgment.

Fuck.

I released her hand and moved back at the same time, breaking the moment before it turned into something we couldn't take back.

She straightened immediately, drawing herself up like armor sliding back into place. One breath. Shoulders squared. Composure restored with practiced ease.

It didn't help me at all.

Because reality had crashed down hard.

There was someone else in her life. Someone she was missing. Someone she might've been crying over only minutes ago. Add that to everything else circling my head, and the situation went from tempting to impossible.

"Hey." My voice came out rougher than I intended, but I wasn't apologizing for it. "Come say hello to Caleb."

She blinked, clearly caught off guard by the request. Or maybe by how close we'd just come to crossing a line.

"He's had a rough day. You wouldn't know it to look at him. But I can tell, and I know he'd get a kick out of seeing you."

"Oh." Her expression shifted, tension melting into something warm and sincere. "Would that be okay? He seems like such a good kid. And he was so nice to me."

"He's an incredible kid." The words came without hesitation. "And yeah. It would mean a lot."

She nodded, already decided. "Okay. I just need to wash my face first. I don't want to scare him with"—she gestured vaguely —"this."

"You look perfect." The words tumbled out before I could stop them, honest and unfiltered. I took a breath and reined it in. "But do whatever you need."

Her mouth curved, shy now. She ducked her head, then stepped past me into the hallway, moving quickly like she needed the distance as much as I did.

"Jamie."

She turned back, eyes wide. "Yeah?"

"My parents are here." I fell into step beside her, close enough to catch her if she stumbled. "Maybe don't mention how hard Caleb was flirting with you yesterday. My mom still thinks he's her sweet baby boy."

She laughed, lighter this time. "I think I can manage that. But can he?"

I huffed. "Good point."

"I'll be right back." She angled toward the washrooms. "Wait for me?"

"Of course." The answer came easy, automatic. "I'll be right here whenever you're ready."

And I meant it. In more ways than one.

She disappeared down the hall, taking the warmth with her. I stayed where I was, leaning against the wall, watching the space she'd just left like I could will her back faster.

For the first time all day—hell, maybe months—my head wasn't full of cancer treatments or worst-case scenarios.

It was full of a woman with tear-stained cheeks, a sharp laugh, and a hand that had branded itself over my heart.

And how easily she'd made everything else fall away.

CHAPTER FOUR

JAMIE

Eric waited exactly where he'd promised, and relief flooded through me at the sight of him.

Not just because he was devastatingly good to look at, but because having him there made facing Caleb feel possible. In my head, all I could picture was the vibrant teenager reduced to a hospital bed, surrounded by beeping machines, looking too much like my father.

The pain slammed back into my chest, sharp and relentless.

I pressed my hand over my heart, half-expecting it to leap free. The tremor in my hands was so violent I could feel it against my breastbone.

Please don't let it show.

The thought of Caleb seeing how terrified I was turned my legs to lead.

Eric's hand settled at the small of my back, light but deliberate in a way that felt almost…protective? Possessive? I couldn't tell, but whatever it was made my pulse skip as he guided me forward with that same quiet confidence I'd noticed before.

He was barely touching me, and still, I had trouble focusing on anything else.

But maybe that was the point.

"Look who I found," Eric called as we stepped into the room.

Three faces turned toward us.

Relief hit first. Caleb looked the same as I remembered. Yes, he was in a hospital bed with machines clustered around him, tubes snaking everywhere, still bald and pale and undeniably sick. But none of that registered first.

It was the grin. Brilliant, mischievous, completely at odds with his surroundings. The kind of smile that made it impossible to forget the clever, vibrant kid underneath all the medical equipment.

His parents were another story.

They both looked confused, their surprise dulled by exhaustion etched deep into their faces. His mother most of all. She looked wrung out, every nerve stretched past breaking and still expected to hold.

Suddenly, I understood why Eric wanted me here.

"Wow! My day is complete." Caleb might've been a little too pleased to see me, judging by the sharp look his mother shot him.

"*Mon beau*, who is this?" she asked Eric, her accent thick and unmistakably Francophone, before turning her beautiful hazel eyes on me.

She was stunning. Even under harsh hospital lighting, her thick dark hair shone, her features striking in a way that felt effortless. Perfectly shaped brows, strong cheekbones, the kind of woman who turned heads without trying.

"Mom. Dad." Caleb's eyes danced with mischief. "Let me introduce you to the prettiest woman in this godforsaken hospital. I found her yesterday."

His infectious smile burned off the last of my nerves.

"Gorgeous." He nodded at me like it was a title I'd earned. "May I present my parents, Sylvie and Glenn Alexander."

I blinked. What was the appropriate response to that? A handshake felt wildly insufficient. With Caleb's theatrical flair, a full curtsy almost seemed expected.

"Hello." I managed a stilted wave. If nothing else, it felt safer than fainting.

"Caleb, you suck at introductions." Eric's low chuckle vibrated through me as he nudged me deeper into the room.

"Oh, come on," Caleb protested.

"Mom, Dad, this is Jamie," Eric continued. "I rescued her from your youngest son yesterday. He assaulted her with a pudding cup."

Caleb gasped in exaggerated offense. "Liar."

A laugh slipped out before I could stop it. "Actually, I think Caleb rescued me. I was feeling a bit low, but he helped cheer me up. And I'm fairly certain I was the one who assaulted the pudding."

Smiles spread around the room, but Sylvie's stood out. It softened and warmed, like she was filing the moment away somewhere precious.

"This is his habit. Cheering people up." Her eyes shone as she focused on me. "It's very nice to meet you, Jamie."

"Yes," Glenn's voice was unexpectedly rich, smooth and refined despite his quiet demeanor. He wasn't unattractive, but next to his wife, he faded slightly into the background. "Very nice to meet you. And may I say, Caleb is quite right. You're a very striking young woman. I don't believe I've seen a prettier face in this hospital."

My pulse stuttered. *Oh no.*

He cleared his throat, glancing quickly at his wife. "Except for you, of course, my dear."

I stood there, suddenly hyperaware of my hands, my posture, my face. Was I supposed to laugh? Deflect? Thank him? With this family, it felt like there might be a correct response and I was already a step behind.

Then everyone else started laughing. Everyone, including his wife.

"Nice job trying to save yourself, Dad," Caleb teased. "You almost fooled her."

"What?" Glenn scoffed. "I'm allowed to notice these things. She's a lovely girl. And your mother knows how much I adore her."

"Mom also knows how to lock you out of the bedroom." Eric was clearly enjoying himself.

Sylvie flushed but waved it off. "*Oui*, but your father also knows to properly beg forgiveness. He's never spent an entire night on the couch."

"Eww." Caleb's nose scrunched up. "TMI, Mom. T. M. Freakin' I."

Laughter filled the room, easy and unrestrained, washing away the last of my awkwardness and loosening the knot in my chest.

This wasn't what I'd expected. Eric's parents weren't stiff or formal. They were relaxed, playful even. Open with their affection, teasing each other like people who'd spent years choosing each other again and again.

And the way they folded their sons into that warmth and affection felt effortless.

Standing in the middle of it was strange. Not wrong, just… bigger than what I was used to.

My world was small by necessity. It was just me and Hunter, everything contained and manageable.

This was different. More people, more voices, more love moving in all directions at once.

And it felt good to be inside it, even if just for that moment.

I let myself fall into their easy rhythm—light conversation about weather and headlines. The boys spun into a spirited baseball debate while Sylvie and I exchanged knowing looks like we'd done this a hundred times before.

It was laid-back. Happy, even.

We hadn't forgotten where we were, but for a few minutes, the weight lifted enough to let something hopeful slip in. As if somehow, we all knew we'd be okay.

Maybe.

The conversation lulled and I cleared my throat. "Well, it was really nice to meet you, Mr. and Mrs. Alexander, but I should be going. I just wanted to pop in and say hello to Caleb."

"Please. You make me feel ancient. First names are fine, *mon ange*." Sylvie's voice was warm with invitation. "I hope these rowdy boys didn't scare you off. Having another woman around is nice. You cannot stay?"

I shook my head. "No. It's been wonderful, but I should get back to my father. The nurses can't seem to get him to eat anything, and I thought I might try."

They didn't need my problems. Not on top of everything else they were carrying. And yet the words kept coming, tumbling out before I could stop them.

"He probably won't eat for me either. He's dying, but he's still the most stubborn person I know. He doesn't want me here, but I figure maybe I can blackmail him into eating if I promise to leave when he's done."

They all stared like I'd grown an extra head. And really, who could blame them?

Heat crept up my neck.

Once again, I was too damn much. I'd taken something light and dropped it straight into the deep end.

"You shouldn't give up." Glenn's voice was thoughtful. "I'm sure he wants you here, but perhaps he's feeling vulnerable. Parents are meant to be the caregivers. Accepting a reversal like that can be…difficult."

"Yeah," Caleb agreed. "And he's probably scared."

The word *scared* lodged somewhere deep and stayed there.

I'd been so wrapped up in my own dread, my own history, that I hadn't considered what this felt like from the other side of the bed. From my father's side.

Maybe they were right. My father had pushed me away before, when everything felt out of control. This might not be so different. It could be fear talking. Or even weakness.

Not rejection.

"Thank you." More words tangled between gratitude and regret, but I didn't trust myself to sort them out. "It was nice seeing you again, Caleb."

"The pleasure was all mine." He grinned.

It wasn't the wild, flirtatious smile he'd flashed before. This one was quieter. Genuine. The kind that made my chest ache a little.

I turned to Eric. "Walk me out?"

He nodded once, mouth set in a hard line.

This time, he didn't touch me as we left. He followed a few steps behind, deliberate distance opening between us where there hadn't been any before. The space felt heavy with everything I'd dumped into that room without meaning to.

I'd taken a good moment and bent it into something uncomfortable. Turned their warmth into an opportunity to throw a pity party for myself.

That wasn't who I was. I wasn't fragile or self-absorbed. I was capable and grounded.

Hell, I'd raised a child on my own since I was eighteen.

So why did I feel like I was coming apart now? Over my father, of all people?

The shame settled deep and unwelcome.

The moment we stepped into the hallway, I spun toward him. "I'm sorry."

"No." His voice was firm enough to stop me mid-breath. "You're not doing that."

I froze, my heart stuttering.

"Don't apologize for having feelings. At least you're brave enough to show them." His jaw was tight, tone controlled in a way that felt intentional. "I've been hiding behind fake smiles and bad jokes since Caleb was diagnosed. Yesterday was the first time I smiled for real."

My breath caught. "Yesterday?"

"Yeah." He met my gaze without hesitation. "When I saw you and the awestruck look on my little brother's face. I knew you were the reason he looked so fucking happy. He hasn't looked like that in a long time, Jamie. We've both just been pretending."

"But I didn't do anything. I was wallowing in my own misery. He's the one who made me smile."

"Maybe. But you let him in. You smiled back, and it wasn't out of pity. That mattered."

He crossed his arms, the movement stretching his shirt tight across his chest. "He needs to feel like he can do more than make people cry. He wants to make people laugh. You gave him that."

I swallowed, emotion pressing tight against my ribs.

"Those moments are all we really have," he said. "They're the things that fucking count."

I looked down, shame still circling despite his words. "I still feel like I ruined it."

"You didn't. You reminded us that we're not the only ones hurting in this place."

The corner of his mouth lifted. "You also gave Caleb a new challenge. You left his room looking upset. He's going to make it his personal mission to track you down and fix that."

The thought of Caleb's stubborn optimism tugged a smile out of me, but it was Eric who held it there.

I couldn't remember the last time someone had touched something real in me this quickly. Not with charm or obligation, but with presence. The way he'd held me while I cried—solid, unflinching—had felt like something to grab onto when everything else was slipping.

Which was exactly what made it dangerous.

Men like him didn't just appear when you needed them most. Sincere, self-possessed, and unfairly attractive. The timing felt suspect, like the universe dangling something shiny I wasn't meant to touch.

I drew in a slow breath and blew it out hard, the sound breaking into an unmistakable raspberry. Not graceful, but honest. Besides, he'd already seen me with pudding in my teeth and tears on my cheeks. Any pretense was long gone.

Eric's smile widened, dimples flashing like he knew exactly what they did to me.

God, he really is great to look at.

"Thanks, Eric. For everything."

"Anytime."

I turned toward my father's room, forcing my legs to move.

"Hey."

I glanced back.

He leaned against the doorframe, one arm braced overhead, bicep bulging against his sleeve. His posture was casual in a way that should've been illegal, his gaze steady and unapologetic as it held mine.

"I'll see you around, beautiful Jamie." He winked and backed into Caleb's room without breaking eye contact.

I continued down the hall on rubber legs, with a smile fixed stubbornly on my face. It stayed with me all the way to my father's door.

It was still there when I stepped inside.

Even as I faced the one man who'd spent years breaking my heart.

DAY MINUS 6

CHAPTER FIVE
JAMIE

FIFTH DAY AT THE HOSPITAL, AND NOTHING HAD CHANGED. NOT my father's condition. Certainly not his attitude. I still hadn't managed to get him to eat, and he'd been pointedly ignoring me since yesterday's blowup.

When he wasn't asleep, he stared at the blank television like it had personally wronged him. Every time I asked if he wanted something on, he answered with the same gruff, *no*.

Okay, so he wasn't completely ignoring me. But a single word wasn't much of a conversation, and there was only so much wall-staring I could handle.

I settled into the chair beside his bed and checked Hunter's latest text.

Math was annoying today

My fingers flew over the screen. *Are you still doing fractions?*

I waited, leg bouncing, phone clenched tight, hoping I'd caught him between classes.

Yes they r stupid and boring

A quiet sigh escaped as I typed my reply. *Well, if you want to be an architect and build stuff like you do in Minecraft, you'll need to take a lot of math classes.*

The typing bubble hovered longer than I liked. Long enough for my chest to tighten.

Then his response popped up.

UGH

Silent laughter shook my shoulders.

If it weren't for school and a social life that already outpaced mine, I would've happily texted him all day. To anyone else, our messages probably looked ordinary. To me, they were proof that everything was still intact. That he was okay. That I hadn't broken something by coming back here alone.

Leaving my nine-year-old in Toronto with his best friend's family had felt necessary in the moment. Sensible, even. They'd welcomed him easily, like it wasn't an imposition at all.

My head accepted that. My heart was slower to follow.

What if this dragged on longer than planned? What if he never quite settled, always a little too careful in someone else's space?

I could see him hesitating before asking for what he needed, defaulting to yes when he meant no because he didn't want to be difficult. Because he was awkward like me. I imagined him curled into a bed that didn't smell like home. And the moments when he struggled, the ones no one else would notice, when he might reach for me out of habit and remember I wasn't there.

That was the thought that weighed the most.

So I read every message twice. Took comfort in small details—what he ate, who he sat with, the casual way he told me about his day. Simple things, offered without effort.

So far, they'd kept the panic at bay.

Another text came through, my smile slipping as hospital monitors beeped their steady rhythm around me.

Jackson wants me to join his baseball team

Something about it didn't sit right. Teams and baseball were fine, but Hunter had never shown interest, and his asthma usually kept him sidelined.

Do you want to play baseball?

His reply was immediate and honest. *Not really but he's my best friend I don't wanna let him down*

I guess you have a decision to make. I finally released the breath I'd been holding.

Wow thanks mom. best advice yet

The banter was easy, yet something nagged at me. Not once had he asked when I was coming home. He trusted that I'd do what needed doing. Trusted me even when I didn't trust myself. Somehow, he understood that for now, this was where I was supposed to be.

How did a nine-year-old get so damn wise?

No baseball. But can I take a woodworking class this summer?

My smile widened. *Woodworking?*

Yeah. I wanna learn to build stuff. You could help since you're already good at it.

That sounds awesome, bud. Warmth spread through my chest.

Cool :)

Cool. Now go finish your lunch, you hoodlum.

I sat there for a moment after the screen went dark, still smiling.

I was so damn lucky.

Hunter was the best kid I knew, and it had nothing to do with any exceptional parenting skills on my part. Raising him had been a long, messy experiment. Trial and error, every step of the way. On my own, there was no one to hand him off to when exhausted, no one to consult when I panicked, and no one else to blame when I screwed up.

And I screwed up a lot.

There were no instructions. No roadmap. Only instinct.

So I gave him all the love and kindness I could. Space to be exactly who he was. Those were the things I remembered most about my mom. Not rules or lectures, but how she made me feel safe.

Whenever I doubted myself as a mother, I thought of her. Tried imagining how she would've handled a loud, energetic little boy with a mind of his own. It didn't stop me from wishing she was still here.

But it made me feel less alone. Less afraid.

The motor in my father's bed whirred to life, snapping me back to the moment.

"What are you smiling about?"

I startled. Not just becausc he'd spoken, but because there was no bite to it. No malice. It was the first thing he'd said that didn't feel like an invitation to argue.

"A few things, actually."

"I bet." His mouth twisted. "Can't wait to get rid of me, can you?"

My smile cracked, and with it, my heart. "What?"

"It's okay, James. I don't blame you. I'm a ripe old asshole. Rotten to the damn core. Me being gone will be a blessing. For you and for me."

And just like that, the calm I'd been holding evaporated.

I should've known his civilized approach was just a smokescreen. He'd always liked luring me out into the open so he could cut me down with his hateful words. Even when the negativity was aimed at himself, he had a way of mocking me with it.

Still, he was talking, and maybe that was better than being punished with silence.

"Blessing?" The word burned on the way out. "You think this is a blessing? Sitting here, watching you die, knowing you're perfectly content to let cancer eat you alive? You don't even want to try. You'd rather go out miserable, angry, and alone. Yeah, what a gift."

"Fuck you. I didn't ask you to come here. I didn't need any of this shit. If I want to be done with my sorry goddamn life, that's my prerogative. Who the hell do you think you are to tell me otherwise?"

"Why do you do that?" My chest felt tight, words scraping free. "Why do you always try to push me away?"

"I don't need to push you away. You're good at leaving all on your own. Remember?" His words sliced through me.

I had left. Walked away and hadn't once regretted it.

Did I even have the right to be here? To expect anything from him now?

I'd told myself that facing his own mortality might have softened him, but his body failing hadn't touched his will. Physically weak, yes. But still so goddamn unmovable. Still determined to hold his ground, even if it meant dying on it.

"Dad—"

"Good afternoon, Mr. Hartley. How are you feeling?" Nurse Judy breezed in without the slightest regard for the emotional land mine she'd stepped on. "It's lunchtime, if you think you might feel up to eating."

"I'm not hungry."

I'd watched him bark and bristle at Judy and the other nurses all week, every warning loud and unmistakable. *Stay away. Stay back.* She hadn't flinched once.

"Well, how about some tea or ginger ale?"

"Fine," he grumbled. "Ginger ale."

"Excellent." She beamed like she'd just won something hard-earned. Turning to me, she softened her tone. "Why don't you grab yourself some lunch too, Jamie? You look like you could use it."

"Are you sure I shouldn't stay?"

Leaving felt dangerously close to proving his point. Even if he was right, the stubborn streak I'd inherited from him dug in hard. I wanted to stay out of sheer defiance.

"Get out of here," he muttered. "I don't need a goddamn babysitter."

Ever the poet.

"Okay." I forced my voice steady. "But I'll be back later."

It might've sounded like a concession, but it wasn't. It was a promise. Because I wasn't walking away this time.

I wasn't giving up on us.

CHAPTER SIX

JAMIE

Lunchtime in the hospital cafeteria felt like a bad high school flashback. Same noise, same awkward energy. Except there was less acne and even fewer seating options.

I was seconds away from giving up and taking my tray back to my father's room when the crowd shifted and I saw him.

Eric sat alone in the corner, shoulders squared, posture solid, like he'd carved out the space by sheer presence. His eyes were down, and his expression was locked into something unreadable. Nothing like the easy, smiling version of him that had been living rent-free in my head.

Without second thought, I went to him.

"Hey." I set my tray down at his table. "You up for some company?"

He looked up, surprise flickering before he masked it. The frown eased and he gave me a smile that could've stopped traffic.

But it didn't bring out his dimples. Or reach those intense blue eyes.

And it didn't fool me.

"Hey, beautiful. If you're the one keeping me company, I'm all in."

"Please don't." I kept my voice low, but it still came out sharper than intended.

His brow creased but the smile held. "Don't what?"

"That." I motioned toward his face as I took the seat across from him. "Remember our talk yesterday? The part where you said you'd been hiding behind fake smiles?"

"Ah. That part." His mouth flattened, easy charm gone without a fight. "Yeah, I remember. Guess some habits stick around longer than they should."

"Well, you don't have to do that with me," I said. "You know I understand at least some of what you're dealing with. And after yesterday…"

Gratitude flooded me, sudden and unwieldy. For the way he'd shown up. For the steadiness he'd provided and the strong arms I'd leaned into when I hadn't trusted myself to stand alone.

But I didn't trust my emotions enough to give them the floor. If I wasn't careful, who knew what would come spilling out.

"You helped me when I needed it," I continued, carefully. "If there's any way I can return the favor, I want to. So, talk to me. I'm a great listener."

Eric closed his eyes, head dipping as he let out a long breath. He didn't rush to fill the silence. He owned it, letting it settle until he was ready.

"Caleb started another round of chemo yesterday afternoon. This one's heavy-duty. He has radiation today, and in about a week, a stem-cell transplant."

I didn't understand all the medical details, but I didn't need to. The gravity of it showed in his face.

"The doctor's optimistic," he added. "If everything goes the way he expects, Caleb will be okay. There's been a lot of progress with this kind of cancer. A lot of people with Hodgkin's come out the other side."

He drew a measured breath. "But seeing him in that room. Watching him get pumped full of meds…he looked so young. So fucking vulnerable."

Mouth firm and shoulders set, he paused again, as if centering himself.

It was the most impressive display of self-control I'd ever seen.

"My mom isn't handling it well. Dad and I try to keep it together for her. For Caleb. Not that we don't feel it—we just don't let it run the show. And Caleb…" His gaze drifted, worry carving deeper lines between his brows. "He's already been through so much. There's still a long fight ahead. Things could—"

His jaw locked, cutting the thought short.

The truth of it sat heavy between us.

All his worry was for his brother, but it seemed to me that Eric was the one fighting. Holding the fear, the responsibility, the weight of everyone else's emotions, refusing to let it knock him down.

And somehow, that made him even stronger.

Without thinking, I pushed my sandwich aside and covered his hand with mine.

He looked up, eyes darkened by all the things he hadn't said. A second later, his fingers shifted beneath mine, turning decisively, closing around my hand with quiet certainty.

We stayed like that, hands joined, the cafeteria noise dulling until it faded into something distant and unimportant.

No words were needed. The moment was easy and natural.

Until it wasn't.

The world edged back in the moment his thumb began to move, brushing the back of my hand. The contact sent a jolt up my arm, sharp enough to steal my breath.

I watched his thumb press into my skin, the strength in his

forearm obvious even at rest, muscle defined without effort. Veins popping in a way that was far too sexy for a hospital cafeteria.

With more discipline than should've been necessary, I dragged my gaze up to his face.

The strain had eased. His jaw wasn't locked anymore. His mouth had softened. Hair slightly mussed, like he'd run his hand through it without thinking. He looked calm and anchored.

Dangerously attractive.

There was no point pretending otherwise. The pull was immediate and undeniable, and the timing made me feel like an absolute asshole for noticing it at all.

He'd just opened himself up in ways most men never did. And instead of restraint, my body kept supplying unhelpful suggestions about how much better it would feel to be closer. About how nice it might be to let his quiet control take over.

That was my cue.

I needed to leave before I did something ruinous. Like lean across the table and kiss him.

I started to pull away, but Eric's grip tightened, dragging me forward, stopping my escape and bringing us face-to-face.

His eyes held mine with deadly focus. "Where do you think you're going?"

In another setting, I'd have called his voice seductive.

"What?"

"Where are you running off to?"

"Running off? Nowhere, I just thought…" My gaze bounced around, taking note of all the exits. "I should get back to my dad's room. Check on him."

The words tumbled out, abrupt and clumsy, and I winced at how easily I'd made my own mess sound more urgent. Again.

"How's he doing?" Eric eased his grip but didn't release me.

"I don't really know. Some moments it feels like he's

slipping fast, and then he rallies and sounds almost like himself again. It's harder to watch than I expected."

"Can I meet him?"

I blinked at him. "Why would you want to do that?"

"Because you've met my family. And because I don't think you should have to do this alone." His unyielding gaze held mine. "You're here by yourself, aren't you?"

There wasn't anything clever to say to that, so I nodded.

"Jamie, I may not know much about your situation, but that's a lot to carry on your own. Even for a tough girl."

He wasn't wrong. I'd just been on my own for so long that letting someone step in felt foreign. Reckless, even. Leaning on him meant trusting he wouldn't disappear the second things got too tough. The moment I became too much.

"You've got enough on your plate. I don't want to add to your stress."

His mouth tipped into something like a smile. "You're not. This helps—focusing on you instead of living in my own head. I've been stuck there too long."

It sounded like a handy excuse for avoidance. Hell, maybe it was. But the way he said it made it feel like a decision he'd already made. One I should go along with.

"What do you say, beautiful?" His thumb brushed the back of my hand. "Should we go say hi to your old man?"

The idea of introducing a man to my father made me laugh. "How about you just walk me to his room? No offense, but I doubt he'd be thrilled to meet you. He's not big on strangers. Or people in general."

"Fair enough."

He didn't let go of my hand when we left the cafeteria. Didn't ask if it was okay. Just led the way, unhurried, like we had all the time in the world, his thumb tracing steady circles against my skin.

There was nothing overtly erotic about holding hands in a

hospital corridor, yet my body reacted anyway. Heat settled low. My skin prickled. Every sense tuned to him.

Two days. That's all it had been since we met. It was too soon to feel this close to anyone. Too soon to want this much.

"What are you doing this afternoon?" His voice sliced through the quiet like he could sense I was about to flee.

"Besides hanging out in this place?" I shrugged. "I don't know. I need to stop by my dad's house soon. It's probably a mess. I should figure out what kind of work it'll need. To sell it. Once he's…gone."

My throat tightened.

Eric's firm grip shifted, sliding up around my wrist, drawing me closer. "I'll go with you."

It wasn't a request—more of a declaration. The certainty of it knocked the breath out of me.

He wanted to go with me. To my father's house. To the place I hadn't set foot in for ten years. The place that held too many ghosts.

"I…I don't…you don't." My mind scrambled for a way out. "I mean, you don't have to. I don't even know how bad it is. It'll be boring. Possibly gross. I'll just be making lists—"

"Jamie." He tugged me even closer. "Stop."

The spiral closed off. My mouth snapped shut.

"No more excuses. Let's cut the bullshit with each other. Deal?"

It sounded simple. It felt anything but. I'd been editing myself for so long I wasn't sure what the uncut version even looked like anymore.

"I can do that," I murmured. "At least, I'll try."

"Good." He nodded, assured. "I'm not worried about the details. If you want company, I'll go. If you don't, I'll stay here."

The way he said it made my chest tighten, not with pressure, but with the strange relief of being allowed to choose.

"Don't you want to stay with your family?"

He glanced down at our joined hands, grip still firm. "Honestly? I think I need some space. My brother and sister are on their way. Things are always a bit chaotic with them around."

His thumb shifted against my skin again. "An afternoon out sounds better. Especially if it's with you."

The fact that he wanted to spend that time with me, even as an escape from his burdens, sent a flutter straight to my core.

"Oh." Too anxious to give an answer, I reached for the first diversion I could think of. "How many siblings do you have?"

"Three. Caleb, Celeste, and Marc. I'm the oldest, then Celeste. Marc was the youngest until my parents had their late-in-life surprise." A faint smile crossed his lips. "Caleb."

"The two of you seem really close."

"We are." His tone softened without losing its edge. "I sort of helped raise him. He followed me around so much when he was little, people thought he was my kid."

He shook his head, amusement flickering across his face. "The looks we'd get. I can't imagine being a parent at seventeen. That would've been a nightmare."

Nightmare. The word nearly knocked me back. My steps slowed, my whole body growing rigid.

Eric didn't notice. He was still walking, still talking, unaware of how sharply that single sentence had cut.

But how could he know? He had no idea that I'd been pregnant at seventeen. That I'd seen those looks, felt that judgment, absorbed it all until it felt like part of my identity.

Hunter had never been a mistake. Never a burden. He was the best thing in my life. Protecting him was instinctive.

And right now, I wasn't ready to find out how Eric would react to that part of me.

"This is it." I motioned to my father's room, lifted my gaze to his, and shut the door on the truth about my son. I didn't want to examine why. Not with him standing this close. That was a problem for later, when I was alone.

"You sure you don't want me to go in with you?" He scanned my face like he could read everything I was hiding.

"I'm sure."

The corner of his mouth crooked. "Fine." He reached up and tucked a strand of hair behind my ear. The gesture was maddeningly gentle for someone who radiated control like he did.

I turned toward the door, but his hand closed around mine again, firm and sure.

"Jamie." He didn't wait for me to look back. He stepped closer, close enough that his breath stirred the hair at my temple when he spoke. "I'm coming with you to the house. You're not walking into that place alone."

Every nerve in my body flared. "But—"

"No buts."

When I finally met his eyes, there was nothing wavering there. No softness. No doubt. Just immovable resolve.

"Ten minutes," His thumb brushed mine one last time. "I'll be right here. Then we go."

"Okay," I whispered.

But it wasn't really agreement.

It was surrender.

He let my hand go and leaned back against the wall, arms crossed, waiting like a soldier on watch.

I turned toward my father's door, stride strong and purposeful, but when I reached the doorway, I faltered, looking back for one last dose of moral support.

Eric's gaze lifted immediately, sharp and intent.

Was he checking out my ass?

The corner of his mouth tipped, slow and unapologetic, like he knew exactly what he'd been caught doing and didn't mind one bit.

"Ten minutes." His voice was calm as ever.

I turned and walked into my father's room, his certainty following me like a hand at my back.

He wasn't going anywhere.

And I had a feeling he didn't mind the wait if it meant watching me walk away.

CHAPTER SEVEN

ERIC

JAMIE'S KEY REFUSED TO COOPERATE.

We stood on the front porch of her dad's house, the lock stubborn under her increasingly frantic attempts. Her shoulders tensed, color creeping up her neck in that way that told me she was close to losing it.

"Easy." I covered her hand with mine, stilling her before the key snapped. "Is there another way in?"

She huffed. "We could try the back door."

I stepped aside to let her lead and immediately regretted it.

Watching the sway in her hips as she moved around the side of the house turned my focus traitorous. She'd been under my skin since the hospital, and she clearly wasn't done settling in. Every line of her body claimed my attention whether I wanted to give it or not. And my mind twisted every word she said into unfortunate innuendo.

Try the back door, she said.

Yes. Fucking please.

I forced my gaze forward. Control mattered. Especially now.

She glanced back, caught me watching anyway, and rolled

her eyes like she knew exactly what she was doing to me. Like she'd planned it. That only made the situation worse.

Nothing dulled the attraction. Not the house. Not her father. Not even the thought that she might have someone else—some asshole who probably didn't deserve her.

Caleb talked a lot about living in the moment, but it had never been my style. Standing behind her at the back of the house, keys jangling, frustration humming in the air, I was starting to understand the appeal.

But I wasn't here to make a move. I was here because she needed backup. Because this place came with history, and I wasn't about to let her face it alone. Whatever heat sparked between us could wait.

Jamie shuffled along the back deck, checking under planters and along the windowsills for a spare key. I stayed where I was, breathing slow and controlled, locking down every instinct that told me to close the distance.

My gaze kept landing on her anyway. The glimpse of black lace at her hip when her shirt rode up. The curve of her breast when she bent forward. It was enough to test my discipline.

She muttered another curse under her breath, her shoulders taut and hands clenching.

Done waiting, I moved straight to the sliding glass door and pulled. The damn thing slid open without resistance.

We both froze. She stared at the open doorway like it might bite. I watched her instead, noting how she lingered at the threshold, reluctant to step inside despite nothing blocking her way.

What was she afraid of finding on the other side?

She'd warned me more than once to expect a disaster. I hadn't asked why.

I also hadn't asked about her relationship with her father. I didn't need to. The fact that she didn't know the state of his house, yet prepared for the worst, told me enough. More than she probably realized.

I wanted to ask anyway. I wanted details, context. Everything.

But this wasn't the moment to pry.

"Well?" I stepped aside, motioning toward the open door.

"Yeah. Okay." She sighed. "Let's get it over with."

She went in first. Her soft cry pulled me in after her, fast and alert.

I assessed the room in a single sweep. Nothing looked out of place. The house was clean, orderly, well cared for. Old bones, good ones, paired with modern touches. Stainless steel appliances gleamed in the kitchen where we stood. Everything looked exactly as it should.

Everything except Jamie.

Her face had gone pale, eyes too wide, body tense and shaking.

"Hey." I stepped in, caught her at the elbow, steadying her before she could argue. "Sit down."

"No." The word came out as a whisper. Then, firmer, like she needed to convince herself as much as me, "No. I'm fine. It's just…it looks almost exactly the way I remember."

"And that's a problem?"

She shook her head. "No. It's just surprising."

I let her move ahead, not crowding her but sticking close enough to intervene if needed. I took my time, scanning the unfamiliar house on instinct while keeping her in my peripheral, trying to see it the way she did.

The living room was all warm wood and leather, anchored by a massive stone fireplace that dominated the far wall. It looked comfortable and lived in. The perfect place for a family.

Jamie drifted down the hall on her own. I didn't rush after her. I lingered instead, drawn to the photographs lining the mantel. Professional family portraits. A mother and father flanked by two little girls, with big smiles and polished poses.

The girls looked alike. White-blond hair. Blue eyes.

But Jamie stood out even then. There was something unmistakable about her, even as a child. A brightness that pulled focus without trying.

What caught me more was her parents. The way they leaned toward their daughters with obvious pride. This was the kind of happiness that couldn't be staged.

A strong family. Or at least one that had been.

It didn't match the woman down the hall. It didn't match her warnings, her tension, or her certainty that this place would be falling apart.

Whatever had gone wrong here, it hadn't started with the house.

She drifted back into the room, bewilderment written across her face.

"This place is nice. Your dad lives here alone?"

"Yeah…" Her eyes traced the room again. "He's been alone for a long time now."

"He's taken good care of it."

"I know." Her attention snapped back to me. "I'm shocked. But I'm glad too. This place always meant so much to him. He restored most of it himself. Worked on it for years."

She exhaled, forehead creasing as emotion took hold. "I used to beg him to let me help. Even when the work was complicated, he'd find something for me to do. Always made me feel important."

Her voice softened. "God, I loved those moments. I haven't thought about any of this in years."

I stayed quiet and let her talk, watching the tension ease from her face.

She loved this place. The good memories ran deep. Whatever had gone wrong came later.

"I think his love for it rubbed off on me," she said. "I work in home restoration and remodeling."

That earned a quiet smile from me.

It didn't surprise me at all. Jamie didn't scare easy. She liked getting her hands dirty. Took on work a lot of people shied away from.

Beautiful, yes. But tough. Exactly how I'd pegged her from the start.

"I'm not nearly as good as my dad was." Her mouth curved into a soft smile. "But I love the idea of bringing an old home back to its glory."

"Sounds like real work."

"It is. Honest work but I love it. I just don't get to do much of it." She hesitated, then shrugged. "I've worked with my boss almost five years. He's trusted me with one small remodel. I think I only got it because the clients were difficult. Most days I run the office and handle customer service. It kind of sucks, but gotta pay my dues, right?"

"Fuck that." The thought that she'd been shafted into some bullshit gender role pissed me off. Customer service, my ass. "Your boss sounds like an asshole."

"No." She shook her head at me like I didn't understand. "He's not that bad."

"Really? Because to me, it sounds like he's using you." I didn't bother dressing it up. "You're a pretty face that keeps the clients happy. I've met plenty of guys like him. They don't have the balls to give a woman a real chance in their business."

Her shoulders squared. "So, what, I'm just a pretty face? Nothing more?"

Shit.

"No." I met her gaze and held it. "I'm saying you're wasted where you are. You're smart. You're capable. And given the chance, you'd probably run circles around half the men in your field. Maybe all of them."

She studied me for a long beat. "I know how good I am, Eric. But he gave me a job—one that I really needed. I was grateful for that."

"Fair. Doesn't change the fact that you deserve better."

"Maybe." Her attention drifted back to the room, fingers tracing the edge of a table like she was grounding herself. "Maybe not."

I took the hint, shutting my mouth and letting silence do the work.

A smaller cluster of photos on a side table gave me something else to focus on.

All three were of the same little boy. Dark-blond hair. Brown eyes. The family resemblance was obvious, but the pictures were newer, and he didn't appear anywhere else.

My mind ran through the possibilities—a younger brother, a second family, a secret that explained the tension she'd warned me about.

Or I was inventing problems that didn't exist, and the photos didn't mean a damn thing.

Speculation without facts was useless, and I wasn't about to ask. Not after proving I had a talent for saying the wrong thing around her.

I stepped back from the photos just as Jamie came up beside me.

She looked down at them and froze. The color drained from her face, her hand lifting to her mouth as her eyes filled with tears, too fast to hide them.

So much for the photos meaning nothing.

Instinct took over, the room narrowed, and my attention locked on her. I didn't know the cause, but I knew my role.

She wasn't handling this alone.

"Hey. Come here."

I took her hand and guided her to the couch, sitting first and drawing her down with me. The armrest boxed her in, close enough that retreat wasn't an option.

It still wasn't close enough.

I caught her at the knees and pulled her legs across my lap, turning her toward me until there was nowhere else for her attention to land. Whether the contact was for her or for me didn't matter. It felt necessary.

"Look at me." With a finger under her chin, I urged her gaze up to meet mine.

She held there, breath shallow, pain sitting just under the surface. I wanted to take it from her. All of it.

"Listen." My grip eased, thumb sliding along her cheek instead. "You were there for me this morning. And we made a deal, remember? No more pretending. You don't have to hide how you feel."

She nodded, swallowing hard, but stayed silent.

"I'm here now," I murmured. "You can trust me with this if you want to talk."

I waited, searching her watery blue gaze, giving her space to speak.

Still, she said nothing.

Instead, she leaned in, arms coming around my neck, her face hovering close. Then her mouth found mine, stealing the air from my lungs.

Well, fuck.

CHAPTER EIGHT

JAMIE

THE SECOND MY MOUTH MET HIS, I KNEW I'D CROSSED A LINE.

Eric's hand stayed gentle under my chin, but the rest of him locked down, tension snapping tight beneath my palms.

Damn it. I knew better.

Everything he'd said about trust and feelings hadn't been a prelude to kissing. And yet I'd rushed in anyway, boundaries slipping the second I wanted him badly enough.

His mouth didn't move against mine. The kiss was closed and controlled—our lips touching, nothing more. And still, it was too much.

I was too much.

I pulled back fast, heat flooding my face as I dropped my gaze. "I'm sorry," I muttered. "I don't know why I—"

"Jamie." His low voice cut through my stammering.

I expected distance. A gentle letdown. For him to let me go and ease the moment apart.

Instead, his hand slid into my hair and tightened, halting my retreat. He held me there, the space between us thick and electric. "Look at me."

My eyes snapped up without hesitation. My breath stuttered,

heat blooming between my thighs. The desire in his gaze closed around me, pushing out sadness, confusion, every lingering doubt.

All I could see, all I could feel, was Eric.

I wanted him. Not just his body, but his steadiness. His attention. The way he stayed when things got messy. I wanted to disappear into him for a while and let the rest of the world wait.

His blue eyes searched mine—for what I didn't know, but I was willing to give it, whatever he wanted.

"Fuck it," he growled in a heavy rush.

Then his mouth claimed mine.

This time, there was nothing restrained about it. He took control, tongue sweeping, teeth biting, mouth firm and demanding, setting the pace before I could think to catch up.

Everything narrowed to sensation. His mouth. His hands. The uncompromising way he held me exactly where he wanted me.

His grip in my hair tightened, and a low moan tore from me, soft and helpless.

The kiss branded me. Burned away every other thought. Left only heat and his possession.

And then his mouth was gone.

He pulled back, breath heavy, his expression locked down again, impossible to read.

A taste, just a tiny little taste, was all he'd given me. But God, I wanted so much more.

My stomach tightened, my breath went shallow, and the lump in my throat returned.

I was in the living room of my dying father—the man I'd ignored for ten years—making out with someone I'd met two days ago. Worse, I was the one who'd started it.

What the hell was wrong with me?

A better person would have packed a bag, gone back to

Toronto, and put distance between herself and Eric Alexander, before it was too late.

But I wasn't that person.

Not when I melted under his attention. Not when it felt so good to disappear into a moment and forget everything else existed.

It felt way too good.

Which was exactly why it couldn't happen again. The stakes were too high. I had my son to think about. The life I'd fought to piece together. Losing myself to a man, even one as incredible as Eric, felt like a price I wouldn't survive paying.

Shame crept in, hot and suffocating. I couldn't bring myself to meet his eyes. I stared at his mouth, waiting for the inevitable words of regret.

"Jamie." His low voice was steady, unfazed.

I forced myself to look up.

He was watching me, brow furrowed, like he was waiting for something from me.

Before I could say a word, he spoke again. "Someone's at the door."

And sure enough, when I turned my attention outward, I heard it. A hard, insistent knock at the front door.

Then again, only louder.

"Shit."

I lurched out of Eric's hold, heat still humming under my skin as I smoothed my clothes and ran for the door.

Flight over thought. Always my specialty.

Instead of doing the sensible thing and checking the sidelight first, I yanked the door open.

Such a bad call.

I was greeted by messy, dirty-blond hair, dark brown eyes, a growing arrogant smirk, and a uniform. Wait...

Was that a badge? Who in their right mind would give Dylan McCoy a police badge?

Oh, please don't let him be armed.

There was no universe in which this man-child should ever be trusted with a gun.

"Wow." His eyebrows lifted as his gaze dragged over me, slow and predatory. "You are the last person I expected to find here."

The surprise in his voice didn't dull his wicked grin or the sinful glint in his eyes. If I didn't know better, his intensity might've scared me.

Unfortunately, I knew him far too well.

I knew what he wanted. And I knew exactly how little of it I was willing to give. Ever again.

"Gotta say," he added, all swagger. "You're a really nice surprise."

It had been over a year since I'd last seen my ex. Longer than that since I'd wanted anything to do with him. But he hadn't changed. Same easy charm. Same quick seduction.

If only he'd stop thinking with his dick for once and take me seriously.

Not because I wanted anything from him but because I didn't get the luxury of cutting him out. Because he was the father of my child.

That fact didn't make him any less of an asshat. Just a smooth-talking, frustratingly attractive one who now apparently wore a uniform that did him far too many favors.

"What are you doing here, Princess?"

Princess. Seriously?

This was the problem with Dylan. No matter how many times I'd told him we were done, that the romance and pet names were over, he refused to let it die.

Still, he was asking the same question I'd been asking myself for days.

Why had I bothered coming back here?

"My dad's in the hospital."

"Yeah." His voice dipped, sympathy sliding in alongside the bravado. "I heard. I'm sorry, Princess. I know that can't be easy."

The way he managed to blend empathy and entitlement into a single sentence was almost impressive.

I shrugged, offering him nothing.

Somehow, he took it as permission. His gaze sharpened, hunger flashing across his face like it physically hurt him to hold back, and he took a step closer.

But that single step was as far as he got.

His forward momentum halted. Confusion flickered over his features, followed quickly by irritation, his eyes cutting past me.

"Who's this?" he snapped, the question edged with authority he hadn't earned.

I glanced over my shoulder.

Eric stood a few steps back, posture relaxed, expression flat. He didn't look surprised. He didn't look impressed either. His attention was fixed on Dylan with a calm that felt loaded, like he'd already assessed the situation and found it lacking.

"Oh." I turned back with forced brightness. "Sorry. Dylan, this is my boyfriend. Eric."

My tongue lingered on the word boyfriend.

Dylan's attention jerked back toward me. "What?"

Oh. Shit.

The lie had come out of nowhere. No thought or plan, just pure instinct. Because right now, it was the best shield I had against Dylan McCoy's version of interest.

Fear slid through me as I waited for a reaction. For the lie to break and my pathetic attempt at defense to crumble. For Eric to judge me, deny me, or simply realize I wasn't who he thought. That kissing me really had been a giant mistake.

I didn't hear him move. I felt him.

A solid presence at my side, Eric's arm came around me like it had always belonged there. His big hand settled at my hip, pulling me in close and locking the lie into place without a word.

Boyfriend.

The claim was absolute.

My breath stuttered. For one reckless second, I wished it was real. I wanted to turn into him, plant my lips over his again, and let the world slip away. Damn the consequences.

But Eric was a good man. Better than good. And men like him didn't sign up for lies, chaos, or women whose lives came with this much baggage.

The adrenaline hit all at once. My hands started to shake, chest tightening like it always did when things spiraled too fast.

"Hey." Eric's breath was warm against my ear. "Stay with me."

His arm tightened briefly, a silent reassurance, before he turned his attention to Dylan. "So, is there a problem, Officer?"

"Huh?" Dylan blinked, clearly thrown. His attention slid back to me, searching my face like I was suddenly unfamiliar.

"Well," Eric continued, unbothered, "you were knocking at that door pretty hard."

"Oh. Yeah." Dylan cleared his throat. "A neighbor called it in. Said someone was poking around Frank's house. Given his condition, I figured I should check things out."

"Looks like you've done that." Eric's voice held an edge of warning. "And then some."

Dylan's mouth twitched. "Yeah. I have." His eyes dragged over me again. "Everything's looking good. Really good."

My stomach dropped, anxiety spiked, and all the reasons I'd worked so hard to keep this man out of my life rose to the surface.

"It's just me," I mumbled, the entire situation beginning to feel out of control.

There was too much feeling. Too much pressure. And my body was tipping toward overload.

"Yeah, Jamie." Dylan's voice softened. "I see you."

There was no sneer in it. No mockery. It landed like a sigh pulled straight from his chest, full of things I didn't want to hear. It was a sound that said he wasn't done yet. Not really. No matter who stood at my side.

Eric went utterly still beside me, and the temperature in the room seemed to drop ten degrees.

Blackness swallowed my vision, and whatever strength I had left finally gave way.

CHAPTER NINE

ERIC

JAMIE TIPPED FORWARD, ONE HAND CLUTCHING HER CHEST AS HER knees went soft.

I was already there, my arm locking around her waist before she hit the ground. Dylan reacted too, but he was a moment too late, letting out a disgruntled sound as I scooped her into my arms.

He could make whatever noise he wanted. I didn't give a shit about his ego.

Jamie was mine to protect, not his.

She was light in my arms, her body sagging into mine like she'd run out of energy to hold herself upright. I drew her closer, instinctively shielding her, and kept her there when she started to protest, pushing weakly against my chest.

"I'm fine. You can put me down." Her fingers curled into my shirt, contradicting her words.

"No."

I didn't believe her for a second. Not any more than I believed Dylan had shown up here with innocent intentions.

Jamie wasn't fine.

I knew this posture. This stubborn refusal to admit weakness.

The instinct to smooth things over, to shoulder it alone and keep moving because stopping felt dangerous. I'd lived there. Still did, most days.

She carried her troubles the same way I did—quietly, until they started to break her apart from the inside.

Ignoring her protests, I tightened my hold and carried her into the living room, Dylan on our heels. I set her on the couch where I'd kissed her only minutes earlier.

That kiss still burned through me. Ill-timed, but impossible to regret. I'd crossed the line deliberately, shut out everything else, and followed pure instinct.

Forget morals or consequences. The only thing in my sights was beautiful Jamie.

"I'm okay." She was already trying to sit up.

I kept a hand on her shoulder, firm enough to stop her. She'd bolt if I let her. I could sense that she lived with a constant readiness to flee.

"Not yet." I smoothed her hair back from her face. "Give yourself a minute."

Dylan took a step back like he'd been shut out. Good. Maybe he was getting the fucking hint.

"What can I get you?" I asked her, keeping my focus where it belonged.

"I don't need anything. Honest." She looked more like herself with every breath.

"Then sit up slowly." I slid my hand behind her head, ready to catch her if she tipped again.

I wasn't going anywhere.

In fact, I needed to be closer.

I could've told myself it was to give her something solid to lean on. But the truth was simpler. I wanted her within reach. Her body tucked against mine.

I sat, pulling her gently into my side and wrapping an arm around her before she could argue. "How's that?"

Color crept up her neck, blooming across her cheeks. It might've been embarrassment from almost fainting or the fact that she was beside me again. Didn't matter. I liked the effect either way.

Dylan cleared his throat. "Jamie, you sure you're okay, Princess?"

The asshole was persistent, I'd give him that. Oblivious too. He either didn't notice the way she flinched at the name or didn't care.

"Yes. You just surprised me." She forced a smile, waving him off. "I've been stressed about Dad. It's been a lot. But I guess, since you're here…we should probably talk."

Her gaze flicked to me, uncertain.

"I'll grab you some water." It felt like something a boyfriend would do. And I could play the part.

I'd never really done it before—not long-term, anyway—but I knew how to show up when it mattered. Protecting her already felt instinctive. Being present. Reassuring her without making a production of it.

Those parts came easily.

What didn't make sense was how thoroughly Jamie had gotten under my skin in such a short time. A handful of conversations. A few moments where we'd both let the cracks show. And suddenly I was carrying feelings I couldn't name.

Maybe it was grief. Fallout from everything that had blown apart with Caleb. Maybe I was reaching for connection because I was tired of surviving this all on my own.

Maybe she was just a distraction.

Except she didn't feel like one.

Water took all of thirty seconds to find. There was a neat line of glasses in the first cupboard I opened, and a pitcher of filtered water in the fridge. No effort required.

I hesitated anyway, took my time filling the glass, and listened to their voices carrying through the open doorway.

"Tell me what you need from me." The arrogance was gone from Dylan's voice, replaced by something that sounded like genuine concern.

For a moment, I wondered if I'd misjudged him. If maybe he was more than just a cocky prick.

"It's a little late for that, don't you think?" She sounded tired. Like this was a conversation they'd had before.

"It's never too late, Jamie. I'm here. Right now, I'm here."

"Dylan…" Her voice tightened. "I'm not the one who needs you. How many times do I have to tell you that?"

"Oh, right." His tone flipped, sharp with bitterness. "You don't want me. I'm only good for a nice hard screw every now and then. My mistake. I've never been good enough for you, have I?"

My jaw locked. The idea of him touching her, of her ever letting him close like that, set something hot and ugly loose in my chest. Jealousy wasn't my usual vice, yet it slammed into me without warning.

"If you felt used…" She sighed. "Well, maybe you were. It wasn't intentional, but yeah. I probably was using you in those moments. I'm sorry."

That stopped me cold.

Jamie was tough, resilient in ways that had impressed me from the start. But somewhere along the way, I'd started treating her like she needed protecting. Like she was fragile. Hearing her now, owning her choices without backpedaling or excuses, forced me to confront something uncomfortable.

I hadn't been seeing her as helpless because she was weak. I'd been treating her that way because I wanted her to need me.

That should've eased something in me, but it didn't. Because if I was honest, I wanted what Dylan wanted. Not just her body but her trust. Her reliance. I wanted to be the one she turned to when things got hard.

"There was a time I wanted more from you," she continued. "You know that. But I don't feel that way anymore."

"I know. It's been a long time since there was anything real between us. I get that. I just thought…maybe you'd change your mind."

"I won't," she said. No hesitation. "I just want you to do the right thing."

He sighed. "I don't know how you expect me to do the right thing when you live so far away. I still have a life, Jamie. But I have put thought into it—I just wanted to make the whole thing work, with you too."

Do the right thing? Make the whole thing work? What the hell did that mean?

"I really wasn't prepared for you to have a new guy. He does seem good at taking care of you, though."

"Yeah. Eric is good at that. He's done a lot for me." She hesitated, then added, softer, "He doesn't even realize how much. He's kind of amazing, actually."

Unearned pride surged through me, settling somewhere deep in my chest. She meant it. I could hear it in her voice.

Dylan huffed. "Yeah, I get it. Doesn't mean I'm giving up, though."

"Dylan…"

"Relax. I'm not pushing. But what about Hunter?"

Hunter. My grip tightened around the glass. Was he the other man? The one she'd been missing?

"What about Hunter?" Jamie shot back.

"Does he know what's going on here? You didn't bring him."

"No. I didn't want him here. I didn't know what to expect." Her tone turned protective. Whoever Hunter was, she was shielding him from this mess. "I guess I expected a different kind of fight."

Dylan chuckled. "Things change, Princess. People change."

I'd had enough.

No more standing in the shadows, piecing together her life while he poked at old wounds like he still had the right.

Water in hand, I stepped back into the room and took in the scene.

She'd edged as far back into the couch as she could, arms crossed tight over her chest. Dylan sat on the edge of the coffee table, leaning into her space like he had every right to be there.

They weren't touching, but Dylan could've changed that with the shift of a wrist.

And that pissed me off a hell of a lot more than it should have.

She'd introduced me as her boyfriend. Yes, she'd tossed it out like a shield, a line in the sand, but Dylan had stepped right over it.

Fuck him.

I walked straight over to her and held out the glass. She uncrossed one arm to take it, her fingers brushing mine for a second before she pulled it back in against her chest.

"Thank you, Eric." She broke eye contact with Dylan and looked up at me as she brought the glass to her lips.

Those luscious fucking lips that had been under mine only minutes ago.

Necessary or not, convenient or not, being at her side and standing up for her felt right.

"Okay. Well, I should get going." Dylan stood. "Are you staying here, Jamie?"

"Here?"

"Yes, here. Your dad's place. Are you staying?"

The question hung there, weighted and intrusive.

Jamie hesitated, and I caught a flicker of conflict in her eyes. "I don't know. I'll have to think about it. I'll let you know."

I didn't like that. Cop or not, he didn't need access to her choices. He'd already taken more space than he deserved.

Jamie walked him to the door, and I paced the living room while I waited, tension winding tight.

She came back in wearing a too-bright smile. "Well. That was fun."

The forced cheer didn't match the exhaustion written all over her face.

Fuck, the timing of this was a disaster. Whatever conversation I'd been gearing up for wasn't happening tonight. She didn't have anything left to give. And I sure as fuck wasn't going to take anything from her the way Dylan had.

"I'm guessing you might have questions." She rubbed a hand over her face.

Questions? Plenty. None of them appropriate right now.

"There are a few things I wouldn't mind clearing up. But it's late. We should get back to the hospital." I paused, choosing my words carefully. "Tomorrow, though. We grab food, then talk."

Her shoulders eased a fraction. "I feel like I owe you something. You kind of saved my ass." Guilt crept into her expression. "I panicked. I'm sorry."

"You handled it. But tomorrow, your boyfriend's taking you out for a proper meal."

The word landed between us.

She froze, her eyes going round. "You don't mind keeping up the charade?"

"Is it going to help keep guys like Dylan off your back?"

Her face flushed. "It's been ten years since I was last in this town. And I didn't exactly leave under the best circumstances. So yeah…I wouldn't mind having the backup."

"Then it's a deal."

She laughed. "Okay, boyfriend. Where are you taking me?"

Even joking, hearing it again did something to me.

"You pick. I'll handle the rest."

She grinned. "Fair warning. I get impulsive when I'm hungry. First food sign wins. And you're paying."

"Deal."

She turned for the door, lighter now, some of the strain easing.

I caught up to her in two strides, took her hand, and laced our fingers together without asking.

"Jamie," I murmured at her ear. "It's good to see that smile again."

I squeezed her hand and didn't let go.

DAY MINUS 5

CHAPTER TEN

JAMIE

THE DAY FELT ENDLESS. TIME CRAWLED SO SLOWLY IT sometimes seemed to slip backward altogether.

But I was fine. Everything was okay. The hours only dragged because I was stuck between four hospital walls, watching my father sleep, and Hunter was too busy to reply to my texts.

At least, those were the lies playing on a loop in my head.

Truth was, things were far from fine, and I was nowhere near good. Time felt like a vacuum because worry plagued me, stretching every moment thin.

My father hadn't spoken a word. He hadn't acknowledged me at all. But I'd learned his open eyes didn't mean he was actually with me. Less and less of his time was spent lucid, and I clung to the hope that it was the medication, not the disease.

That uncertainty sent me spiraling back to the same question I'd been asking myself since I arrived. Why was I here without my son? What kind of mother leaves her child behind?

But even those heavy thoughts weren't the ones undoing me most.

No. It was thoughts of Eric pulling me under.

The fact that he occupied so much space in my mind

felt absurd. I barely knew him, and yet I couldn't stop thinking about him. Couldn't stop replaying the kiss we'd shared.

The sensation was imprinted on my lips, my whole body still high from the brief contact.

Worse still was the conversation I'd managed to avoid. Somehow, I'd escaped explaining the mess that was Dylan. My history with him remained buried, and part of me desperately wanted it to stay that way. The idea of laying all of it bare for Eric made my stomach knot.

But without that talk, what chance did I have of ever feeling his mouth on mine again?

That kiss had crowded out everything else. My father. My son. My carefully constructed resolve.

Everything.

The guilt was blinding. But the pleasure…*oh, the pleasure.*

It lingered, vivid and undeniable. Unlike anything I'd felt before. I hated how easily my mind wandered from that single kiss to all the places it could have led, and all the places it still might.

No matter how hard I tried to stop it, the desire refused to loosen its grip.

My thoughts were still drifting somewhere scandalous when Nurse Judy swept into the room, her smile so bright it felt accusatory.

"Jamie dear, it's almost dinnertime, and there's a remarkably handsome young man in the hallway who says he's here to take you out to eat."

"What?"

"I wouldn't keep him waiting if I were you." Her voice dropped to a conspiratorial whisper. "He's a fine-looking man. If you don't hurry, another woman might try and steal him. A woman like me maybe." She laughed, thoroughly pleased with herself.

Not waiting to see if Judy's enthusiasm would wake my father, I slipped into the hall.

Eric was waiting just outside, leaning casually against the wall again, arms crossed over his chest like he owned the space simply by standing in it. The sight of him sent a jolt through me, equal parts relief and excitement.

"What are you doing here?" The question was sharper than I meant it to be, an attempt to mask the ridiculous thrill blooming in my chest.

"It's been less than twenty-four hours, and you've forgotten already?" He smirked, pushing off the wall to move closer. "I promised to feed you. We made a date, remember?"

He looked at me like he always did, like he was reading more than I was saying. Like he knew all the ways I'd been fantasizing about him.

The glint in his eye made my pulse stutter.

Shit. I was such an open book for this man, it was ridiculous.

"I could eat." I shrugged, aiming for casual and missing by miles.

His warm hand closed around mine without hesitation, already turning us toward the elevator like the decision had been made the moment he showed up.

Even as my feet followed him, my mind stayed stubbornly fixed on everything but food.

Somehow, we ended up at a table, drinks sweating onto coasters, a plate set in front of me.

"This is seriously the best hamburger I've ever tasted," I mumbled around a mouthful of half-chewed meat and bun.

Yes, it was a burger place, but not some greasy, overrun chain. It was the kind of place that took its food seriously. Still, the meal wasn't the best part.

Eric watched me eat, openly amused, his attention fixed on me in a way that made my pulse trip. He lifted his milkshake, lips closing around the straw, his gaze never leaving mine as he took a slow sip and dragged his tongue across his lower lip afterward.

My blood pressure spiked. The man had a way of making everything look sexy. Even eating.

And I wasn't the only one who noticed.

A woman at a nearby table kept glancing over, her eyes lingering on the line of his broad shoulders. The server had already made three unnecessary trips to our table, her questions directed at Eric with a smile that was a little too bright. Even the guy at the corner booth had looked up from his phone more than once to steal a glance.

If Eric was aware of the attention, he didn't show it. His focus stayed locked on me, like I was the only person in the room worth looking at.

"I'm glad you're enjoying it." His smile was easy, the look in his eyes making it clear he knew exactly what he was doing to me.

We still hadn't talked about yesterday. He hadn't pushed, but the weight of it sat between us. There was no doubt he'd overheard at least some of my conversation with Dylan. But how much did I need to explain?

How much of myself was I ready to unpack?

Not much, if I was being honest. Still, telling him the truth felt like the right thing to do.

If things were normal, if we hadn't met under fluorescent lights in a hospital cafeteria at one of the worst moments of our lives, I would've already said it all. But my hesitation wasn't just about sparing him my baggage.

The real reason was less noble.

I liked the way he looked at me. The assurance in it. The way he made me feel capable and fragile at the same time, strong without having to pretend I wasn't tired. He held me in a kind of quiet regard that felt rare.

"Can I ask you something?"

I swallowed thickly, the food sliding painfully down my throat and settling heavy in my stomach. I nodded anyway. Whatever he was about to ask felt inevitable.

"Are you really going to stay at your dad's place?"

"I hadn't thought about it before yesterday," I admitted. "But I've got a room up at the resort that I've barely used."

"Copper Ridge Resort?" His tone didn't change, but something in his gaze sharpened.

"Yeah. It's not exactly budget-friendly but I didn't want to be right in town." I exhaled, decision crystallizing. "I think I'll save the money and stay at the house."

"Good." The word came out firm, satisfied. "It seemed to hold some good memories. Being there might help you sort through the rest."

"Maybe." I shrugged. "We'll see."

"I'll take you back to the resort and help you move your things." He said it like it was already decided, like the most natural next step in the world.

The offer was too easy to accept.

And that was the problem.

I couldn't keep relying on him to bail me out of trouble, even with something so simple. I wasn't helpless. I was complicated. And some of those complications weren't pretty.

He deserved better than a half-formed version of me.

He deserved the truth.

Just not here. Not with strangers all around us and no space to breathe. Not with half the restaurant stealing glances at him every few minutes. I needed somewhere I could speak freely, where Eric could react however he wanted, and I could run if needed.

"I'd like to go somewhere else first." I met his gaze, pulse ticking faster. "If that's okay."

He leaned back in his chair, studying me with that intense focus that made me feel like prey. "Yeah. Of course. Where to?"

"Let's go for a walk."

CHAPTER ELEVEN

JAMIE

"This isn't what I expected." Eric's voice carried easily through the pine-scented air as needles softened our steps and trees closed in around us.

I knew it wasn't. This wasn't a waterfront walkway or public beach where everyone else went—locals and tourists drawn to the Bay the second spring arrived. Those places were crowded. Families with strollers. Couples pretending not to watch each other. Runners, dogs, cameras, noise. The whole town spilling out to be seen.

Not ideal when I was trying to avoid public scrutiny. The secrets I needed to share were better said in private.

Mills Conservation Area wasn't empty, but it was big enough to feel secluded. Trails cut through rock and trees, winding along the river and climbing the natural rise of the Niagara Escarpment until they reached the lookout perched above the valley.

His arm brushed mine, warm and solid, and I forced myself to focus on the view instead of the contact. "Not a nature guy?"

"It's great. Just not what I grew up with. I've spent most of my life in the city."

"Toronto?"

"Montreal. Born and raised." He stepped over a root without breaking stride. "After university, I moved to Manhattan to work for my uncle. I've only been in Copper Ridge about five months. My parents and Caleb moved here four years ago. My sister's in Toronto, though."

"That's where I live. But being back here feels…good. I missed all this green."

I drew in a deep breath, clean air filling my lungs in a way the city never quite managed. "If you think this part's impressive, wait until you see what's next."

We crested the rise as I said it. The trees thinned, then fell away entirely, and the lookout spread open beneath the sky. Golden evening light poured across the rise like it had been waiting for us.

Eric stopped behind me, close but not touching. For a moment, the world narrowed to wind in the trees and the steady sound of his breathing at my back.

The view tugged at something deep in my chest, memories flooding me all at once. I was eight again. Then fifteen. Standing here and pretending the valley below was a kingdom and I was something untouchable.

Princess.

Like a whisper from the past, Dylan's annoying nickname echoed through my mind, making my skin crawl.

What would've happened if Eric hadn't been there yesterday? If I'd been alone with Dylan?

There was no point lying to myself. I probably would've let him touch me. Let him pull me back into the same tired loop we'd been circling for years.

I'd always justified it. We had history. A child. He knew me better than anyone. He was easy and familiar. All the excuses I hid behind so I didn't have to call it what it was.

Loneliness.

Dylan had always been convenient.

The truth wasn't just embarrassing. It was ugly. I hadn't misread him. I'd seen exactly who he was and chose not to look too closely. He still believed in us. In some version of a future I'd already left behind.

And I let him. Strung him along because it felt safer than standing on my own.

The firm weight of Eric's hand settled on my shoulder. "Hey, where'd you go?"

"Sorry. Got lost in thought."

"Thoughts about what?"

There it was. The opening I'd been working up to.

I drew in a breath and let it out all at once. "About that explanation I owe you."

No one else had ever stepped in for me the way Eric had. He was the only one who'd ever taken control when I needed someone. On fake-boyfriend credentials alone, he'd earned the truth.

It was now or never.

"I can practically hear the gears grinding in your head." His thumb brushed my collarbone in a slow, absent sweep that made stepping away feel impossible.

My pulse kicked hard as a breathless laugh escaped me.

"I'm not going to pretend I'm not curious. But I won't corner you into saying something you're not ready to."

Of course he wouldn't.

He was infuriatingly decent, and all I'd given him so far were fragments and half-truths wrapped in avoidance.

I shook my head. "I want to tell you."

His jaw tightened, but he waited.

"Dylan was my first boyfriend. We started dating when we were fifteen." My voice sounded steady, but it didn't feel that way. "We thought we were in love. Mostly we were just young. And stupid."

Eric's hand slid from my shoulder down my arm, fingers closing around mine with quiet authority.

"I stayed at his place whenever being at home felt… unbearable." My eyes closed and lips pressed together, the words hard to get out.

Eric tugged on my hand, guiding me to one of the benches overlooking the trail. The motion was decisive, and I obeyed without thought.

"Talk to me." Our thighs brushed as he sat next to me. "I've seen the photos. I know it wasn't always like that. Tell me what changed."

"It's a lot. Too much. It's all tangled."

Silence stretched between us, but he didn't rush to fill it. He just waited.

And somehow, that gave me the strength to go on. "My mom and sister died in a car accident when I was thirteen. My sister died on impact. My mom didn't. She was kept alive in a coma for just over three weeks."

Saying it out loud still felt unreal, like I was reciting facts from someone else's life.

"For twenty-three days, my dad and I sat beside her. She was broken, bruised, and unconscious. We watched machines breathe for her and told ourselves it would be okay. That she'd wake up. That she'd come back to us." My throat tightened. "She never did."

His grip firmed, thumb tracing slow circles over my wrist. A reminder I wasn't alone.

"The coma was induced. The doctors said it was the only way to try to save her. But after three weeks, it wasn't her anymore. Just machines." I swallowed hard. "They told us she was brain dead. There was no real choice left, but it was my dad who had to make it."

My chest burned as the memory pressed down hard.

"He signed the paperwork. Less than twenty-four hours later, she was gone."

"Fuck, Jamie. I'm so sorry."

"I don't deserve your sympathy." My voice cracked as the first tear slipped free. "I blamed him. Screamed at him and called him a murderer."

The pain that gripped my chest was sharp and old, nothing like the dull ache I'd been carrying. This one had teeth—grief that had never been processed or even named.

"What I didn't understand was that the doctors would've done it anyway. That the decision my dad made was probably the hardest one he'd ever face."

The lump in my throat swelled until it hurt to breathe. "He did it out of love. Out of mercy. He donated her organs. He spared us weeks of watching her fade."

Tears slid freely now, no point fighting them.

"He never defended himself. Never corrected me. Never told me the facts. He just let me hate him."

"Come here." Eric didn't wait for permission. He pulled me into him, like he'd already decided this was where I belonged.

I let myself lean into him. I hadn't earned this. Didn't deserve the way he held me like I was something worth protecting. I took it anyway.

"We were both drowning," I said, my voice cracking. "But instead of holding onto each other, we just…shut down."

Eric's arm tightened around me, and I curled my legs onto the bench, pressing my cheek to his shoulder.

"He started drinking. I'd come home from school and find him passed out. Sometimes in his own mess." My stomach knotted. "When he wasn't out cold, he was furious. Everything set him off. I cleaned him up when I could. Avoided him when I couldn't. And that became the norm somehow."

Silence settled around us, but my thoughts hadn't stilled.

Coming back here, I was prepared for that version of my

father. For the mess. The quiet dread of walking through the door.

Instead, I'd found a man who seemed…functional. When had he clawed his way out? And how had I missed it?

"Did he hurt you?" Eric's voice wasn't loud, but the words were hard.

"He slapped me once. But the first time he hit me was the last time he ever got the chance."

My chest burned as the memory surfaced. The crack of skin on skin. The sting that lingered long after my face stopped throbbing.

"So you started running to Dylan." It wasn't a question, and it didn't sound like an accusation, either. Eric stated it like a fact. "That was your out."

"Yes. He was my escape." A bitter, breathy laugh slipped free. "I really believed he was going to save me."

God, I'd been so young. So desperate. I'd wrapped my future around a boy who cared more about sneaking booze and getting me into bed than getting me out of anything. He talked pretty, and I'd listened.

Like a fool.

"But he didn't."

"No," I agreed. "He didn't."

He exhaled, slow and measured. "Okay. My turn."

I blinked. "What?"

"You gave me something real." His gaze didn't waver. "More than I expected. Now it's my turn. And if you decide you're done after that, I'll respect it."

"No, Eric. I should just finish. I should tell you everything."

He leaned in, close enough that his breath brushed my cheek. "Hey, beautiful girl, you're stealing my spotlight."

I almost laughed despite myself.

"I'm an unemployed thirty-one-year-old man who, until five

months ago, had my entire life mapped out." The way he said it made it clear he wasn't asking for pity.

"I built that plan myself," he continued, his jaw tightening. "But every step was calculated to meet the expectations I thought my parents had for me. Corporate accounting at my uncle's pharmaceutical company, the right apartment in Manhattan, the right connections. I told myself I was in control, that I was choosing my path."

He dragged a hand through his hair, fingers curling hard at the ends like he needed the pain to keep him present. "But I hated every damn day of it. Manhattan felt like a trap, not an opportunity. I just didn't let myself think about it until Caleb got sick. Then suddenly all that careful planning felt pointless. I'd been wasting my time. My fucking life."

His eyes locked on mine.

"So I walked away. Left the job, the apartment, my friends, everything I'd worked for without a backward glance. My uncle still thinks I'm coming back to work. But I've already decided—I'm done living someone else's version of success."

I pulled back enough to see his face clearly. "There's nothing shameful about that. You're an adult who made a choice. I left home at seventeen because I didn't think I had one."

"Seventeen?" he repeated, brows lifting. "For real?"

"Yeah. My dad pushed me past the point of no return. He threatened me. He threatened Dylan…" I swallowed hard, fear trying to cut off the words. "And my baby."

Eric tensed, his breath held and body tight.

"Dylan gave me an ultimatum. And like an idiot, I went to my father for help."

"What do you mean?"

"Do you remember that picture you were looking at? At my dad's house. The one of the little boy?"

My lips curved despite the tremor in them. My son's grin

flashed through my mind, bright and unstoppable. "That's my son."

The shock on Eric's face cut deep. I'd told myself the omission was harmless. Seeing his reaction proved otherwise.

"Dylan's his father," I said, because there was no turning back now. "When I told him I was pregnant, his reaction wasn't exactly supportive. He made it clear I could keep him or keep the baby. Not both."

Saying it out loud still hurt. And yet, the more I spoke, the stronger I felt.

"I was terrified. So I went to my dad." My fingers dug into my jeans. "He called me a whore and hit me. That's when I packed a bag. Took his car. His credit card. No plan. No goodbye. I just walked out. And I never came back."

"You have a kid?" Eric's voice was calm. Too calm. Something dangerous simmered beneath it.

"Yes." I lifted my chin, even with tears still falling.

"Dylan's the father."

"Yes," I whispered.

"You were a teenager. You stole a car. Left home. And raised a child on your own."

I nodded. "Mostly."

The silence that followed was nothing like before. Not peaceful. Not shared. It pressed in, heavy. Eric stared out over the trees, jaw ticking, breath shallow, like he was holding something back.

I couldn't sit inside it.

I slid out from under his arm and stood. It was a relief to have the truth out in the open. It felt better to be honest. Better to be the real me.

The rest I could survive.

Rejection was familiar. Expected, even. Fake or not, this thing between us had always been fragile. There'd always been an end in sight.

It was time for me to go.

CHAPTER TWELVE

JAMIE

"WHAT THE HELL, JAMIE? WHERE DO YOU THINK YOU'RE going?"

I barely had time to turn before his hand closed around my arm and yanked me back. Hard.

I stumbled, momentum carrying me straight into him. He caught me easily, arm locking around my waist, planting me back onto the bench like he owned every inch of me.

"You think you can just drop that and walk away?" His voice was controlled, but there was an edge to it that sent heat spiraling down my spine. "You think you've ruined something here, so you'll run before you have to face it?"

His grip didn't loosen. Neither did his stare. "What are you so afraid I'm going to see?"

The question pinned me in place.

Was it wrong that this turned me on?

My pulse skidded as I licked my lips, nerves and heat tangling together. His eyes followed the motion, darkening, attention sharpening like I'd just issued an invitation.

He bent close, his mouth brushing my ear. "You are the most

amazing woman I've ever met. Do not even think about walking away from me."

The words shot through me like lightning, igniting every nerve ending along the way.

"Do you have a real boyfriend, Jamie?"

The laugh that escaped me was thin and shaky. "No."

"The guy waiting for you in Toronto—that's your son?"

"Yes." My pulse was racing now. "His name's Hunter."

He pulled back to study me, gaze intense and searching, like he was mapping me from the inside out.

God, I'd never felt more exposed. So stripped bare.

And I didn't hate it.

"When I kissed you before, did you want that?"

My face flamed as a strangled whimper crawled up my throat.

His brow lifted, the corner of his mouth curving. "I'll take that as a yes, beautiful."

"Yes," I breathed.

"Good." His voice dropped to something dangerous. "Would it be alright if I kissed you again?"

"God, yes. Please."

Something broke loose in his expression. A sound rumbled out of him, low and hungry. But he didn't close the distance the way I expected.

Instead, his hands gripped my waist and lifted me with effortless strength, repositioning me before I could process it. Suddenly I was straddling him, legs braced on either side of his thighs.

Heat pooled low as tingles raced through me.

He slid his hands up my sides, unhurried, reverent. Over my ribs. My shoulders. He framed my face, fingers threading into my hair, thumb brushing my mouth like he was testing my reaction.

"You amaze me." His eyes searched mine, intense enough to steal my breath.

I didn't have the clarity to question it.

He drew me down slowly, deliberately, letting the anticipation stretch until it hurt. Just before our mouths met, he stopped, holding me there, breath mingling with mine.

"No more pretending." The command vibrated against my lips.

Then he surged forward and kissed me, leaving no doubt that he meant exactly what he said.

Our mouths met, and my body lit up. Heat snapped through me all at once, like every cell had been waiting for this exact moment.

Strangely, my mind went quiet. No noise. No doubt. Nothing but clean, steady calm as I melted into him.

My fingers slid into his hair, luxuriating in its thickness, one hand trailing down the back of his neck, over the solid span of his shoulders. I knew, with sudden certainty, that if all I ever did was kiss him like this, it would be enough.

His arm locked around my waist and drew me closer, and we sank down against the back of the bench. He took his time, lips moving with intent, tongue brushing mine in a slow, seeking sweep.

I answered without hesitation.

The sound that tore out of me was unfiltered and helpless. Any softness vanished. Eric's mouth turned hungry, demanding. He traced a path along my jaw, down my neck, his breath hot against my skin, leaving me aching.

I felt his need as clearly as my own. It wasn't gentle. It was focused. Urgent.

I pressed closer, unable to stop myself, hips shifting instinctively, chasing friction. His grip tightened as I ground down over his erection, the contact stealing what little control I had left.

This. This was what I'd been craving. The electricity. The heat. The way my body finally made sense.

"Fuck." He broke away, stealing a sharp, final kiss. His hands clamped firmly onto my hips, halting my movements.

"Jamie." His mouth hovered over mine.

I hummed a sound that might've been an answer.

"Beautiful, beautiful girl. You are fucking killing me."

"You said a swear!" The shrill voice hit like an alarm.

I yelped, jerking back in surprise, nearly tumbling out of Eric's arms as I twisted around. He stiffened behind me, attention snapping to the interruption.

A little girl stood there, hands planted on her hips, glaring at us with unmistakable disapproval.

If I hadn't already been flushed from everything that had just happened, I would've been red with embarrassment. "Well, hello there. You scared me half to death."

Eric, entirely unapologetic, still had my leg draped over his lap, one hand secure at my thigh, the other locked around my waist like our audience was only a minor inconvenience. His shoulders shook with silent laughter.

"You said a swear." The little girl's finger stabbed in Eric's direction. "I heard you."

"Me?" His eyes narrowed as if genuinely offended. "Impossible."

"You did. The big one. The one that starts with F. Mommy told me it's not a nice word and you shouldn't never say it."

They stared each other down. A full-on standoff. Alpha male versus pint-sized moral authority.

I glanced around, suddenly aware of how alone we were. Where had this little hellion come from?

"Hey, sweetie," I said, leaning into my friendliest voice. "Is your mommy or daddy somewhere nearby?"

"Nope. Mommy's home with my new brother, Benjamin,"

she announced proudly. "Daddy's carrying Bella up the mountain. I told him I was the fastest. I am."

"You definitely are." Eric's amusement was thick in his voice.

"Kara." A man's voice boomed across the space as a tall, exhausted-looking figure stepped up to the lookout, a squirming toddler balanced on his hip.

Relief and irritation battled across his face when he saw his daughter. "I told you to stay with me." Then his gaze slid to us. To Eric's arm still around my waist. To my leg still very much over his lap.

His expression hardened.

"Come here, Kara. Leave these people alone."

"But Daddy—"

"It's okay." I tried to ease out of Eric's hold.

The man's eyes flicked pointedly to our tangled lower halves. "Perhaps you two could…relocate. I'm sure there are better places to enjoy the birds and the bees."

I jumped to my feet, grabbing Eric's hand and tugging him along with me.

"Daddy, I don't see the bees."

Eric barked out a laugh so loud and sudden I lost it, giggles spilling out of me as we started down the trail.

The man just stared after us, unimpressed, exhausted, and possibly a little envious.

"Thank you. Goodbye." I called over my shoulder.

Eric didn't slow until we were clear of the lookout, fingers still laced with mine, laughter still shaking his chest.

And somehow, even as I fled downhill, embarrassed and red-faced, I was still turned on.

CHAPTER THIRTEEN

ERIC

BY THE TIME WE WERE OUT OF VIEW OF THE LOOKOUT, SHE WAS breathless.

Not from the hike. From laughing.

Jamie had cracked jokes the entire way through the woods. Dirty ones. Creative ones. Delivered without an ounce of shame.

The girl was trouble. Exactly my kind.

And she wasn't taken. No boyfriend. No invisible boundary I had to respect.

Which meant the only thing holding me back was my own fucking restraint. And whatever it was that Jamie wanted. Hopefully, it was the same thing I did.

"I just have to know..." Laughter still bubbled in her voice as we stopped beside a trickling waterfall. "Were you holding my leg over your lap to hide your erection?"

I held her gaze. "It wasn't obvious, was it?"

Her grin widened. "Oh, I noticed. Kara's dad might've been suspicious, but I couldn't tell if that look on his face was disapproval or jealousy."

"You think he was jealous of my poorly timed wood?"

"Oh my God. You brought your own wood to the woods." She doubled over laughing, and I couldn't help joining her. "Seriously, though. You should put up a billboard. You've got a lot to be proud of there."

A sly little smile curved her mouth. Then she winked.

Fuck me. She was complimenting my dick. And she hadn't even seen it in action.

I just stared at her, speechless for once, pulse hammering in my ears.

"I thought I was going to die of embarrassment at first. I've never been caught like that. But it was kind of exciting, wasn't it?"

I stepped into her space, caught her around the waist, and drew her flush against me. Nothing between us but heat and too many layers of clothing.

"You liked that, beautiful girl?" My mouth brushed her ear. "Did getting caught turn you on?"

Her breath hitched. "Yes."

The blush spreading over her neck had nothing to do with the hike. Knowing I'd put it there sparked something prideful and possessive inside me.

My hand slid over her ass, pressing her closer so she couldn't miss what she'd been joking about.

She let out a gasp, and that was all the invitation I needed.

My mouth met hers in a slow, controlled kiss. But I forced myself to pull back before I lost my composure. Because if I let myself take what I really wanted right now, I wouldn't stop.

Jamie's eyes were still closed, lips parted, like she was under a spell.

For a moment, I understood exactly why Dylan kept circling her.

How do you walk away from a woman like this? Even a bruised ego would be worth it.

"I have a lot of memories of this place," she murmured, still dazed. "But I think this one's going to be the second-best."

"Second-best?"

Her eyes snapped open. "Oh shit."

"Too late, beautiful. You brought it up. You owe me the story."

"Our deal?"

"You're catching on."

She looked at me like I was pushing her too far.

Hell, maybe I was. But I was eager for more of her. For the parts she kept hidden. And I wasn't backing off.

She exhaled. "When I was little, I came up here with my family. I wasn't much older than Kara, the language patrol kid." She huffed a laugh. "Honestly, how did her parents manage two more with her around?"

I smiled at her joke but folded my arms and waited.

The scowl she shot me could've scorched bark off a tree.

"Fine," she muttered. "We were on a hike, but I was playing in my own little world. I kept drifting farther behind. My mom was annoyed with me, but she was busy arguing with my sister about hiking shoes that weren't pink enough."

Her voice softened as she talked about them. The bickering. The rhythm of it. The normalcy.

I didn't interrupt.

"My mom lost track of me, and my dad was way ahead, doing his leader-of-the-pack thing."

I reached for her hand without thinking.

"I didn't even notice at first. I just remember looking up and suddenly realizing I was alone."

"Your best memory of this place is getting lost?" The breeze caught a piece of her hair, and I brushed it back.

"That's not the good part." She shook her head, eyes drifting past me to the waterfall. "I was scared for a second. But I remembered what my dad taught me. I stayed put and trusted he'd find me.

"I pretended I was a forest princess on a stone throne. When he showed up, he was my knight. That's why it's my favorite memory. He was my hero."

Her fingers tightened around mine, her smile faltering. "He taught me to be brave and strong, but turns out, he was the thing I couldn't survive."

The ache in her voice settled deep.

She still loved him. That was the part that hurt. Not anger. Not resentment. Love. Even after he'd become something she had to escape.

"He found me that day. But after my mom and sister died... we both got lost. And I think I was supposed to find him this time." Her breath hitched. "I was supposed to save him. Instead, I ran."

Her words splintered. "I ran. And I've felt lost ever since."

She'd decided it was her job to fix him. To carry him. To be stronger than the man who raised her. And when she couldn't, she called it failure.

"You're not lost, Jamie." I didn't soften the words. If I did, she'd twist them into pity. "You took a detour. That's not the same thing."

She looked at me like she wanted to believe it, but believing meant letting go of the blame.

Silence stretched between us—too thick, too unsettled.

I shifted before it could swallow us whole. "Guess I owe you a secret now."

She swiped at her eyes, mouth twitching. "I believe a little secret-telling is in order. Cough it up, big boy."

Big boy.

My grin widened despite myself. "Alright. That billboard idea of yours? I didn't rent space, but my dick's already had its fifteen minutes."

She blinked. "What?"

"An ex took a few photos, then decided to share them. They made the rounds. Ended up on some nude selfie site. She thought it was hilarious."

I hadn't. But that part didn't matter right now.

"Oh my God, Eric. That's awful. Are they still up?"

"Yeah. Once something's online, it stays online."

"And you didn't know she'd taken them?"

"I knew." My jaw tightened. "I just didn't think they'd leave her phone."

Her expression shifted, amusement fading. "That's such a violation."

"It was. But I'm still here."

"Just think of all the creeps who've seen them. Gross." She wrinkled her nose. "What site did you say that was? You know… in case I get bored later."

The laugh that escaped her was bright and wicked. And I liked it a whole hell of a lot.

"You don't need to go digging through the internet. I'm right here. I can give you a private showing. No search bar required."

Her fingers curled into my shirt, tugging me toward her. "Oh really?"

I slid an arm around her neck, close enough to feel her breath catch. My teeth grazed the line of her jaw. "Name the time and place, beautiful."

She laughed and pushed me back a step. But when she looked up, the laughter was gone.

"Eric. This thing with you and me…I don't know what this is."

She held my gaze. "I like you. And I really want to fuck you. But this was supposed to be a fake relationship. I don't know if I'm ready for it to be anything more than that."

My first instinct was to close the distance and take the choice out of her hands. Not because I didn't respect her boundary but because I hated that she thought she needed one.

But she didn't know me. Not really. With the mess we were both standing in and the history she was still carrying, it made sense that she wanted to protect herself.

"You're afraid it'll get bigger than you can handle."

Her chin lifted, defiance flashing. "Of course I'm afraid, Eric. I don't know what the hell I'm doing."

"You don't need to have it figured out." I stepped back into her space, my hand settling at her waist with quiet authority. "In public, I'm your boyfriend. I'll play the part."

I drew her closer until there wasn't room for doubt. "That doesn't mean pressure. Or promises. But we agreed—no more pretending. So don't hide behind the word fake when what you really mean is you're scared. Okay?"

She leaned in, her arms coming up around my neck. "Okay."

"I'm not going to lie to you, Jamie. I probably want you a little too fucking much."

She sucked in a sharp breath, her eyes going wide. Even caught off guard, she was stunning.

Done with negotiating, I leaned in and took her mouth again.

This time, I didn't hold back. Fuck restraint. Forget being careful. I said no more pretending, and I meant it.

She met my lips with enthusiasm, letting out a soft, needy sound that went straight to my cock. Her mouth would either be my death or my salvation—I hadn't decided.

She'd joked about the thrill of getting caught, but I doubted public sex was on the table. I tore my mouth from hers with a low groan and forced a sliver of distance between us. My chest heaved, body already tight and aching.

She looked just as wrecked. Good.

I scrubbed a hand through my hair, adjusted myself without apology, and met her eyes again. "I hope you don't think I'm going to let that other thing you said slide."

Her brow furrowed. "What thing?"

"The part where you said you want to fuck me."

Color climbed back into her cheeks. "Oh."

"Honestly, that's the only part I really heard. Everything else you said was just blah, blah, blah…so much talking."

She laughed, breath still uneven. "Who was talking? I only remember kissing."

CHAPTER FOURTEEN

JAMIE

ERIC DIDN'T QUESTION WHEN I GUIDED HIM OFF THE TRAIL, deeper into the trees.

Even people who thought they loved adventure didn't usually stray this far from the path. But Eric followed without hesitation, stepping over roots and rocks like he trusted me to know where I was going.

This forest and I were like old friends. Getting lost here, intentionally or not, was something I'd done often.

This time, I knew exactly where I was going, but I planned for us to get lost together all the same.

I stepped over a fallen log and ducked beneath the angled trunk that leaned against a rock overhang, creating what looked like the mouth of a cave. It wasn't a cave, but it was a hidden pocket carved out by time and gravity and luck.

The waterfall was close enough that the rush of water still filled the air, soft and constant. But the trees muffled everything else, making it feel private.

Inside, the space narrowed. A curved rock wall rose along one side, evergreens crowding in from the other. The fallen trunk sealed off the entrance behind us, leaving only open sky above.

I'd hidden here as a kid. Cried here as a teen. But I'd never brought anyone with me. Especially not for this.

Eric squeezed in behind me, shoulders nearly brushing the rock, and the space shrank instantly. Or maybe it just felt that way because he took up so much of it.

"Is this your secret clubhouse?"

"Why?" I turned slowly, forcing myself not to react to how all-encompassing his presence was. "Do you want to join my club?"

"Hell yes, beautiful. That's an offer no sane man would refuse. What's the admission price?"

My pulse raced. "Why don't you show me what you've got, and I'll let you know if it's enough."

I slid two fingers into the waistband of his jeans and dragged him closer, popping the button with my thumb. Forget the teasing preamble. I wanted him to know exactly what I was doing.

I'd never been shy about sex. But with Eric, it felt different. I felt bolder somehow, like he'd knocked down some invisible wall and stepped back to see what I'd do with the space.

And what I wanted was to take the lead.

Power hummed low in my veins as I eased his zipper down, watching his face.

God, that look. A little dark, a lot devious, and, best of all, patient.

Until he brought his hand down hard on my ass. Not a slap exactly, but a claim.

He slid his other hand into my hair, fisting it at the base of my skull. Every little tug sent a riot of sensation rippling through me, skittering down my spine and making my nipples pebble.

He wouldn't hurt me. Not unless I asked him to. That conviction steadied the rush, giving me something I could lean into instead of fear.

And it gave me the nerve to keep going, to act like I was

setting the pace, even though we both knew damn well he was the one in charge.

I tugged at his jeans, my gaze dropping to the band of his boxers, pulse thudding, body coiling tight.

"Jamie." His voice rumbled against my ear. "Give me your mouth."

Heat pulsed between my thighs, and I almost sank to my knees. But he was guiding my head up, not down.

I lifted my face and lunged for him.

He caught my mouth in a quick, deliberate kiss, then pulled back to drag his tongue over my bottom lip. When he slid back in, he deepened the kiss with lazy control, taking his time like he had nowhere else to be.

If he thought he could undo me with slow burning desire…he was absolutely right.

My fingers skimmed down his stomach, nails grazing lightly over the hard plane of muscle. His abs flexed under my touch, a subtle reaction I felt more than saw.

But his mouth…

Dear God, his mouth.

It was overwhelming and addictive. Every slow sweep of his tongue, every measured pull of his hand in my hair, kept me right where he wanted me.

Casually, like I wasn't trembling inside, I curved my hand over the elastic of his boxers and worked them down inch by inch, my fingers brushing over his cock as I exposed him.

One second his mouth was on mine. The next, he was breaking away with a growl and grabbing my wrists.

My breath caught as he lifted both my hands over my head and pinned me back against the rock, his body pressing in, locking me in place.

"You first." His breath was heavy, eyes dark.

Keeping my wrists secured in one hand, he dragged the other slowly down my arm. Over my shoulder. Across my collarbone.

His fingertips skimmed the curve of my breast, light enough to tease.

My chest arched toward him, chasing his touch, and his mouth curved into something devilish. His hand came back, full this time, cupping and squeezing until a low moan escaped me.

His hand left my breast on a pained protest that died the moment he reached the hem of my shirt. The second my wrists were free, he stripped it over my head, his gaze never leaving my face.

I wrapped my arms around his neck without thinking, holding him there.

"Look at you." He watched his fingers trail over my skin. "All flushed."

"It's your fault."

"Good. I like it." The corner of his mouth lifted. "You're fucking sexy."

His hand slid down again, dragging the cup of my bra aside before he bent his head. The first brush of his mouth against my nipple sent a sharp pulse straight through me to my aching core.

My fingers fisted in his hair, but he didn't rush.

He took his time, tongue circling, drawing out every reaction, his fingers working the other peak with slow, knowing pressure.

I writhed against him, caught between wanting more and wanting to make it last.

Slow and gentle gave way to something more demanding. His mouth grew more insistent. His grip firmer. The measured control turning rougher as I arched further into him.

"Eric. Oh God. I need… I need…" The words fell apart as his mouth moved up my neck, and whatever grip I had on myself unraveled fast.

"I've got you, beautiful girl. I know exactly what you need."

Before I could catch my breath, he pressed in closer, grinding his hard body against mine, reminding me exactly what I'd started. His hand slid down, possessive and sure, slipping beneath the waistband of my leggings. Heat flared as he pushed past my thong, slicking his hand through my folds, and discovered exactly how worked up I was.

A pleased-sounding growl rumbled through his chest, and I whimpered as he circled my clit.

My hips lifted on instinct, but he didn't let me rush him. He took his time, stroking, teasing, drawing out the ecstasy until I wasn't sure I could handle any more.

By the time he finally pushed one finger, and then a second, inside of me, I was ready to combust.

My fingers dug into his shoulders as he set the pace, watching my face like he was studying every reaction.

The world narrowed to his hand. His mouth at my throat. The solid rock at my back.

"Fuck, that's it, Jamie. Let me feel it."

I barely registered the scrape of stone against my spine or how loud I'd gotten. Nothing existed outside the rhythm he controlled.

Embarrassment didn't stand a chance.

I spread my legs wider, silently demanding more.

He answered by tightening his grip and driving me right to the edge, slow enough to make me beg, steady enough to prove he wasn't losing control.

He had me. And he knew it.

"You like that, beautiful?"

"Yes," I moaned.

I was right there. Balanced on the edge. His voice in my ear, low and filthy, the steady, deliberate way he touched me like he knew exactly how far to push. It wasn't just what he was doing. It was how focused he was. Like my pleasure was the only thing in the world that mattered.

"That's it. Come on my hand, beautiful girl."

The command made my knees week. But I didn't want to leave him behind.

My hand slid between us, finding his hard cock. I wrapped my fingers around him and stroked in rhythm with the pace he'd set, determined to give back even a fraction of what he was doing to me.

His head tipped back slightly. "Fuck. Don't stop."

The sound of his hunger. The weight of his body braced around mine. The pressure building inside me with nowhere left to go.

It was too much.

"Eric—"

My body seized as release tore through me, hard and blinding. Every muscle tightened, then shuddered. I clung to him, riding out the waves as he held me steady, not letting me slip, not letting me collapse.

"That's it. Good girl."

The world slowly came back into focus. My pulse thundered in my ears. My back still pressed to stone. His hand eased away.

But I didn't let go of him. I'd come but he hadn't.

I lifted my head and kissed him, tasting the smug satisfaction on his mouth.

"Your turn," I whispered, and dropped to my knees before he could protest.

With my gaze held to his, I licked him from root to tip, watching as the most glorious man I'd ever laid eyes on took pleasure from my mouth. Arms braced against the rock. Chest rising and falling. Eyes dark and blown wide.

He was too big to take fully, but I hollowed my cheeks and sucked him down until I gagged and pulled back. Then I did it again.

At first, he tried to hold back—one hand in my hair, breathing hard but keeping still. Like he was worried about pushing me too far.

But I didn't want him to be sweet. I liked him dirty. I wanted him real.

"Use me," I pleaded, spit trailing down my chin.

Finally, he let go, the look on his face collapsing to dark, greedy lust. His grip turned rough. His breathing ragged. The controlled pace dissolved into something more instinctual.

He thrust himself into my mouth, forcing me to take what I could.

And God, it was fucking perfect.

I moaned around him and that was it.

The sound of my name in his mouth as he lost it, sent heat straight through me. He tried to pull back at the last second, but I held on, determined to take every drop as he came down my throat.

When it was over, he sagged slightly against the rock, chest heaving, and satisfaction settled over me. The air between us shifted as the rush faded. My skin cooled and pulse steadied.

This was the part that could have turned awkward.

But it didn't.

He looked at me like I was something to be handled carefully now, not because I was fragile, but because the moment mattered. His thumb brushed the corner of my mouth, and then he kissed me without hesitation.

I pressed back into him, kissing him deeper, needing to anchor myself. The contact should have felt simple. This was only meant to be physical—just two bodies working out tension.

So why did kissing him feel like stepping onto something unstable?

The lines weren't supposed to blur. This thing could only be temporary.

I had a son. A life I'd built with careful, deliberate boundaries. The past week had already turned that world into a minefield. One wrong move and everything could detonate.

Wanting Eric the way I did…that was already dangerous.

Feeling anything more than that? That could be catastrophic.

Still, I couldn't pretend this was just sex anymore. Something had shifted. Something that wasn't going to disappear just because we'd both come.

Call it fear. Call it self-preservation. I wasn't ready for anything bigger than this. My life didn't have room for complicated. Not now.

But my body hadn't gotten that memo.

What we'd just done felt like a beginning, not a finish. A taste. Enough to wake the hunger, not quiet it.

My mouth left his on a slow exhale, and his finger traced down the side of my face.

"I think I like being in your club."

A laugh burst out of me, sharp and reckless. I slipped my hand under his shirt and pinched his nipple hard.

"Fuck." He jerked. "That hurt."

"Who said you're in?"

His eyes narrowed in mock offense, but there was heat under it. "I thought an orgasm was the price of admission."

"You thought one would do it?" I smiled as I adjusted my bra, reaching for my shirt where it hung from an evergreen branch.

He stepped closer as I pulled it over my head, crowding my space without touching me. "So what's the buy-in?"

"New deal." I met his gaze. "You get temporary full-time membership, along with all the usual rights and privileges. Revocable at my discretion. But you have to come back to my room at the resort, right now. We skip the hospital until tomorrow."

The playful edge in his expression faded just enough for me to see the calculation behind it. "I can live with that. But one question first."

"Of course."

"How many members are in this club?"

I lifted a brow. "Past or present?"

"Both."

"You really want my entire sexual history right now? That's a heavy conversation for a man I barely know."

"I'd argue you know parts of me pretty damn well." His jaw flexed as he seemed to come to a silent decision. "Fine. Past can wait. But present is non-negotiable."

It wasn't jealousy or insecurity talking. Eric had standards. And even though I was slightly worried about not living up to them, I had to admit I was glad he did.

"That's fair. For almost a year and a half, there's only been one member."

His expression sharpened. "Dylan?"

The name hung between us.

And for the first time since we'd started this little game, Eric wasn't smiling. Maybe there was a hint of jealousy there after all.

"No. Not Dylan."

His hand stilled at my waist.

"Who?" The word wasn't loud and yet it was still an uncompromising demand.

One that sent a whole new surge of heat rushing through me.

"Me. I'm the best partner I've ever had."

I meant it as a joke. Mostly. But despite the slow smile spreading across his lips, the heated amusement lighting his eyes, he didn't laugh.

"I'm serious, Eric. I haven't had sex in almost two years."

"Two years?" His gaze dragged over me like he wasn't just assessing but appreciating. Claiming. "That sounds like a challenge, beautiful girl."

"Does it?" I lifted my chin, stomach flipping. "Funny. It just sounds like honesty to me. No pretending, remember?"

[illegible]

Eventually, and my [illegible] sexual history, right [illegible] One [illegible] baby [illegible]

[illegible]

[illegible]

[illegible]

[illegible]

[illegible]

And for the first time since [illegible]

[illegible]

[illegible]

[illegible]

[illegible]

[illegible]

[illegible]

[illegible]

[illegible]

CHAPTER FIFTEEN

JAMIE

THE CAB OF ERIC'S TRUCK SHOULD'VE BEEN THICK WITH HEAT. Instead, guilt slid up beside me and buckled itself in.

He still looked unfairly good behind the wheel. Forearms flexing as he shifted into gear, jaw set, eyes focused.

If not for the steady hum of the engine and the fact that we were about to merge into traffic, I might've been tempted to climb straight into his lap. Consequences be damned.

But the voice in the back of my mind wouldn't shut up.

It started as a gentle whisper, reminding me to be careful. Then quickly, that little voice became a loud, impatient bitch, shaming my carelessness.

Eric was brushing off time with his brother for me, while I forgot about my own responsibilities. The guilt had been easy to mute when he was touching me. We hadn't even pulled out of the parking lot before I was calculating how long it would be until his hands were on me again.

But that nagging voice wasn't wrong. We couldn't just pretend the rest of the world didn't exist because it felt good to get off with each other.

"If we're not stopping at the hospital. I should probably call and check in."

"Good idea. Set your mind at ease. See if you can get an update for me too." There was no resistance or frustration in his tone. Only support.

And that only made the guilt sharper.

The nurse who answered seemed bored by my concern. My father's condition was the same. He was stable, she said, and they'd call if that changed.

I put the phone on speaker so Eric could hear about Caleb. If he was carrying the same guilt clawing at me, he didn't show it.

Before I could linger on it, his hand settled on my upper thigh. His fingers spread slowly and squeezed. The pressure pulled me right back to thoughts of what we'd been doing earlier, to the way those same fingers had owned my body.

But I still had one more call to make, and I couldn't do it with my mind on sex.

I eased his hand away, not rejecting him, just reclaiming enough space to think. He didn't fight it, understanding more than I said out loud.

Calling Hunter always settled me. Right now, it made the guilt worse.

He answered with his usual explosion of energy. I barely managed a hello before he launched into stories about school, Minecraft, band practice, and subtle campaigning for the dog he was convinced we needed. His voice was bright, and for a moment, the chaos of the past week faded.

Then he asked about me. About the hospital.

"Everything's fine." I hated how automatic it sounded. "How about you? Everything still good with Jackson's parents? Maybe I should speak with them again."

"Everything's fine, Mom. I'm tired though, so I think I'm just going to bed."

My stomach pulled tight.

It was too early. My kid negotiated bedtime like it was a hostage situation. He didn't volunteer for it.

"Okay, bud. But you know, if there's anything you need to talk about, I'm here for you. No matter what. Okay?"

"I know, Mom. I love you."

"I love you too, Hunter. Have a good sleep. I'll talk to you again tomorrow."

But before I could hang up, he called out, "Mom?"

A lump formed in my throat. "Yeah, sweetie. What's the matter?"

"When are you coming home?"

My heart was already cracked from being away from him, but his question finished the job.

All the earlier guilt, the quiet shame about the hospital, about Eric, about distraction, splintered into something jagged. Raw, twisting anguish.

With a tear trailing down my face, I answered, "I don't know yet, but I really miss you. Maybe you should come here for the weekend."

"No, I don't want to. I just miss you. A lot." The smallness in his voice hollowed me out.

"I miss you too. So much."

For a second after the call ended, I just stared at the screen, like I could somehow pull him back through it.

Eric's hand closed around my knee. "You okay, beautiful?"

"Yeah." My voice cracked anyway. "He misses me."

"Of course, he does."

"This is different. I shouldn't have left him there. I'm a horrible mother."

"I have a hard time believing you're anything but a damn good mother."

I shook my head. "You don't know that."

"I know you. And I know you wouldn't have left him unless you had a reason."

A reason.

What was the reason? I couldn't find it. My thoughts spiraled, fast and vicious.

Hunter was my world. My whole entire world. And I'd walked away from him. Left him with people I barely knew. For a week. A fucking week.

My chest tightened.

Oh God.

How long did I have to stay here? What if he needed me right now? What if something happened and I wasn't there?

The tingling started in my fingers. Then my toes. My heart raced, tripping over itself, as my breath came too fast, too shallow.

"Jamie." Eric's voice cut through the spiral. "Goddammit, beautiful. Don't make me pull this truck over. Just breathe."

Shit.

I'd spent years making lists, planning contingencies, worrying about every possible disaster. I hadn't expected anxiety to be the thing that took me down.

Crappy daughter. Horrible mother. Now I couldn't even keep my own body under control.

I dragged in a shaky breath, forcing myself to focus on him.

"It's alright. I've got you. Just keep breathing." His hand stayed firm on my thigh, thumb moving slowly back and forth in a steady rhythm.

I latched onto it, using the consistent motion to help me focus. To center myself. I did what he told me and breathed.

In. Out. In.

"I've got you," he repeated.

Gradually, the pressure in my chest eased. The tingling faded. The world stopped tilting.

When I looked at him, he was still driving, still calm. Simply unwavering.

"Thank you," I whispered as the last tear slipped free.

He shot me a sideways glance. “No need. I can’t have you passing out on me again.”

Despite everything, a breathy laugh escaped me. “I didn’t pass out.”

“No. But you’re carrying too much. You need to let someone help you with it.” His hand squeezed my leg once for emphasis. “You don’t have to do everything alone.”

I stared out the windshield. “Maybe you’re right. I’ve just always felt like it was up to me. Like if I didn’t hold everything together, it would fall apart.”

“What about Dylan?”

“What about him?”

“Hasn’t he taken care of Hunter? Brought him here for visits? Been involved?”

I shook my head. “He visits us three or four times a year. That’s about it. He’s not exactly father of the year. But to be fair, I haven’t made it easy.”

“Bullshit.” His hand tightened on the wheel, knuckles going white. “If I had a kid, nothing would keep me away. Not distance. Not pride. Not a complicated relationship with his mother. You don’t check out on your kid because of inconvenience or hurt feelings.”

From the way Eric had dropped everything to be there for Caleb, I didn’t doubt him. Family wasn’t a talking point for him. It was action.

Hunter deserved that kind of devotion from someone other than me. He deserved a father who showed up without being chased.

“Dylan and I have had similar conversations. But I think it’s harder for him. His parents had a rough marriage—his dad left eventually, and his mom didn’t handle it well. She got remarried, but Dylan’s never been close to his stepdad. He never had the best role models—”

“Don’t make excuses for him,” Eric cut in. “You didn’t have

a perfect blueprint either. You still stepped up. You raised your kid. On your own. That's not an accident."

The conviction in his voice steadied me more than the earlier breathing exercise had.

"And wasn't he part of the reason you ran?"

"Yeah."

"Then stop protecting him from the consequences of that."

How did he always manage to cut straight through the noise in my head? He didn't coddle. He didn't judge. He just… anchored. Being near him felt like stepping into something solid. Like my thoughts lined up better when he was around.

The panic had burned off. The sexual tension had quieted. But he was still there, under my skin in a different way now.

He eased the truck into the resort parking lot. "So, are you bringing Hunter here this weekend?"

"He didn't want to come. So, I don't know."

He killed the engine and turned toward me. "Jamie, if you need help—with anything—you just ask me. Okay?"

I nodded, not trusting my voice to hold steady.

"No matter what happens between us, I'll do what I can for you." He held my gaze. "I mean it. We're friends first. I don't have many. The ones I do, I take care of. That's not conditional."

There it was again. That unwavering thing in him.

I offered him a small, grateful smile, and slipped out of the truck before I did something reckless like reach for him and never let go.

I'd almost made it through the front doors to the lobby when Eric caught up beside me.

"Don't disappear on me yet."

"I'm not disappearing. I'm collapsing."

He huffed a faint laugh. "The bar's open, and my cousin Zane should be on shift."

"Your cousin works here?"

A flicker of something unreadable crossed his face. "Yeah. My family owns the place."

Owns.

The word snagged in my head.

The entire sprawling resort with its polished stone floors, sweeping lake views, and staff who moved like a synchronized orchestra? His family owned all of this?

I slowed without meaning to, suddenly hyperaware of the marble beneath my feet, the crystal chandelier overhead, the understated luxury I'd been too distracted to fully notice before.

He'd said it casually, like mentioning the weather. Like it wasn't a monumental detail that reframed everything I thought I knew about him.

But I was too exhausted to process the implications. Too emotionally scraped raw to follow the thread of what that meant about money, about security, about the vast chasm between the world he came from and the one I'd clawed my way through.

"I am not up for meeting any more of your family right now." Although a drink didn't sound terrible.

"It's not meeting family. It's one drink at the bar with me. And a man who thinks he's God's gift to women. You'll be entertained. I promise."

"Fine. One drink."

The bar sat just off the lobby, all warm lighting and low music. Everything here probably cost more than my monthly rent, but Eric moved through it like he belonged. Because he did. Hell, this place was probably like a second home to him.

Zane spotted Eric immediately and leaned across the polished counter like he'd been waiting for a cue.

"Well, hello there," he drawled when Eric introduced us. "Nice to finally have someone worth looking at. I was tired of this guy's ugly mug."

"Careful. She bites." Eric's hand slid to the small of my back, possessive and sure.

Zane's grin widened. "I'm willing to risk it."

I should have rolled my eyes. Instead, I laughed.

Zane flirted shamelessly while mixing our drinks, inventing outrageous stories about Eric's teenage disasters—stories that took place right here, where he'd spent childhood summers and family vacations with lake views and room service at his fingertips.

Eric didn't rise to the bait. He just sat close, one hand warm and steady at my back, occasionally cutting in with a dry correction that only made Zane louder.

For those few minutes, the hospital felt farther away. The guilt softened at the edges. Hunter's voice in my head quieted to something manageable.

I wasn't spiraling anymore. I was smiling.

When Eric decided time was up, he didn't ask. He finished his drink, thanked his cousin, and guided me toward the elevators.

Zane called after us that he expected a full report later.

Eric didn't dignify it with a response. He just pressed the elevator button and looked down at me, satisfied. "Better?"

And annoyingly, wonderfully, I was. A little tipsy, completely worn out…but better.

The warmth didn't last long. By the time we stepped into my room, the weight of the day settled back into my bones, and my feet dragged across the carpet.

"Why don't we take a hot shower and then get some sleep?" His hands settled on my shoulders.

His thumbs dug in, kneading out tension I hadn't even realized I was holding.

"I don't know if I can stand that long. I know this was my idea, but I'm exhausted."

"I'll hold you up." There was no teasing in it. No room for debate, either.

He took my hand and guided me toward the bathroom before

I could argue, already turning on the water, already in motion. He moved with the assuredness of someone used to taking care of things. Of taking care of people.

He stripped off his shirt, then the rest, efficient and not at all self-conscious.

Even through the haze of exhaustion, the sight of him lit me up. Broad shoulders. Strong back. Muscle shifting under skin with power and purpose. Dark ink covered his entire left shoulder—bold lines and curves that wrapped around the muscle, telling a story I couldn't read from this angle.

With his back to me, he adjusted the water temperature while I let my gaze wander lower, appreciating the view without apology.

He turned and caught me staring. A slow smirk curved his mouth. "You need help over there?"

Before I could answer, he crossed the space between us in a single stride.

I closed my eyes, expecting the brush of his hands.

Instead, I felt fabric loosen and fall. Piece by piece, he undressed me without grazing my skin, without giving me what I expected. The restraint made my pulse jump harder than if he'd touched me.

When the last layer slipped away, I stood there bare, eyes still closed, suddenly aware of everything. My stomach. My hips. The stretch marks, and the C-section scar I rarely thought about until moments like this.

"Jamie." His voice wasn't playful or hungry. It was sure. "Don't hide those pretty blues from me. Open your eyes."

I did.

Slowly, I lifted my gaze from beneath my lashes.

Eric wasn't looking over my body the way I'd feared. He wasn't cataloging flaws or tracing my scar with his eyes. He was looking at my face.

No, it went deeper than that. His gaze held mine with an intensity that made my breath hitch.

"You're gorgeous. You know that, right?"

His fingers tucked a strand of hair behind my ear, then slid down along my jaw, steady and warm. He tipped my chin up, aligning our mouths.

"And I'm not just talking about your body. Though that part of you is pretty damn incredible too."

"Eric," I breathed, half protest, half plea.

"Shh." His thumb brushed my lower lip before he kissed me. "Let's not waste all the hot water."

I'd assumed the shower suggestion came with certain expectations. But I was wrong.

He kept it simple, practical. We washed separately, trading places under the spray. No wandering hands. No escalation. Just the quiet intimacy of shared space.

When he stepped behind me, I tensed on instinct, but his hands slid into my hair and began working the shampoo in with firm, steady pressure. He massaged my scalp like he meant to untangle more than just knots, and by the time he rinsed it out, my muscles had gone slack.

I was barely upright.

But before I could sway, his arm wrapped around my waist, holding me securely as he guided me out of the tub. He wrapped a towel around me and dried me with the same deliberate attention he seemed to give everything.

"Feel better?" he murmured against the shell of my ear.

"Mm-hmm," was all I could manage.

In one smooth movement, he scooped me up and carried me to the bed, laying me down like I weighed nothing at all. I was vaguely aware of him finishing the job with the towel and tucking me under the covers. At some point, the room dimmed. Then my eyes closed.

I didn't notice if he took a moment for himself. I only noticed when he slid in beside me.

A faint, ridiculous voice in the back of my mind scolded me for falling asleep next to a perfect, naked man without taking advantage of the opportunity.

But exhaustion won.

The last thing I registered was the solid warmth of his chest under my cheek, the steady rise and fall of his breathing beneath my ear.

For once, I wasn't alone in the dark.

DAY MINUS 4

CHAPTER SIXTEEN

ERIC

It was past midnight, and Jamie was curled against me, naked and trusting, her breathing deep and even.

This should have been simple. Count the minutes until I could wake her, watch her face transform with pleasure again. Or better yet, sleep. Dream about the way she'd fallen apart for me only hours ago.

Instead, I stared at the ceiling, my mind circling back to her story about being lost in those woods.

Christ, how had she done it? Stripped me bare with a few simple sentences about hiking trails and panic. It was the feeling of being utterly lost without even realizing it, of looking up one day and not recognizing anything around you.

Every word had hit like a physical blow because it was my fucking life in a nutshell.

I'd spent years building what everyone called the perfect life in Manhattan. When I walked away from it all, I told myself I was finally free. But I'd just traded one cage for another. Instead of chasing someone else's definition of success, I'd thrown myself into being the perfect caretaker, the reliable brother, the one who held it all together.

I'd been so busy taking care of everyone else that I'd never stopped to ask what I wanted.

Until now. Until her.

Jamie had somehow opened a door I didn't even know was locked. Every moment with her felt like stepping into sunlight after years underground—first in Manhattan's shadows, then under the suffocating weight of responsibility.

The fear. The anger. The long, numb stretch of living on autopilot. It all dropped away.

With her, I felt present.

Fucking alive.

Was it possible for a blow job to lead to an epiphany? Ridiculous sounding, but here I was, feeling like I'd experienced a seismic shift in my existence.

At some point, while I was still dissecting my own existence like a damn philosopher, sleep must have taken me.

I woke to soft morning light filtering through the curtains and Jamie's spectacular ass cradling my semi-hard cock.

"Mmm…" Jamie moaned, low and throaty.

I swept her hair off her shoulder and leaned in to kiss the curve of her neck. Her skin was like silk, and she smelled like honey and desire and everything I wanted to wake up to for the rest of my life.

The thought should have scared the hell out of me. Instead, I filed it away and focused on the woman in my arms.

I trailed light kisses up her neck while my hand moved in the opposite direction, skimming down her arm, her hip, grabbing a handful of that perfect ass I couldn't stop thinking about.

When she moaned again, I brought my lips to her ear. "Good morning, beautiful girl."

She tilted her head back, sleepy and pliant, offering her mouth without opening her eyes.

I took it.

Her kiss was pure seduction. It started slow, still heavy with sleep, but within seconds, her tongue was pushing into my mouth like she couldn't get enough.

Yesterday, she'd been the one calling the shots, and I'd loved watching her take what she wanted. Nothing was sexier than a woman who wasn't afraid to demand pleasure.

But this morning? This morning was all mine.

I took control of the kiss, my hand tightening in her hair. She made a sound of approval that shot straight to my cock.

Grabbing her hip, I pulled her back toward me, grinding against her ass. The friction was phenomenal, but I needed more.

I slid my hand between her legs, running my fingers over her pussy, lightly circling her clit before dipping down to tease her opening. When I found her wet and ready, satisfaction rolled through me.

I broke away from her mouth. "I need you now, beautiful girl."

It wasn't a request.

Jamie opened her eyes, pinning me with a look of pure need, and lifted her leg over my thigh, opening herself to me.

She was so small in my arms, but her body fit against mine like we'd been designed for each other. I kissed her again while my hand drifted up to tease her nipple with feathery touches.

Her breathing turned ragged, little moans escaping with each touch.

"You want me?" I circled the tight peak of her breast.

"Yes," she breathed.

I dragged my cock through her wetness, coating myself, making her gasp. She was so slick and hot, I wanted to bury myself inside her and never come out.

But then reality crashed in.

No condom.

How the fuck had I forgotten? I'd never been this careless, never lost control like this. Not with so much at stake.

Jamie noticed my hesitation, her hands grasping at my dick, trying to guide me home.

"Stop." The command was too sharp, but I needed her to listen. "We need a condom."

She froze, and for a moment we just breathed together, suspended between need and responsibility.

"Oh. I have some." She bolted upright. "Let me get them."

She was up and gone before I could respond, and I watched that gorgeous ass jiggle as she ran for the bathroom.

Fuck, I needed her back here, now.

She returned in seconds, bouncing onto the bed with a strip of condoms. "Here. My doctor always gives me samples. I keep telling her I don't need them, but I'm going to thank her next time."

I ripped one off and tossed the rest across the mattress. "You can thank her for me too."

Jamie sat back on her heels, watching intently as I rolled the condom on. Her lust-filled eyes tracking my every movement made my cock twitch.

"Come here," I commanded, my voice rough with need. "Right back where you were."

Her smile was sin incarnate as she slowly crawled the short distance on her hands and knees. Like a cat, she arched her back and stretched out beside me, pushing that perfect ass toward me.

She was gorgeous. And right now, she was all mine.

I pulled her tightly against me, earning a yelp that quickly became a moan of satisfaction.

Now Jamie was the impatient one, throwing her leg over my hip, grinding against my straining cock.

"Take me," she gasped, tilting her head to look at me. "Don't hold back. Just take me."

Her permission unleashed something primal in me. "You want it hard and fast?" I guided myself to her entrance, barely holding back.

"God, yes."

I lifted her leg higher and began pushing into her heat. Slowly. Inch by fucking inch. The torture was exquisite.

With her eyes closed and mouth open, Jamie cried out as I filled her.

Tight, wet, and perfect, she felt like home wrapped around me. I pulled out slowly, gripped her tighter, and pushed in again. Slow and deep. She was trembling, her sounds of pleasure pushing me to the edge of my control.

I wanted to pound into her like an animal, but the slow burn was building something devastating between us. Something that would shatter us both when we let go.

When I slicked my fingers through her wetness and began rubbing her clit, her eyes flew open, breath catching.

"You like that, beautiful?"

"Yes, Eric, don't stop. Please."

"I thought you wanted it hard and fast?" I kept my rhythm slow and steady. "Change your mind?"

"I don't care. It feels good. Don't stop."

"Good girl. Hang on tight." I kissed her deeply, our tongues tangling, stoking the fire burning through my veins.

Then, without warning, I rolled us both to our knees. Keeping her back to my front, I sat on my haunches and pulled her down over my lap, her legs falling to either side of mine as I impaled her.

Her cry was loud and lustful. Exactly what I wanted.

My hand returned to her clit as she rocked over me, taking everything I gave her. Her cries turned sharp and desperate as I met her thrust for thrust.

She was close—her body tensing, her head falling back to my shoulder.

I bit her neck and growled against her ear. "That's it, beautiful girl. Come on my cock."

I pulled her hair, turning her face toward me as I took her mouth.

She exploded.

Unable to maintain the kiss, Jamie's head fell back as she screamed her release.

She was still shaking when her orgasm triggered mine. But I had other plans.

I pulled out and pushed her flat to her stomach in one smooth motion, ripping off the condom so I could mark that amazing ass with my cum.

"Don't move." I leaned down to kiss her cheek. "I'll clean you up."

When I returned with a warm cloth, Jamie was giggling.

"What's so funny?"

"My God, Eric. We just woke up the entire hotel. It's only six-thirty, and you had me screaming like the building was on fire."

"Maybe we did set it on fire. It's still pretty hot in here." My face hurt from smiling.

This playful side of Jamie was everything I didn't know I needed. Her quick wit and easy laughter made me think life with her would be an adventure worth taking.

Life with her. The thought settled in my chest like it belonged there.

My existence had been about surviving day to day, not making plans beyond Caleb's next procedure. Thinking about the future had been too overwhelming.

But Jamie made me want to plan. Want to hope. Want to believe that maybe, just fucking maybe, I could have something good.

After cleaning her up, I trailed kisses up her shoulders and neck. She rolled over, pulling me down for a kiss that was soft and deep and perfect.

"I'm sorry about the condom situation." I searched her eyes. "I've never been that careless before."

"Neither have I. We both got carried away."

"I trust you completely, but I can't take chances. Not with—"

"I understand. And just so you know, I'm extremely careful with birth control. Hunter was...well, I had no backup protection. One condom malfunction later and I was pregnant."

"Thanks for telling me. But this isn't about trust. It's about being responsible for both of us."

The way she looked at me then, like I was someone worth trusting with her life, hit me hard. Considering the men in her past, her willingness to believe in me was staggering.

I cradled her face. "Do you want to try sleeping for a few more hours?"

"No."

"Breakfast?"

"No." She sighed contentedly. "I just want to stay here with you. Like this."

"Escaping reality?" I understood the appeal. Right now, this felt like the safest place in the world.

"Maybe. I just like the way you make me feel." A wicked smile bloomed on her face. "And I like the way I can make you feel too."

"Really? Tell me more."

She pushed against my chest, rolling me to my back before straddling my waist. The demanding, take-charge Jamie was back, and I was already halfway hard again.

"I want to ride you until I come again," she purred, squeezing me between her thighs. "Then I want to suck you off…you can come on my tits this time."

Christ, this woman. "Sounds perfect. But here's what's going to happen first."

Her eyebrows raised at my tone, and I felt her grow wetter against me.

"First, you're going to sit on my face. I'm going to lick your pussy until you scream some more. We'll wake up anyone who managed to sleep through round one." I gripped her hips, already guiding her where I wanted her. "Then you can ride me however you want. Deal?"

Her smile turned feral. "Deal."

She started moving up my body, and I felt like I was about to receive communion. When I finally got my mouth on her, all my earlier thoughts were confirmed. She was like honey, the sweetest thing I'd ever tasted.

I treated her like my last meal, feasting on her, fucking her with my tongue, devouring her with my lips. She came so hard she pulled my hair, her legs locking around my head, her body shaking with aftershocks.

And she did it all while screaming my name.

CHAPTER SEVENTEEN

JAMIE

Playing hooky had never felt so good.

It shouldn't have. Skipping out on our responsibilities bordered on reckless. The things we were avoiding were literally life or death.

But wrapped up with Eric, it was easy to forget the world outside those four walls.

We'd already spent the morning tangled together, and I lay there now, loose and warm, my body pleasantly spent. I kept waiting for awkwardness to creep in, for that sharp reminder that this had been way too impulsive.

It never came. If anything, being with him felt easier the longer we stayed in bed.

How many more hours could we steal away?

Eric shifted beside me, his wide chest rising and falling with each heavy breath. Despite the soreness between my legs, that simple movement sparked need all over again. The brush of his thigh against mine. The slow stretch of his arm above his head.

God, everything this man did turned me on.

Was this how addicts felt, always craving another hit?

Maybe it was the result of going without sex for so long. Or maybe this was simply what happened after being with Eric, experiencing intimacy the way it was meant to be.

My stomach growled loudly, cutting straight through my spiral of thoughts.

"Sounds like it's time to feed you again." Eric laughed and slid an arm around my waist, drawing me closer before kissing me, his smile lingering against my lips.

I kissed him back and swung my leg over his hip, fitting myself against him without hesitation. When our mouths finally broke apart, I murmured, "If I had to choose between food and sex, I'd probably starve."

"Sex in general?" His hand trailed over the curve of my ass, igniting another wave of desire.

"Well, sex in general is nice, but ice cream usually wins that battle. No, I meant sex with you. In that case, Rocky Road doesn't stand a chance."

His grin spread wide, dimples flashing, blue eyes bright. That smile warmed me in a way that had nothing to do with lust. It reached deeper, pulling something tight inside my chest.

He shifted us smoothly, rolling me onto my back and settling between my thighs with quiet authority. He was hard again, and I couldn't help the satisfied breath that left me.

"Luckily, no one's making us choose." He reached for a condom from the bedside table.

Unhurried, he rolled the condom on like it was a strip tease in reverse, before returning his focus to me. "You feel so fucking good." He groaned, pushing into me.

"You do too. Amazing." My breath hitched as he buried himself deep inside me.

"Let's never leave this bed. Let's just do this forever."

Forever.

I'd thought it too, in passing. In reckless flashes. But hearing him say it out loud sent a jolt of panic running through me.

Forever meant always, and permanence was only a fantasy.

Nothing ever lasted. Not family, not safety, not love. God, we weren't even in a real relationship. We'd agreed no plans or promises.

This thing between us—fake or not—would eventually have to end.

"I don't know about forever. But we've got today." I pulled him closer, needing the weight of him, the certainty of this moment and nothing more.

"Fucking right we do." His hips punched forward, his cock hitting deep. "Better make good use of the time."

What was slow and steady turned urgent, almost defiant. Not frantic but driven. Like we were trying to outrun the ticking clock neither of us wanted to acknowledge.

His control didn't disappear. If anything, it sharpened. Every movement was deliberate. Every glide of his cock, every stroke of his hand, intentional.

He wasn't chasing his own release. He was focused on mine.

I tried to stretch it out, to savor it, but the build was relentless. And as the orgasm ripped through my body, I screamed.

"Fuck, yes," Eric shouted.

His own release followed close behind, his breath ragged against my skin as he held me through the last of the tremors.

For a few suspended seconds, there was nothing but us. Heat, heartbeats, and the illusion that the world outside didn't exist.

Then a door slammed somewhere nearby.

The spell cracked.

"I don't want to hear any more of your excuses, Rick," a woman's voice snapped from just outside our door. "There's always an excuse."

"Sweet Pea, you know it's not an excuse," a man shot back, voice defensive and tired. "I didn't get any sleep. What do you expect?"

"Once. Just once. I expect something other than

disappointment. I want you to make me scream like the chick we heard this morning. You've never done that for me. She gets it three times in one damn day. Me? Not once."

She stormed off down the hall, leaving her man, Rick, mumbling to himself about sleepless nights, men who used Viagra, and wives who watch too much reality TV.

I buried my face in Eric's shoulder, shaking with laughter.

In my head, I pictured Rick standing outside our door, debating whether to knock and start a fight or ask for tips.

A few seconds later, footsteps shuffled past, and a low, irritated, "Thanks a lot, asshole," carried through the wood.

"Oh my God," I gasped between laughs. "Did that actually just happen? We're absolutely getting kicked out."

Eric was laughing too, with one arm draped over his eyes. "Relax. My family owns the place—remember? Poor bastard probably doesn't even know who to complain to. I do feel a little guilty for making him look bad, though."

"You make every man look bad."

"If you keep saying shit like that, Jamie, I'm going to have no choice but to throw you down and prove myself all over again."

"What? It's a compliment. What on earth do you think you have left to prove?"

"I'm a man. There's always something to prove." The way he said it made heat curl through me.

"Save it for later." I forced myself to sit up. "You wore me out. I'm going to feel this for a week."

He watched me as I swung my legs over the edge of the bed, the humor fading from his expression. "Where are you going?"

"I need a shower." I stretched carefully, my muscles protesting. "I plan to be fully clothed when the manager comes knocking. And you promised me breakfast."

"I did?"

"Well, it was implied. Unless you plan on going naked, I suggest you hop in the shower with me."

Eric seemed just as worn out as I felt. The cocky comments about proving himself disappeared the second we stepped under the hot spray.

We moved leisurely, not worrying about complaints being issued to hotel management. In fact, I wasn't worried about anything.

Three rounds of sex. Two showers. One night wrapped up naked together. Somehow, it had reset me. The problems waiting outside that room hadn't vanished, but they didn't feel as suffocating anymore.

The only things missing from this perfect start to the day were coffee and Hunter's smiling face.

I still missed him fiercely, but the panic had eased. It wasn't the sharp, breathless fear it had been before. This was a week, not a lifetime. Parents sent their kids to camp for entire summers. I could survive a few days.

And if I was honest, the anxiety hadn't been only about whether he needed me.

Hunter depended on me, yes. That was natural. But somewhere along the way, I'd started depending on him too. On his company. On the way our routines filled my days. He hadn't just been my responsibility. He'd been my comfort. My only real friend.

That wasn't fair to him. Or to me.

One day soon, he'd be a teenager with his own priorities. A life that didn't revolve around his mom. I couldn't cling to him as my only source of happiness and expect it to end well.

As risky and self-indulgent as it felt to want something beyond my obligation to my son, maybe it was necessary. Maybe taking care of myself didn't have to distract from being a good mother.

Maybe it could make me a better one.

The shower left me clearheaded, steadier than I'd felt in days.

Eric and I moved around the room, gathering my things. We completed the task in silence, oddly in sync. He grabbed my razor and toothbrush from the bathroom, without me asking. I glanced under the bed while he cleared the nightstand. We worked side by side in quiet rhythm, no awkwardness, no missteps, just easy coordination.

It might've been melodramatic, but moving beyond that room felt like taking the next step—a step forward.

In the elevator, Eric slipped his hand into mine. His grip was warm, steady, and certain. He didn't say anything about the future, didn't make promises. He just held on. And I let him.

And yes, I was absolutely thinking about breakfast. I was starving.

CHAPTER EIGHTEEN

ERIC

MIRACULOUSLY, WE GOT JAMIE CHECKED OUT WITHOUT A SINGLE complaint to management.

The desk clerk shot me a look I couldn't decipher—probably recognition, since most of the staff knew exactly who I was—but I didn't care to analyze it. Focusing on anything other than Jamie was pointless.

Every word, every smile, every tiny expression captivated me. I was obsessed.

Especially after spending the morning in bed with her. Hell, fucking her might've only made it worse.

After securing her bags in the back of my truck, we climbed in, ready to head to the café Jamie insisted had the best coffee around.

"Well, that was awkward," Jamie said as we pulled away from the resort.

"What was?"

"Seriously? The way that clerk was flirting with you?"

"She was? I didn't notice. I was just happy we got you out without any trouble."

The tension radiating from her was palpable. "Eric, she asked you for your phone number."

"Isn't that normal for a hotel?"

"Why would that be normal? You weren't even on the guest list. The room was under my name, and they already had my number." Her voice sharpened, a hint of possessiveness creeping in that sent a thrill through me. "And I can assure you she did not lick her lips like that when she asked for my ID at check-in."

I grinned as I pulled into the café parking lot. "Huh. I guess it's a good thing you wouldn't let me give it to her, then."

"Wait." She studied my face. "She knew who you were, didn't she?"

"Maybe."

She turned away from me with a huff and got out of the truck, slamming the door. "Still didn't give her the right. Lecherous whore. What kind of woman does that? Hits on a man who's clearly taken?"

Taken. Christ, she had no idea how right she was.

Panic flickered across her face after the words left her mouth. "Not that you're taken. I didn't mean it like that."

"I don't know..." Heat rushed through me at the thought of her wanting to claim me. "I seem to recall something about a secret club. If I remember correctly, I was given full rights and privileges as part of my membership."

I caught her around the waist, pulling her to my side. "I'm all yours as long as you want me, beautiful."

She smiled and ducked her head, color rising in her cheeks. I pulled her closer as we walked into the café, and she settled against me like we'd done this a million times.

After the last twenty-four hours, telling Jamie I didn't want anyone else felt natural. How could I possibly want another woman when she was around?

The only thing I wanted was more of her—her mind, her

body, and perhaps a piece of her soul to keep when it came time for her to leave.

She hadn't lied about the coffee. It was better than average, and after days of hospital sludge, it hit the spot. With bagels and coffee filling us up, I relaxed again.

Not that I'd forgotten the obligations waiting at the hospital. I could never forget about Caleb, but my worry over him felt less consuming. A sense of optimism hung in the air.

Somewhere deep inside, I believed he'd be okay.

"So, what's the plan for today?" I reached across the table, needing the contact of her fingers against mine.

"I don't know. Shouldn't we be heading back to the hospital?"

"Well, I was thinking…" I rubbed my thumb across her knuckles, anchoring myself to this moment instead of the sterile hell waiting for us. "My brother and sister should be here by now. Caleb's going to have company all day, and he's still got four more days until his transplant. Once we hit Day Zero, I won't be able to leave. He'll be in isolation, but I'm going to be caged in that hospital for days, possibly weeks."

"Day Zero?"

"Transplant day. We're on a countdown. Like we're dropping a fucking bomb or something." The bitter laugh that escaped me held no humor. Four days. Four days of pretending I wasn't fucking terrified.

"Well, that's ominous, isn't it?" Jamie winced at her own words. "Sorry, I'm just ignorant to the whole thing. You say transplant, and I picture blood-dripping organs, ice packed into coolers."

"It's a bone marrow transplant. He'll get an infusion into his center line—that big ugly catheter tube sticking out of his chest. And then we sit and wait, hoping the stem cells start making new white blood cells for him."

"And he has to be in isolation?" Her hand tightened around mine.

"For a while. Infection is a big risk. It's all a waiting game. He'll probably need blood transfusions and antibiotics as well. But it takes weeks before the new cells start to form."

Her eyes grew wide. "Wow. He's such a brave kid."

Braver than me. I was the one running away, stealing time with her when I should be holding vigil at his bedside.

But what good was I doing there? Sitting in that chair, watching him sleep, counting down to Day Zero like some kind of death march?

"He is." I forced myself to meet her eyes. "But my point—until Day Zero, I'm kind of useless. Maybe you and I could spend more time together. We could stay out in the world a little longer. The hospital will still be there tomorrow."

The words felt like both confession and justification. I needed her to understand that this wasn't abandonment. It was survival.

"I like the sound of this idea, but I'd really like it if you'd call Caleb first, just to be sure."

So, I did. When Caleb heard I'd be spending time with Jamie, he responded, "You better be talking about me the whole time." He also made me promise to bring her by first thing the next morning.

The relief that flooded through me was immediate. My little brother was giving me permission to be human.

Maybe it was irresponsible. Maybe my optimism was misplaced. Hell, I could've been in complete denial.

I didn't care.

Part of my daily routine was focusing on what mattered. Today, spending time with Jamie felt crucial. Knowing our secret club meeting could end just as quickly as it began drove me to make the most of the moment.

The sun was shining. The spring weather was more like early summer. Life outside the hospital was vibrant and active.

I needed this. I needed to feel like a real person instead of a zombie. I needed to watch Jamie as she shed her fears and anxieties, stepping into the world of the living.

The world of the sick and dying would still be there, waiting. Jamie and I weren't dead yet. We just needed to remind ourselves of that.

When I suggested the beach for our next excursion, Jamie agreed without hesitation. I wanted to see the Bay up close.

I hadn't been to the shore once in the five months since I'd moved here. Considering my parents' home was only a fifteen-minute walk from the beach, it felt ridiculous that I hadn't managed the trip.

"Do you think it's too early for swimming?" I stood on the boardwalk, looking out at the smooth, calm waters.

"Umm, yeah. You'd freeze your nuts off." Her tone was saucy, like she thought I should've known better.

"You make it sound so enticing." I laughed, but the sun was hot against my back, and the water looked tempting. Irresistible, even. "I think I'm going to chance it."

"What?"

I was already pulling my shirt over my head, enjoying the way her eyes tracked the movement. "Come on, how many opportunities do you get to do something fun like this?"

"Fun? You think jumping into an ice bath is fun? Eric, there's no way you're dragging me into that water."

"Jamie, Jamie, Jamie." I stepped closer, watching her pupils dilate. "I'll make a deal with you."

"No. No more deals." But her voice lacked conviction, and she didn't move away when I invaded her personal space.

"I seem to recall our last deal worked out in your favor. How many orgasms were involved? Three or four?"

"Eric." She looked around, as if someone might be listening. "That was different. Besides, our last deal worked out in your favor too. I highly doubt this one will be enjoyable for either of us."

"So quick to assume. You know what they say about assumptions…" I could see her preparing to object, so I reached out, catching her chin between my fingers. "You can always say no, but you have to hear my offer first."

The way she melted into my touch sent satisfaction coursing through me.

"The deal is, you agree to get in that water with me." I held up my hand, stopping her protest. "You only have to go up to your knees. If you make it that far with me, then later, when we head over to your dad's place, I'll help you make some new memories of your childhood home."

She looked skeptical, so I leaned closer, my thumb brushing across her bottom lip. "We could give that cozy little twin bed of yours some action. I bet I can fuck you hard enough to break it. Want to find out?"

She was blushing again, and I refused to believe it was just the sun's heat. She sucked her bottom lip between her teeth, and if she wasn't careful, I'd be dragging her into the water and trying to make her come at the same time.

"Well, beautiful? What do you say to that deal?"

"I think you've got your work cut out for you. My childhood bed is a double, not a twin." She practically moaned the words.

We raced each other to the shore, tossing our shoes and socks aside. When we reached the water, Jamie stalled to roll up her pant legs, but I hoisted her over my shoulder, carrying her in as she squealed.

Only seconds later, I wanted to squeal too. "Shit, it's cold."

Jamie only laughed. Perched over my shoulder, she was unaffected by the frigid temperature.

It felt like a million tiny knives were poking at my legs, but I refused to back down, plowing on until the water reached my knees.

"What's the matter? Is the water a little chilly?"

"Why don't you find out?" I grunted, tipping forward and dumping her into the lake.

I made sure she went in feet first—I wasn't a complete asshole—but she stumbled on the landing, her ass hitting the water before I could steady her.

"Motherfucker. That's fucking cold."

It was the foulest language I'd heard from her, and it was adorable. But I was in just as much pain as she was. My balls were nowhere near the water, but they were in jeopardy of freezing off, just like she'd predicted.

"Sorry." I stepped toward her, determined to carry her back out of the ice, but the little devil splashed me, right in the face.

"Oops, sorry." Her giggles were infectious.

That was it. Deal or no deal, she was going to get it. But when I bent to splash her back, she took off running.

"I don't think so." My height advantage made it easy to catch her.

Scooping her back into my arms, I ran toward the beach, kicking up as much surf as possible and soaking us both in the process.

Our antics and laughter attracted an audience. As we made it back to the sand, we were greeted with looks of bewilderment and humor.

One asshole leered at Jamie in her wet T-shirt. I caught his eye and held it. Whatever he read there made him decide he had somewhere else to be.

Most of the other onlookers dispersed after realizing we were okay, but an older couple lingered, watching as we shook ourselves off like wet dogs and jumped around to warm up.

"Looks like you were having fun," the lady called.

"I'm not sure if getting hypothermia can be classified as a good time." Jamie laughed.

The lady ignored Jamie's sarcasm and turned to her husband. "Remember when we used to fool around like that?"

"What do you mean? I chased you around the condo just last night." He winked.

"Oh, yes. That was fun. Still, it's nice to see young people being so carefree," she said as they wandered away.

Carefree?

Was this what Caleb raved about—living in the moment? If so, I wanted a whole fucking lot more of it.

Watching Jamie pull her wet hair into a messy knot, that delirious smile lighting up her face, I felt something I'd almost forgotten existed. Pure happiness. The kind that had nothing to do with responsibility or obligation or keeping everyone else afloat.

It wasn't possible for Jamie and me to be completely carefree with so much waiting for us in the real world. But for now, everything felt right. As long as we kept the darkness at bay, we could have this.

Taking Jamie's hand in mine, I led her back up the beach to the boardwalk. "Come on, beautiful girl. I owe you."

CHAPTER NINETEEN

JAMIE

ERIC SPENT THE REST OF THE DAY IN FULL REDEMPTION MODE after his water torture.

Not that I minded. I'd survived plenty of polar bear dips growing up, dared by friends who thought ice water was the ultimate test of courage. May was practically tropical compared to those January plunges.

But Eric looked so determined to atone for his sins, his protective instincts kicked into overdrive every time I so much as shivered. Who was I to deny him the chance to play knight in shining armor?

Despite my protests, he bought a sweater just so he could wrap it around my shoulders, his hands lingering possessively at my collar as he adjusted it. The way he watched me—intense, focused, like I might disappear if he looked away—sent warmth spiraling through my chest.

We wandered Copper Ridge for hours, with his fingers laced through mine. Every few blocks, he'd pull me closer, his arm sliding around my waist with casual ownership that made my pulse skip.

The town had grown in my absence. New storefronts lined

streets I used to know by heart. Unfamiliar faces moved through spaces that once belonged to childhood friends.

But underneath the changes, something fundamental remained untouched. The rhythm of it, the way afternoon light slanted across Main Street. All of it wrapped around me like a memory brought to life.

And a dangerous sense of belonging I'd spent years trying to bury surfaced.

Eric must have sensed my mood shift because he stopped mid-stride, turning me to face him.

"You okay?" His thumb traced my cheekbone, the simple touch grounding me.

"Yeah. Just remembering."

His eyes darkened with understanding, and he pulled me against his chest, his chin resting on top of my head. The protective gesture was so natural, so right, that I let myself melt into him.

We talked about everything and nothing. Music, movies, the historic romance novels I couldn't stop reading. Eric's knowledge of bodice-ripper terminology was both impressive and mortifying.

"Seriously, how do you know the term throbbing manhood?" I demanded, heat flooding my cheeks.

His grin was wicked. "My college roommate had a girlfriend who left her books everywhere. I might've read one or two." He leaned closer, voice dropping in an intimate way that made my pulse race. "And now that I know you're into them, I might just read a few more."

The conversation drifted naturally from the lighthearted to the serious. Hunter. My job. The way my boss treated me like I was disposable. Eric's expression darkened as I spoke, his jaw clenching whenever I mentioned the man.

"He has no right to treat you like that." Eric's voice carried an edge that made me shiver. "You deserve better."

The fierce protectiveness in his tone made my stomach flutter. No one had ever been angry on my behalf before. The feeling was intoxicating.

We avoided the heavy topics by unspoken agreement—cancer, uncertain futures, what came next.

Instead, we kissed. A lot.

Against storefronts, on park benches, wherever Eric decided he needed to taste me. Each kiss felt like a claim, his hands framing my face or fisting in my hair with barely restrained hunger.

By the time we made it back to my father's house, I was drunk on his attention.

The kitchen felt different with Eric's presence filling the space. He moved around me with purpose. His body heat a constant presence as we searched for dinner ingredients. Every casual touch felt exhilarating. His hand on my lower back as he reached around me. His fingers brushing mine as he passed me something.

"Here." He handed me Mom's old yellow colander, his fingers covering mine for a beat longer than necessary.

"God, this thing's indestructible. I think it was my grandmother's."

"Must've been the era. Mine had the same one." Eric was already rummaging through drawers with the confidence of someone who belonged here. The domesticity of it stole my breath.

We moved around each other like we'd done this dance a hundred times. His hip bumped mine as he reached for plates. I pressed against his back, inhaling his scent while he stirred sauce. When I stretched to reach the pasta bowls, his hand settled on my waist, steadying me.

This felt dangerous. Too easy. Too right.

At the breakfast bar, Eric claimed the stool next to mine, pulling it close enough that our thighs pressed together. His arm brushed mine every time he reached for his water. When he leaned forward to take a bite, his shoulder bumped against me. Every time he lifted his fork, I watched the muscles in his forearms flex.

The man was pure temptation, and he knew it.

"Have you thought more about what you'll do with this place?"

The question hit like a cold splash of reality. I wasn't ready for this conversation, wasn't ready to think about owning this house or what that would mean.

"Nope." I turned the tables before he could push. "What about you? You've told me you don't want to go back to work for your uncle, but what do you want? What's in your future?"

Eric shifted, his discomfort obvious. Good. He could squirm for once.

"I haven't allowed myself to really think that far ahead."

"There's got to be something. What did you want before you got all responsible?" My teasing smile masked genuine curiosity.

"Nothing serious. I liked art."

I waited, eyebrows raised. When he just sat there looking smug, I leaned forward.

"That's it? Come on, Eric. I entertained all your job advice. Don't I deserve more than *I liked art*?"

His deep chuckle vibrated through me. "Fine. Photography, mostly."

Still holding back. The man enjoyed riling me up, making me beg for more. When I maintained my patient smile, he sighed and raked his fingers through his hair.

"I loved taking pictures." His voice dropped, becoming reverent. "Something about being behind a lens. Seeing the world through a hidden eye. You might see something every day, but when it's captured with the right light, the right angle, on the right film, it becomes something new. I could tell whole stories with a single shot. Create new realities."

The passion in his voice, the way his eyes lit up. This was Eric stripped bare. Not the corporate drone or the dutiful son, but the artist he'd buried beneath obligation.

"I'd love to see your work."

"I haven't touched a camera in years. There's nothing to show you."

"Take one now." I nodded toward his phone.

He laughed, the sound rough. "With that?"

"Why not?"

Eric studied me, something shifting in his expression. When he looked at his phone then back at me, heat flared in his eyes. "Okay. But you're going to be my subject."

My stomach dropped. Me and cameras were natural enemies. I always looked ridiculous.

Eric must have read my hesitation because he stood, suddenly towering over me. His hand wrapped around my wrist, not quite gentle, and pulled me to my feet.

"Come on." His voice was pure command, leaving no room for argument. "You're going to lose some of those clothes."

My forgotten dinner seemed irrelevant as I let him lead me toward my bedroom, my pulse hammering at the promise in his voice.

CHAPTER TWENTY

JAMIE

EVEN WITH A SIMPLE PHONE CAMERA, ERIC'S PHOTOS WERE gorgeous. Somehow, he managed to make me look not just normal, but actually pretty.

I'd worried he might push for something smutty—and honestly, I wouldn't have argued too hard—but he kept things classy. Despite being in my bedroom, I never felt objectified.

He really was an artist, and the dimpled smile lighting his face told me that tapping into his creativity made him incredibly happy.

This was what he should have been doing all along, not analyzing profit margins for Big Pharma in New York.

With just one impromptu photo session, he transformed into someone lighter, more alive. It was impossible not to get swept up in his enthusiasm.

This whole day had been perfect. If anyone had told me yesterday that I'd feel this uplifted and guilt-free, I'd never have believed them.

Maybe it was finally being comfortable in my hometown again, or maybe all the amazing sex had knocked something loose in my brain. My disposition had shifted so dramatically I could barely keep up with myself.

Worry seemed like something I should be doing but couldn't remember why.

Eric seemed just as uplifted. The only shadow I'd seen cross his face was during our early morning talk about Caleb and Day Zero. That was some seriously scary stuff. No wonder he'd been doing whatever he could to distract himself.

What kind of state would I be in if our roles were reversed?

I couldn't imagine. But I understood his need to stay occupied, to focus on something other than medical jargon and battling a disease with willpower alone.

I hoped I'd been a decent distraction. I hoped I could continue being that for him, even if only for one more night.

We crawled into bed exhausted from our early morning activities and busy day. I'd chosen underwear and a T-shirt for sleeping. Maybe it was being in my father's house, or maybe we were both tired, but assuming anything more than sleep seemed wrong.

It wasn't that I didn't want him. God, I hadn't stopped wanting him.

But I didn't know how Eric felt about carrying this beyond tonight. The last day and a half seemed like it had existed in a different dimension, and once we left it—once we woke up—we'd be back on the other side where our troubles waited. Where focusing on anything other than sickness and death would be impossible.

Where futures were unpredictable.

Fear crept in that this thing between us, whatever it was, couldn't possibly continue beyond this one perfect day.

Eric had been scrolling through the photos he'd taken, critiquing angles and lighting, explaining what he'd do differently with better equipment.

But now he slipped his phone onto the dresser and turned his attention to me. "You're pretty quiet over there. Did you fall asleep?"

"Sorry. I was just thinking."

He pulled me closer, lips brushing my ear. "You aren't thinking about our deal, are you?"

"Well, I wasn't. But now that you've mentioned it, I won't be able to think about anything else."

"Let everything else wait until tomorrow." His hand slid down my back, claiming and possessive. "Let me stay focused on you."

How did he always know exactly what was on my mind?

"You're right. I'm falling back into worries about tomorrow."

"Here and now, Jamie." He kissed my jaw, then my lips, light and teasing. "I can't guarantee tomorrow will be better, but I can guarantee you this." His hand moved to cup my ass, pulling me against him. "I made you a promise. I keep my promises."

Heat pooled low in my center. "What are those favorite words of yours? A deal's a deal?"

"A deal is sacred." His voice dropped in that intimate way that made my pulse race. "Sort of like how Lannisters always pay their debts."

"You sneaky liar. You did watch it."

"Nope. Read the books." He winked before capturing my mouth with his.

Within moments Eric had rid me of my clothes, leaving only my worry as a barrier between us.

He pulled back to look at me, sapphire eyes dark with desire. "Come here, beautiful. I want to give you something."

"Is it your cock? Because that's the only thing I really want right now."

Despite our teasing, his kiss had kindled an aching burn throughout my body. Desire took over, ridding me of inhibitions.

"Christ, Jamie." His voice was rough with need. "You have a fantastic way with words."

He kissed me again, tongue diving deep, thrusting into my mouth the way I craved his hard length inside me. When he broke away, I protested with a soft whimper.

"Want more of my mouth?"

"Yes. It's very talented. I like how it makes me feel."

"I thought you wanted my cock." His lust was barely hidden behind playful words as he reached for the box of condoms.

My hand roamed down the hard planes of his stomach, fingers trailing over defined abs that twitched under my touch. Following the light line of hair from his navel, I wrapped my hand around the thick base of his shaft and pumped once—deliciously slow.

"Looks like I have what I want right in the palm of my hand."

"Your hand isn't where that belongs right now." His voice turned commanding as he found my soaking center. "This is where my cock belongs." He slid fingers into me, making me gasp.

"Or here." He kissed me deeply, reminding me how much I loved his cock in my mouth.

"Or here." His other hand gripped my ass, fingers stroking over the tight ring of muscle.

"Those are your choices. Which one's it going to be?"

I shivered at the filthy images his words produced. The weight of him in my hand, knowing how it felt to have him buried deep inside me, made me squirm with anticipation.

"Why do I have to choose? Why can't we do all of it?"

Eric's groan was desperate, needy. "I don't think I'd last long enough." He sheathed himself quickly. "I'd love to have your lips wrapped around me while I get you off with my mouth. But I couldn't handle it right now. Just the thought has me on edge. I have no self-control around you."

"Do you know how much that turns me on?" Heat flooded through me. "Knowing I drive you so wild you can't control yourself? You make me feel the same. I love that we can take each other there."

Something flashed hot and wild in Eric's eyes. Suddenly I was pinned beneath him, arms trapped at my sides by his powerful embrace. When he slammed into me, the force was almost painful.

It was the best feeling in the world.

With only a few furious strokes, a powerful orgasm ripped through me. My body convulsed, aftershocks continuing long after the initial eruption.

"Gorgeous." He traced a finger over my lips.

As I came down, Eric slowed his movements, kissing me languorously. Still connected, he rolled us to our sides, hands roaming over my hair, down my neck, cupping my breast. His touches were featherlight, mapping my body with sweet provocation.

He started moving inside me again—slow, tender, different than before. This felt like something more. Like he was speaking without words, telling me the connection growing between us could be real.

His blue eyes held my gaze as he slowly worked me back to the brink. With my face captured in his big hand, he forced me to maintain our stare.

The intimacy built as our shared breath fanned around us, and Eric increased pressure with each thrust.

My leg wrapped around his waist, fingers digging into his back, heart beating erratically as Eric dragged another exquisite orgasm from me. It wasn't as strong as the first, but I closed my eyes and cried out softly when bliss washed over me.

Seconds later, eyes wide open to witness, Eric followed me over the edge. Tension dropped from his features, ecstasy clear in his groan of satisfaction.

As he kissed me tenderly, tired contentment took over. We weren't going to break the bed tonight.

And I was entirely okay with that.

DAY MINUS 3

CHAPTER TWENTY-ONE

ERIC

THE FAMILIAR PAIN STARTED AT THE BASE OF MY NECK THE moment we walked through the hospital doors. Harsh fluorescents, antiseptic smell, the hum of too many conversations—all of it building pressure behind my eyes.

I should have expected my sister would be here, ready to make it worse.

Celeste stood outside Caleb's room, arms crossed, red nails tapping against her sleeve, disapproval sharpening her features. When she spotted Jamie's hand in mine, her scowl deepened.

Christ. So much for easing back into this.

I stroked my thumb over Jamie's wrist. It was an attachment I hadn't been able to break since checking her out of her room at the resort. A connection I might never want to break.

"Where the hell have you been?" Same old Celeste. Even her questions sounded like accusations, but she wasn't looking for answers. She was looking for a fight.

Thing was, her bite had never worked on me. I'd been handling her long before she'd learned to weaponize guilt.

"Hi, sis. Nice to see you too." I let cheerful sarcasm drip from every word. "How've you been?"

Jamie shifted beside me but didn't pull away. She leaned closer, her free hand coming to rest on my stomach, fingers spreading against my shirt. Claiming me right in front of Celeste.

Heat bloomed through my chest, and the pounding in my head quieted.

"You've got a lot of nerve waltzing in here after being missing for a day and a half, acting like you don't have a care in the world." Celeste's voice echoed off the sterile walls. "And who is this girl hanging on you, Eric?"

Now Jamie started to retreat. Her hold on me loosened and she took a step back.

No. Not fucking happening. I tightened my grip on her hand, anchoring her to my side where she belonged.

"Celeste, this is Jamie. If you haven't heard about her yet, get prepared. Caleb and our parents are in love with her."

"Hello." Jamie's voice had gone quiet, careful. Nothing like the bold woman I'd walked in here with.

"Hi." Celeste barely spared her a glance.

"Jamie's a twenty-seven-year-old single mother who's smart, strong, and compassionate," I said, cutting off my sister's trademark interrogation before it could start. "I offered to help her with a problem, and she's been kind enough to share her time with me. We're both dealing with some pretty momentous shit in our lives, so it's been nice to lean on each other."

"Eric..." Jamie whispered.

Celeste's expression shifted, worry creeping into the lines around her eyes. That was the thing about my sister's bitchiness—underneath it all was love. She might try to knock me down, but she'd be the first one throwing punches if anyone else tried it.

"Despite whatever crisis you're having, big brother, you had no business running off and leaving Mom and Dad here alone. By the time Marc and I got in, Mom was in full panic mode. Dad was beyond himself trying to console her. You should have been here."

The guilt hit exactly where she'd aimed it. But I'd been carrying that weight for months now. One more day wouldn't break me. "I have been here, Celeste. I've been here for the past five months helping them manage."

"They needed you yesterday. You need to get your priorities straight. No offense to you Jamie, but Eric, the last thing you need to do is go running around with someone you just met."

My jaw tightened, but I forced myself to stay calm. Celeste was scared. Scared for Caleb, scared for our parents, scared that everything was spiraling out of her control. She was lashing out because that's what she did when she was terrified.

But I wasn't going to let her take it out on Jamie.

"You're right about one thing. I do need to get my priorities straight." I paused, letting that sink in. "And Jamie is one of them now. Just like you are. Just like Caleb and Mom and Dad."

Jamie tensed beside me, but I kept my focus on Celeste.

"Since Caleb adores her, and she's been nothing but kind to our family, maybe you could try extending the same courtesy." I kept my voice even, but there was steel underneath. "Because if you scare her away, you'll have one very sad little brother on your hands. And one very pissed off older brother."

Celeste's face scrunched like she was about to throw a tantrum. It reminded me of when she was five, standing with her hands on her hips, furious that the world wasn't bending to her will. Sort of like the kid Jamie and I had encountered at the lookout yesterday.

"Well, get your shit together before you come in here," Celeste snapped. "Caleb's not feeling well, and Marc helped Dad take Mom home for a sedative and rest. It's just you and me. Caleb doesn't need this drama." With a frustrated sigh, she turned and marched into Caleb's room.

The mention of Caleb not feeling well hit like a punch to the gut. Everything else became background noise.

"Maybe I should just go see my dad and let you deal with things here. I don't want to cause trouble, especially not if Caleb's feeling bad." Jamie was already pulling away, ready to run.

That frustrated me more than anything Celeste had said.

"No." It wasn't an argument. It was a demand. No way in hell was I letting her leave now. "Come in and say hello to him. It'll help him feel better."

"But what about your sister?"

"What about her?" I cupped her face in my hands, forcing her to look at me. "You think I can't handle her?"

"I don't want her to hate me. And I don't want her to take it out on you."

Her concern for me, even after Celeste's attack, made something fierce and possessive roar to life in my chest.

"Worried about me, beautiful girl?"

"Of course I am. Spending time together was supposed to help, not make things worse. I don't want to be the cause of any more problems for you."

She thought she was the problem. Christ, this woman was going to be the death of me.

"The only thing to worry about is making sure I get to leave here with you." I kissed her softly. "I can't get enough of you."

Her body melted into mine, arms wrapping around my waist. "I haven't had enough of you yet, either."

That word. *Yet.*

My heart went cold even as my body heated from her touch. I'd done this to myself. Agreed to temporary. Agreed to living in the moment without looking ahead. Given her the power to walk away whenever she decided she'd had enough.

What happened when that day came? When the only thing holding her here was no longer a factor?

And what happened if I didn't want to let her go?

CHAPTER TWENTY-TWO

JAMIE

INTERLOPER. FRAUD. LIAR.

So many names to call myself, but none of them were harsh enough.

Eric and I had agreed to stop pretending, but holding his hand while acting like I wanted nothing more than friendship and sex made me feel like a con artist.

No matter how many times I reminded myself this wasn't my real life—real life was waiting for me back in Toronto—I couldn't stop daydreaming about the possibility of something more.

Celeste's accusations may have been directed at Eric, but the guilt belonged to me. I'd been selfish, stealing his time, keeping him from his family. The idea that I was helping him by keeping his mind off his troubles seemed ludicrous now.

All I'd done was play house with a man who was possibly in a worse situation than me.

If I was decent, I'd walk away before it was too late. Before I hurt him.

Before I hurt myself.

Walking into Caleb's room, my nerves spiked again. This

time I knew Celeste's condemnation would be waiting along with whatever we'd find behind that door.

Eric's hand anchored me. Without him, I wouldn't have the strength to face this. But the moment I saw Caleb—drained of color, curled under blankets, visibly shaking—I knew that strength needed to flow the other way. I couldn't steal it from Eric when he needed it most.

Caleb's eyes were screwed shut, fighting pain instead of resting. This wasn't the vivacious troublemaker I'd met before. This was a sick child who needed love.

"I brought you a visitor." Eric's voice dropped to barely a whisper.

Caleb's eyes fluttered open. He struggled to smile, game face sliding into place. "I knew you'd be back. I'm too damn irresistible."

"You're too damn something." Celeste's scolding cut through the moment. "You need to rest, Caleb. Visiting isn't on the agenda."

"Lighten up, Cece." Caleb's sigh held exhaustion. "I've been tied to this bed for days. All the resting is making me stir-crazy. Besides, having a visit from this angel is already making me feel better."

Celeste shot Eric a look like he was somehow responsible for Caleb's defiance. Eric's smile tightened, his posture shifting into something unmistakably protective.

I stopped watching their silent standoff. Caleb had his eyes fixed on me, trying to convince me he was fine when clearly, he wasn't.

I squeezed Eric's hand once before letting go and moving to Caleb's bedside. His skin was clammy when I took his fingers in mine, his grip weak.

"I don't have any pudding to share." I laced our fingers together.

Tears filled his eyes before he squeezed them shut.

"But I'll do whatever I can to see your real smile again."

"As long as you keep smiling, then I will too." His voice came out hoarse. "Are you done missing that other guy yet?"

"No. But I'll never be done missing him. He's pretty special. Do you want to hear about him?"

"Is he going to make me as jealous as Eric does?"

"Maybe." The thought of how alike they were made me smile. "His name is Hunter. He's nine years old. He's my son, and aside from meeting you and your brother, he's the best thing that's ever happened to me."

"Really?" His smile almost brightened. "Meeting me is the second-best thing?"

"Open your ears, dude." Eric's teasing carried warmth. "She said meeting you and me."

"Yeah, yeah, whatever, Eric. We all know she just threw you in there to make you feel better." Despite the strain in his voice, Caleb's sarcasm was still on point. "Tell me all about him, Jamie. Please?"

With a light laugh, I launched into stories about Hunter.

I wiped sweat from Caleb's face while describing how Hunter loved music and played in the school band, how he definitely hadn't inherited any musical ability from me. I fed him ice chips while listing the pros and cons of letting my son have a dog. I rubbed his back as I explained why Hunter wouldn't be a flirt but would break hearts with his devotion to one woman. I tried getting Caleb's perspective on baseball versus woodworking class, but he fell asleep mid-sentence.

He looked so young. So innocent.

Gratitude overwhelmed me suddenly. This boy had chosen me. This incredibly sick child had recognized my loneliness and set his own suffering aside for me. He was amazing, and thinking about how fragile he was, how precarious his situation, made me sick.

God, his poor parents.

I didn't know how they managed. If it was Hunter lying in that bed, waiting for treatment that could either save or kill him…

No. I couldn't even think it.

Just being separated from Hunter had sent me into a tailspin. If something this horrible happened to him, I'd lose my mind.

At least the Alexanders had each other. They might not always agree, but they were here together. Even Celeste, with her sharp edges, genuinely cared about her family's well-being.

They had love. I had no doubt, all six of them made a strong unit.

"You're really good with him." Celeste's murmur came from the corner.

For over an hour, I'd been the only one talking while Eric and Celeste listened to me chat Caleb's ear off.

"I think he was exhausted. Maybe his body will heal while he sleeps." I had no idea if it was true, but we all needed the reassurance.

"No, Jamie. Cece's right." Eric's voice carried conviction. "You're so natural with him. Making him feel like it was just a normal conversation."

"It was. He's a normal kid. Why wouldn't I have a normal conversation with him?"

"Excuse me." Celeste's voice cracked, tears threatening. "I'm just going to use the washroom. Maybe call home. Will you be here later, Jamie?"

"I don't think so. I need to see my father."

"Oh. Well, thank you." Her brows drew tight, sharp lines forming. "I wasn't expecting you to be so…compassionate. Maybe I'll see you another time."

She rushed out, leaving Eric and me alone with sleeping Caleb.

"Did I upset her?" Worry twisted through me.

"She feels bad about being rude earlier. You just proved why my family loves you."

"Your family barely knows me, Eric. I met your parents once."

"They loved you. Even Cece will now, and she's impossible to please. Trust me."

"I do trust you, but I think you're building me up too much. Your parents couldn't pick me out of a lineup. If I was in their shoes…"

The words died. If I were in their shoes, I'd be sitting in this room alone, dying a little more each day.

Eric's arms wrapped around my shoulders, pulling me into his embrace. I wanted to stay and pretend everything was fine—that my dad wasn't dying, that Caleb wasn't suffering, that Eric and I had a real chance.

But I'd promised Eric I'd stop pretending. Wasn't it time I got real with myself?

"Thank you for believing in me, Eric."

"Thank you for trusting me, Jamie."

"Didn't we already cover the trust thing?" I managed a smile.

"Yeah, you're right. Is that strange?"

"What?"

"That we trust each other so completely, so fast?"

I hadn't considered it before. Trusting Eric felt effortless. He'd been protecting me, watching over me from the moment we met.

But what reason had I given him to trust me?

"Maybe. It probably has to do with all the drama you've seen me go through. You've witnessed my ugly side."

"Even your ugly side is beautiful." His voice dropped, intimate and full of meaning as he leaned closer.

Heat flooded my cheeks at his words, and the way he looked at me.

Then his lips were on mine, fast as lightning. His kiss ignited something fierce and burning deep within me, threatening to consume everything I thought I knew about myself.

My core turned molten, and I kissed him back with an abandon I didn't know I possessed.

God, the things he made me feel.

Terrifying things. Things that pushed every boundary I'd built, shifted my understanding of the world, changed the entire balance of my carefully constructed life. Feelings that would mark me permanently, long after we were done.

But how was I supposed to go back to Toronto and pretend none of this happened? How had I managed to make everything even more complicated than before?

CHAPTER TWENTY-THREE

JAMIE

My dad looked dead. In five hours, he'd barely stirred, and it was freaking me out.

It reminded me of Hunter as a newborn and how I'd check to make sure he was still breathing whenever he fell asleep. It was embarrassing to admit the number of times I woke him, just to be sure he was still alive.

I was tempted to do the same with my father now, except the monitor showed he wasn't dead yet, and I wasn't insane enough to disturb him. Waking him would mean facing him again.

Although maybe that wouldn't be such a bad thing.

He wasn't going to last much longer. All I could do was find peace with it.

With him.

I needed to make amends. I had no idea how or if it was even possible, but I wanted to try. Seeing how he'd taken care of the house, knowing how good things were before we lost Mom and Trina—there had to be something salvageable between us.

I just hoped it wasn't too late.

Maybe if I reconciled with Dad, I could send for Hunter. My

father and son should meet at least once. My decisions had impacted them both so deeply.

I'd probably done Hunter a disservice keeping him from this place. He'd never experienced life outside Toronto's rat race. Never seen the forests surrounding this place, gone to a real farmer's market, or skied at the resort. He'd never had a backyard to play in. And he'd never spent a lazy Sunday watching old movies with his whole family.

He might not ever get some of those moments, and most of that was my fault. I'd robbed him of what could've been the best parts of his childhood.

Pain bloomed in my chest, indecision cracking my heart.

Part of me wanted to run back to the life I'd built over the last decade. Back to the predictable. The safe. I could pack up, leave Copper Ridge in the rearview mirror, and pretend this detour had never happened.

But that part of me was operating out of fear.

Fear that I might want to stay and make a new life here. For me and my son.

Toronto had lost some of its luster compared to Copper Ridge. The nostalgia and longing for this place were easy to ignore when I wasn't immersed in it. But being here again—breathing this air, walking these streets—made the lie harder to hold.

I'd missed it. The town. The people. The version of myself I'd once been.

And if I left now, I'd miss Eric most of all. I wasn't ready to move on without him.

Maybe this thing between us was purely circumstance, a forced connection built on need and fear. Two exhausted people clinging to comfort. Maybe the pull between us was just adrenaline and grief masquerading as chemistry.

Hell, under normal circumstances, we might bore each other senseless.

Maybe.

But when I'd woken this morning with my cheek pressed to his chest, his arm heavy and sure around my waist, everything had felt right. Not dramatic. Not reckless. Just…right.

He made staying feel possible.

Every reason I had to leave blurred when he touched me. The past didn't disappear, but it didn't feel as unmanageable when I was in his arms.

The sound of footsteps in the hallway pulled me from my thoughts. Dylan appeared in the doorway, strutting into my father's hospital room like he belonged there. Like he owned the damn place.

"Hey there, Princess. You're looking good this evening." Cocky as always.

"What are you doing here?" If I wasn't worried about waking my dad, I might've yelled.

"Thought I'd check in, see how you're holding up." He smiled like this was normal. "How's he doing?"

"I don't know. Fine, I guess. He's been sleeping all day. But, really Dylan, why are you here?"

"Just finished my shift. Thought we could talk." He hesitated, staring like he was daring me to make the first move.

"You want to talk again?"

"I was hoping we could continue our conversation from the other day."

Thirty seconds in the room and I'd had enough. Talking wasn't something we'd ever done successfully, even as a couple.

"I wanted you to know you were right." His gaze dropped. "I should be taking more responsibility for Hunter. I want to. I've just been afraid. I don't know what I'm doing. I wasn't prepared to be a dad."

Finally. After ten years, he was finally admitting what I'd been saying all along. The validation should have been sweet, but all I felt was exhaustion.

"Welcome to parenthood, Dylan. You think I had the first clue about being a mom? You think I was prepared? What kind of excuse is that?"

Dylan glanced at my sleeping father. "You're right, Princess. I have no excuse."

"Stop calling me that. I'm not your princess. I never was, and I never will be."

"Calm down." He sighed, exasperated. "It's just a nickname. You might not like it, but you're still a princess in my mind. You can't force me to think differently."

If only it were that easy.

"But I'll try to respect your feelings about it. It's just another reminder that you're too good for me."

"God, Dylan, give it a rest. I'm not the bad guy because I refuse to accept the way you treat me."

"No. I'm the bad guy. That's what I'm saying. I don't deserve someone like you. I've been an asshole, I know it. I'm worried I'm not good enough for our son either. But I want to move forward. Do the right thing. Earn the right to have him call me Dad."

"Well, it's about goddamn time," my father drawled sleepily.

"Dad… I'm sorry, I didn't mean to wake you. We'll take this conversation out to the hall."

"No, you will not." Although weak, he still had a way of asserting his authority. "You think I don't have a right to know what's going on? This is my grandson you're talking about. You're my daughter—like it or not."

The possessiveness in his voice caught me off guard. After years of silence, he was suddenly claiming ownership of my life, my decisions, my child.

"Mr. Hartley, I guess I owe you an apology too." Dylan had the sense to look contrite. "I realize I need to step up. I've been disrespectful to you and to your daughter. I plan to make up for that."

"You gonna start helping her out more?"

"Yes, sir, if she'll let me."

"You gonna do more than visit a few times a year and send a cheque once a month? Actually get involved with your son?"

"Yes, sir. That's what I want."

They were discussing me, my life, like I wasn't even in the room. Like I was some incapable heroine in need of rescue. As if either of them had any business trying to make decisions on my behalf.

I'd raised Hunter alone for ten years. I'd built a career, maintained a home, made every major decision without input from either of these men. What the hell gave them the right to start caring now? And how the hell did my father know so much about me and Dylan?

The irony wasn't lost on me—I'd spent years wanting both of them to step up, and now that they were trying, all I felt was bitter.

"What do you say, Jamie?" Dad asked quietly. "You gonna give him a chance to make things right?"

"With Hunter, yes." I turned to Dylan. "I'd never hold you back from your son. But Hunter needs to be the priority, not your feelings. He barely knows you. It'll take time."

"What about with you, James? You gonna let him make things right with you?"

I wasn't sure how my father had become the facilitator, but I didn't like it. I never wanted to disappoint him, even now. Still, this felt like a setup.

Instead of answering his invasive question, I fired back my own. "How did you know Dylan sends me a check every month? How do you know how often he visits? And who gave you those pictures of Hunter in your living room?"

"Jesus Christ, child." His attempt to yell dissolved into coughing.

Dylan answered instead. "He knows because I tell him."

"So you've been conspiring behind my back? You thought you'd cozy up to Dad so he could convince me to go back to you?"

"You really are paranoid and defensive." Dylan's accusation stung. "I kept in touch because he's your father. Since you weren't talking to him, someone should. He deserves to know about you and his grandkid. I thought he should have pictures and stories about your life."

Stories about my life from a man who only showed up when it suited him. I was aghast at the lengths Dylan had gone to behind my back.

Dad stopped coughing. "You still didn't answer my question. You gonna let Dylan make things right with you?"

Hell no.

Dylan spoke before I could. "All Jamie wants from me is doing right by our son, Mr. Hartley. She's determined we won't have a relationship beyond Hunter. Beyond friendship."

"Jamie?" My dad looked at me like I'd broken some cardinal rule. "You not going to give Dylan a second chance? Don't you think your boy should have a real family?"

"Dad." I sighed, tired and frustrated. "Dylan and I discussed this. Hunter needs two strong parents who love him. Us being together won't make things better. It would make them worse."

"James." His tone grew stern.

Dylan cut him off. "Mr. Hartley, Jamie's got a point. We don't love each other. That's no way to raise a kid. Trust me—that's the home I grew up in, and it sucked."

Dylan admitting he didn't love me felt surprisingly good. I'd been afraid I'd damaged him beyond repair. Maybe something I'd said had finally sunk in.

"Besides," he continued, "Jamie has a new man. I met him the other day. Seems like a good guy. But I'm still running a background check to make sure he's safe around Hunter. I plan to be thorough."

"New guy? How come I didn't know about this?" Dad coughed, looking at Dylan accusingly. "And if he's such a good guy, where is he?"

Shit. This was where lying got you.

How was I supposed to dig out of this without revealing my dishonesty?

I felt like the asshole now. I'd lied to everyone, including myself, and now I had to explain it all to my dying father.

What would Eric think if he were here right now? What would he do? What would he expect me to do? Honesty was best —I just needed the strength to say it.

"He's—"

My phone rang, Hunter's number lighting the screen.

I checked the time. Much later than his normal call. I'd been so caught up I'd missed that my son hadn't checked in.

"Hunter?"

"Hi, Mom." His voice was small and stressed.

"Hey bud, I was just talking about you. What's up?"

"Mom, something's happened and I need you to come get me."

Panic invaded every molecule of my being. "What? Are you okay? What's going on?"

"Jackson's parents want to talk to you. They want me to leave, but I wanted to talk to you first. I didn't do anything wrong. It's a misunderstanding. Trust me, okay?"

"Of course, bud. I always trust you. Put them on the phone. I'll sort this out."

Outrage and terror warred in my chest. What could my kid have possibly done to get kicked out? Were they sick of him? Had his smart mouth gotten him in trouble?

Jackson's mother came on the line, and I went immediately defensive.

"Hello, Jamie. I'm so sorry about this."

"It's fine, Vanessa. Please tell me what's going on."

"Ron and I feel awful about this, truly. We realize it's terrible timing. However, after discussing it with the boys, then privately, we've decided it would be best if Hunter didn't stay with us any longer. We simply can't tolerate this behavior."

Her sickly-sweet voice and holier-than-thou attitude made me want to jump in my car and make the drive just to tell her off face-to-face. She'd always looked down on me, but I'd overlooked it because our kids were inseparable. Her fake empathy turned my stomach.

"Please tell me what happened." Gritted teeth barely contained my rage.

"Well, it seems Hunter has a problem with stealing."

"Pardon me?"

"I know it's shocking, but the police brought our boys home after school today. Hunter got caught shoplifting from the corner store. Poor Jackson got accused as well."

"Wait a minute." I was barely maintaining control. "Both children were picked up for shoplifting, but you believe it was all Hunter's fault? And the police brought them home after school, but you didn't call me right away?"

"When you put it that way, I could see why you might be upset. But really, Jamie, we wouldn't have agreed to keep your child if we'd known he was so untrustworthy."

Assholes. I'd trusted these people with my kid. I knew it was a mistake and ignored my instincts. I should've known trusting someone would end this way. Trust always screwed me.

"Vanessa, it would be my utmost pleasure to release you from your caretaker duty. Hunter will be collected this evening. This I assure you."

"Thank you, Jamie. I hope you understand why we're uncomfortable having him here."

"Oh yes, I understand. I'm also very uncomfortable knowing my son will need to spend any more time in your home." Sarcasm slipped out despite my efforts. "Now, if you don't mind,

I'd like to speak to someone with common sense. Could you please put my son back on the phone?"

Vanessa's squawk of indignation made it clear she'd caught my barb. Why couldn't I ever control myself?

Hunter whispered when he returned, "Mom, what did you say to her? I think you made her cry."

"It doesn't matter. We have a problem to solve. She can deal with her own hurt feelings."

"She's searching my bag to make sure I'm not stealing anything. What should I do?"

Hunter sounded calmer than me. He was direct and composed while I was frazzled and rude. I'd been on Dylan's case about parenting, yet I was the one whose poor decisions had put our child at risk.

"Is that my grandson?" Dad croaked. "Jamie, give me the phone."

Did I look as bad as I sounded? From the way Dad and Dylan were eyeing me, you'd think I was having a breakdown. Compared to my episode in Eric's truck, I felt downright calm.

Still, my struggle to maintain composure must've been obvious. "It's okay, Dad."

"Mom, what should I do?" Hunter asked.

"Jamie, give me the phone." Dad barked with authority.

He looked ferocious, like a man ready to tear into someone with his bare hands. It reminded me of his drunken moments.

Would he yell at me? Berate me for being worthless?

"It's okay, bud, don't worry." A tear slipped down my face as I tried soothing Hunter.

Was I reassuring my son or myself?

"James." Dad yelled again.

"Hunter, do me a favor. Say hello to your grandfather. He'd really like to talk to you. I'll figure out what to do, okay?"

Hunter agreed, and against my better judgment, I handed my father the phone.

When Frank Hartley spoke to his grandson for the first time, something shifted. A universal realignment, or a shift in my perspective. Either way, it was monumental.

"Hello, Hunter? Yes, this is your grandfather. Tell me what happened." His tone held genuine care. The asshole I'd accepted lifted his veil, revealing the father I used to know. Suddenly, he was the good guy, my rescuer, the daddy I'd loved and adored.

My body trembled with silent tears as I watched his transformation. Had he been hidden in plain sight all this time?

"Okay. No need to worry. Here's what we'll do. Stay calm. Go sit at the kitchen table where they can see you. Let your friend's mom search whatever she wants. She can pack it all back up too. Don't move until you see your dad's badge at the door. You're going to be fine. We'll set things straight."

Dylan pulled out his phone, asking for the address. Once he had it typed in, he left to get our son.

"Yes, your dad will bring you here," my father promised. "Your mom will be really happy to see you."

The circumstances were shit, but my boy was coming home. Bittersweet relief flooded me. My boy was coming home. *Home.*

Dad continued talking softly with Hunter, offering him reassurances like a grandfather should. Like they were family instead of strangers.

His final words before hanging up caught my breath. "You'll be fine as long as you stay put. Your dad will come find you. We'll bring you home."

I contemplated this strange turn of events, wondering how it was possible to feel like a little girl all over again, with my dad coming to save the day.

CHAPTER TWENTY-FOUR

ERIC

WATCHING CALEB SUFFER WAS ITS OWN KIND OF TORTURE. HE'D drifted in and out of sleep all day, never fully settling, his body too exhausted to fight and too wired to surrender.

Celeste and I had sat on either side of him while his temperature climbed to frightening heights. The nurses moved in and out with steady efficiency, adjusting meds, monitoring every change, and a few hours ago the fever had finally broken.

Now the room was quiet. Celeste had stepped out, leaving me alone to keep watch, to listen to the rhythm of his breathing and pretend I wasn't on edge, anticipating the next complication.

He shifted, his eyes fluttering open. "Where did Jamie go?"

The worry in his question caught me off guard. Even sick as hell, he was thinking about her. About whether she was okay.

"To her dad. She'll be back."

"Was I dreaming or did you kiss her?" His brow furrowed. "If it was a dream, it was a vivid one. I swear you kissed her right in front of me like I wasn't even here."

Heat crawled up my neck. I'd been so fucking lost in her that I'd forgotten where we were. That kiss had been desperate with the need to comfort her, to ground myself, and my sick brother had caught every second of it.

"So much for being asleep."

"I was drifting but still managed to catch the show." He waggled his eyebrows weakly. "You were really into it. Thanks for rubbing your victory in my face."

Victory. The word sat wrong. There was nothing victorious about any of this. Not his illness, not her pain, not the way I was grasping for something good in the middle of so much fear.

"I'd say sorry but you're such a little perv, you probably enjoyed it."

"It's okay. I can live vicariously through you. Tell me what it's like."

The eagerness in his voice hit me. This was what his illness had stolen from him—his own experiences, his own chances. The unfairness of it made something violent twist in my chest.

"You want to know what it's like to kiss Jamie?"

"Yes. Absolutely, yes. Tell me it's as incredible as I imagine."

"Not happening. I don't mind talking about girls in general, but my sex life is off limits."

Caleb gasped. "You had sex with her?"

"That's not what I meant." Christ, how did I get myself into this conversation. And how the hell did I get out? "And that's really fucking personal. I'm sure she doesn't want me discussing it with you."

"Are you in love with her?"

My breath stalled, chest tight and heart slamming hard. "This isn't a fairy tale, Caleb. Love takes time, knowing someone inside and out. People don't fall in love after a few days."

"Don't you dare fuck this up."

I stared at him, shocked not just by his language but by the conviction behind it.

"If you break her heart, I will be seriously pissed. Like seriously, seriously pissed."

"Relax. No one's breaking hearts. We're taking things slow. No commitments on either side."

"That's bullshit and you know it. You're obviously in love with her. You're just too scared to admit it."

The accusation hung between us like a challenge.

Was I just scared?

I did have strong feelings for her. Strong, unconditional, unwavering, un-fucking-relenting emotions that had been gnawing away at my insides for days.

They'd been there from the moment I first held her. They made my heart race, my stomach churn, made me want to vomit every time I thought about her leaving. Feelings that turned me into a walking cliché ready to make over-the-top declarations.

Fuck.

Maybe he was right. Maybe I was falling in love with her.

"I'm not scared to admit anything," I lied through my teeth. "But jumping in prematurely could hurt us both. I care about her a lot, but I won't claim love until I'm sure. Right now? Hell, right now I don't know much."

"Haven't you learned anything from me, big brother?" He frowned. "There's no time to be wasted. Why do you think I took the chance to talk to her in the first place?"

"Because you're an unrelenting flirt who couldn't pass up the opportunity to torment a beautiful woman."

"Okay, yes, there's that," he agreed with a quirk of his lips. "But it's so much more. When I see a woman like Jamie, I see a chance to make a good memory, and I never know which one might be my last."

"Don't talk like that." My hands clenched, the need to fight something, anything, building like pressure inside me. "You're going to have plenty of chances. You can't give up."

"I'll never give up, but that's the point. I hope to have years and years of chances. But just in case, I want to make as many good memories as possible while I can. Time is precious. You should remember that, too."

"I love you, Caleb. You're too smart for your own good, and you make me look like an ass. But I really love you."

"You're supposed to say that to Jamie, not me. But I love you back." His grin was genuine, practically pain-free. "And you can thank me for introducing you in your wedding speech."

I wished Jamie was here to see his smile. Once again, it was because of her that light had found its way back into this room.

"Now you're jumping way ahead. Like I said, it's not a fairy tale."

"What's not a fairy tale?" Celeste asked, walking back into the room.

"Eric and Jamie," Caleb said before I could get out a word.

Meddling little shit.

"What about them?" Celeste persisted.

"Eric's in love with her."

"Yeah, so?" Even in question, she managed to scowl. "I thought we already knew this. Why is it big news?"

Apparently, I was obvious to everyone but myself. Was I this transparent to Jamie?

"Will you both give it a rest? I don't need you convincing me you know my feelings better than I do. Topic closed."

A soft knock interrupted us. Jamie stood in the doorway, tears sparkling in her eyes.

My heart soared and plummeted simultaneously. How much had she heard? But more importantly, why did she look so devastated?

"Sorry to intrude." Her voice wavered.

"Hey, Jamie." Caleb called as I moved toward her. "We were just talking about you."

I shot him a warning look but kept my focus on Jamie, concern overriding annoyance.

"Hi." She gave them a weak smile. "I need to borrow Eric."

I didn't wait for their response, ushering her into the hallway away from prying eyes and big mouths. "What's going on?"

"I need you to meet my father."

Fuck. Jamie wouldn't ask this lightly. Something big had happened, and it made me uneasy as hell.

"You want me to meet your dad?"

"I know it's out of line, but he wants to meet you. It's a long story but basically, Dylan was here. He left to get Hunter, but he said things and now Dad thinks you're my boyfriend. I'm sorry. I don't know what to say. I don't know if everything's falling apart or coming together. I just know he's dying, and I really want him to be happy with me before he goes. I need my last memories of him to be good ones, Eric."

She was breathless, distraught, with fear shadowing her features. It was like she had no idea I'd do absolutely anything for her.

"Come here." I pulled her against me, pressing a kiss to her ear. "I'd be honored to meet him."

"Really?" She sucked in a sob.

"Of course. That's what we do for each other."

I didn't love lying to a dying man, but Jamie needed this. And I'd already agreed to be her fake boyfriend. Making her happy was reason enough.

Walking into her father's room felt like facing a firing squad. I was prepared to lie my ass off, but when we approached his bedside, he was asleep.

He was imposing even in illness, cancer eating away at him. I couldn't help comparing him to Caleb, and I was morbidly relieved my brother didn't look this bad.

My beautiful girl was going to lose her father soon.

I hoped I could hold her through it. Part of me knew helping her was selfish—I wanted to prove I wouldn't abandon her.

Wanted to show her I could do better than the other men in her life.

I wanted to give her reason to stay.

"Thanks, Eric. I pulled you away for nothing." She turned those sad blue eyes to me.

"How many times do I have to tell you? I'm here for you."

"I feel bad you're missing time with Caleb. He needs you."

"Caleb has me, but right now you need me. He understands. I'm not abandoning him—I'm doing right by both of you."

"You're too good to me."

"Not possible, beautiful girl. I wish I could fix everything for you."

"I like this guy." Her father's weak voice startled us both.

"Dad, sorry. I woke you again."

He looked ready to drift off but remained lucid. "Is this him?"

"Yeah, this is Eric." Jamie gestured between us. "Eric, my father, Frank Hartley."

Fuck. I hadn't even known her last name.

There were still countless things I didn't know about her, but it didn't change that I was falling in love.

"Nice to meet you, Mr. Hartley." My voice was stiff, and way too fucking formal. Meeting her father on his deathbed while everything was so intense had me off-balance.

Despite his medicated haze, Frank noticed my discomfort. "James. I need a minute with this one. Alone."

Jamie looked panicked. "What? Why?"

I wanted to echo her questions, but this was my chance to prove myself. To show Jamie she could rely on me.

"It's okay," I told her. "Go spend time with Caleb. I'll find you when we're done."

After shooting warning glares at both of us, Jamie left.

I hoped this wouldn't backfire. My siblings might not keep

quiet about our earlier conversation, and Frank might not like what I had to say.

"Sit down and listen up. I don't have strength to yell across the room." Frank Hartley might be dying, but he was still demanding. I could feel a lecture brewing, but I'd listen for Jamie's sake.

I sat, bracing for his attack.

"You're not really her boyfriend, are you?"

Not what I'd expected.

When I stayed silent, he closed his eyes on a heavy sigh. "Didn't think so. Seemed too convenient."

"If it makes any difference, this is my fourth day as her fake boyfriend, and it's been the best four days of my life."

Eyes still closed, he laughed.

Frank Hartley—the alcoholic father who'd driven his pregnant teenage daughter away—was laughing at me.

My jaw tightened. "She's special."

"Damn right she is." His eyes flew open, and he stared me down. "She's the best thing I ever did. Worthless as I am, at least I'm leaving something good behind."

I stared back without flinching. "No offense, but do you really have the right to take credit for how amazing she is?"

His eyes flashed murder. Jamie said he wasn't violent, but I could feel rage rolling off him. If illness hadn't robbed his strength, he'd probably try to kill me.

"You're brave." He groaned, pain evident. "She needs someone brave. Someone like you. Don't let her run from you."

Frank was full of surprises. He and Jamie were both complicated, with striking similarities.

"That might be easier said than done. I'm at the worst point in my life and finding her has been the best damn thing. She's given me reason to look toward the future. I don't want to give that up, but she might not give me a choice. Your daughter's stubborn."

Silence stretched between us before I realized he'd fallen asleep again. My confession had fallen on deaf ears.

Maybe that was good. I needed to tell his daughter everything on my mind. Needed to honor our deal and stop fucking pretending.

But my timing was shit.

Her son was coming. With his father.

Jamie claimed she was done with Dylan, but with him reasserting himself, would she second-guess? Hunter's wellbeing was her driving force. If she thought Dylan was best for Hunter, would she take him back?

I needed to know. Needed to take the chance.

But first, I had to meet her son. I had no shot if he didn't approve.

Frank startled awake, seeming confused to see me. "You're still here?"

"You were only out a few minutes."

"Shit. Stop wasting time I don't have. Go tell her how you feel, jackass."

"What if she runs?"

"Then you better promise to chase her."

So I made a promise to a dying man. For the first time in five months, I had more than Day Zero on my horizon. I had a goal beyond surviving each day.

I had a plan.

DAY MINUS 2

CHAPTER TWENTY-FIVE

JAMIE

It was after one in the morning when I finally heard the car pull into the driveway.

I'd been restless, waiting for Dylan to arrive with Hunter, spending the past hour preparing Trina's old room. But instead of easing my anxiety, it had unleashed an overwhelming sense of loss.

Trina and I were never close. A four year age difference and her relentless teen angst had created distance. But that hadn't stopped me from missing her. From wondering what kind of relationship we might have had.

Would we have grown closer as adults? Would she have married, had children, pursued that fashion career she'd dreamed about? Questions that would never be answered. Her life cut too short.

Those faded memories left me drowning in melancholy. I missed what we'd shared. Even the hair-pulling fights and name-calling felt precious now. But what hurt most were the uncelebrated milestones that would never happen. Moments that would only ever exist in my imagination.

How was it possible to miss something I'd never had?

It might've just been an empty room, but being in it hurt.

Maybe it was because the walls were still the god-awful bubblegum-pink she'd begged Dad to paint them. The frilly white lace curtains Mom had sewn were still in the window. It looked identical to my childhood, like stepping back in time, except most of her personal things were gone and she wasn't screaming at me to get out.

But it was her notebooks on the bedside table that nearly broke me. Those books were more like a diary than Trina ever admitted. She'd protected them fiercely, never letting anyone peek.

Seeing them now, dust-free and in a neat stack, made me wonder if Dad spent time reading her words, remembering the brilliant, beautiful, demanding daughter he'd lost.

Would it be wrong if I did the same?

Maybe I would, but not tonight. I couldn't handle any more torment.

The room was ready—blue sheets closer to Hunter's favorite shade, stuffed animals hidden in the closet. It was only a place to sleep, but I wanted him comfortable.

I wanted him home.

Dylan had called hours ago with details. Vanessa and Ron were shocked when Hunter's father showed up instead of me. Apparently, they'd assumed I didn't know who Hunter's father was.

God, they really were assholes.

And they'd been even more surprised to learn Dylan was a cop. They felt compelled to explain their version of events, which didn't match the official report Dylan got from his Toronto contact.

No shit.

At first, I'd worried I was naïve for trusting Hunter when he said it was a misunderstanding. Dylan's report proved I wasn't.

Vanessa and Ron blamed the entire incident on Hunter, when

the store clerk reported it was Jackson who'd been caught stuffing candy in his pocket. Their handling of the situation proved that being older didn't make someone a better parent. If you were an asshole, you'd be bad at it regardless.

I might not have had guidance raising Hunter, but I'd never blame someone else's kid for my own child's actions. I trusted Hunter while knowing kids made mistakes.

Despite reassurances from Dylan, Hunter, and Eric, I couldn't relax. I wouldn't trust my child was fine until I could see him myself. Until I could hug the little troublemaker hard enough for him to complain about broken ribs.

The worry wasn't only about Hunter's arrival, though.

I was nervous because Eric was here.

He'd insisted on bringing me home from the hospital. When I suggested he stay with Caleb, he'd refused outright. Called Marc to stay overnight with Caleb, then attached himself to me.

He didn't want me alone.

I was grateful for his presence, even though he was currently asleep in my bedroom—his big, beautiful body consuming the entire double mattress. But what would Hunter think?

I'd never had a man stay overnight. Even Dylan used hotels when visiting us in Toronto. Introducing my son to a new man this way seemed intense, especially when I had no idea what the future held for us.

How could I explain it to Hunter when I couldn't explain it to myself?

But the moment I opened the door and saw my wonderful boy, anxiety evaporated.

Dylan struggled carrying a semiconscious Hunter from the car. At nine, he was too big for me to lift, but half-asleep in his father's arms, he looked like my baby.

"How is he?" I grabbed the bags from Dylan.

"Heavy as hell." Dylan grunted up the front steps. "He's fine. Talked my ear off for an hour, then slept the rest."

"Was he upset?"

"A little. More worried about Jackson than himself. But he was too busy explaining Minecraft to obsess over much else. Well…there was one other thing. He worked pretty hard winning me over to his cause."

Dread settled in my stomach. "What cause?"

"I'm sorry." He cringed. "I agreed to pay for it."

"What did you do?" I asked, even though I already knew the answer.

"It'll be good for him. He's such a good kid, Jamie. He deserves a dog, don't you think?"

At the magic word, Hunter perked up. "I'm getting a dog?" His smile was sweet and sleepy. My wonderful, troublemaking angel.

Dylan set Hunter on his feet, gazing down with love in his eyes. "Is that really the first thing you want to say to your mom after a whole week apart?"

"No." Hunter launched into me, wrapping his arms around my neck and burrowing into my shoulder. "I love you, Mom."

"I love you back, you little hoodlum."

Holding my child, I watched Dylan's tired smile. He'd made real effort tonight. Hell, he'd used my actual name instead of calling me princess. That progress alone made me optimistic about his promises to be there for his son.

"I hope you know…if I agree to this dog, it goes wherever Hunter goes. Including visits with you."

"So I really can get a dog?" Hunter squealed.

"We'll talk in the morning. You need sleep—you're falling over. Come on, I made you a place."

When Dylan said goodnight, Hunter surprised us both with a giant hug, thanking him for the rescue. For two people who barely knew each other, they seemed to be building something meaningful.

I only hoped it would last.

Tucking Hunter into bed reminded me of when he was small, before he'd declared himself too old for tuck-ins. Now he closed his eyes and accepted my goodnight kiss with a huge smile.

"Mom, I missed you." His voice was heavy with sleep.

"I missed you too, bud. So, so much."

"Thanks for believing me today. If I can't get a dog, I understand. Even though I really, really want one."

Dylan was right. Hunter was a good kid. Good enough to tolerate a dog in our tiny Toronto apartment? I wasn't convinced, but he deserved something. Maybe I could negotiate for a cat.

"Sleep now. We'll talk tomorrow. Good night, sweet boy."

He was unconscious before I left the room.

Now that he was here, exhaustion hit like a freight train. Nervous anticipation had been the only thing keeping me upright.

The past week had been the longest of my life.

But I wasn't complaining.

It had been filled with some of the best moments I'd ever experienced. Having Hunter here made everything better.

Dark spots still hung overhead, but they'd have to wait. I couldn't keep my eyes open long enough to deal with anything else.

Back in my room, I crawled over Eric, wedging myself between his sprawled body and the wall. The instant I hit the mattress, he made space, pulling me into warm, protective arms without waking. Like he was aware of me even in his dreams.

Maybe it was exhaustion, but curled up in a tiny bed with Eric, I was more comfortable than I'd ever been.

I snuggled against him and surrendered to sleep.

CHAPTER TWENTY-SIX

ERIC

I FELT LIKE A TOTAL ASS FOR FALLING ASLEEP ON JAMIE.

She'd waited up late for Hunter's arrival, and I'd wanted to stay awake with her. But after the day we'd both endured, exhaustion had won.

Still, I wished I'd been able to distract her. Especially with so many effective techniques at my disposal. I could have easily taken her mind off her worries.

Letting her sleep in this morning seemed like the least I could do. Besides, she looked breathtaking with her hair spread across the pillow, dark lashes fanned against her cheeks.

Utter fucking perfection.

The house was quiet, yet I found myself surprisingly comfortable making coffee and breakfast. Almost like I belonged.

I was relaxing with my first cup when Hunter stumbled into the room.

Rubbing sleep from his eyes, he shuffled toward me with a giant yawn, blond curls sticking up everywhere.

When he noticed me staring, he seemed anything but awkward.

"Good morning," he said, like finding a strange guy in his kitchen wasn't at all unusual.

For a moment, I wondered if it was normal, then dismissed the thought. Jamie was nothing but responsible when it came to her son. He was her priority. No way was she subjecting him to random men.

Although right now, I was categorically random.

"Morning." I felt awkward myself, unsure how to proceed.

Jamie and I hadn't discussed this meeting. I didn't know how she wanted me to explain things, or if she wanted explanations at all.

Did she even want me to meet him? Maybe she'd expected me to sneak out before he woke up.

But he was important to her, which made him important to me. If I had any hope with Jamie, I'd need her son's approval.

"Is there cereal or anything? I'm starving." He stretched, drawing out his starvation into four long syllables.

I chuckled at his exaggerated hunger, pulling open the cupboard where Jamie and I had stored groceries.

Our groceries. The thought sent satisfaction through me.

"No cereal, but we've got bagels. There's butter in the fridge. Juice too."

"Oh, thank goodness." He dragged himself to the fridge. "Orange juice. My favorite."

He poured himself some juice, then fixed me with curious eyes. "So…I'm Hunter. Who the heck are you?"

Holy shit. He was a mini-Jamie, and I wanted to laugh and hug him for being so damn awesome.

"I'm Eric. I'm a friend of your mom's. Just helping her out."

"I didn't know my mom had friends here. Are you friends with my dad too? Did you know her from before?"

"Actually, I just met your mom six days ago. Your dad and I aren't friends yet, but I've met him."

"Yeah, my dad and I aren't really friends yet either. But he's trying to help me get a dog, so I guess he's kind of cool." He examined me over his orange juice as we waited for his bagel to toast. "Do you like dogs?"

"Of course. Who doesn't like dogs?"

"Exactly. This is what I keep telling my mom. I know she likes them, but she keeps saying no. She just won't give in, even though I think she'd like to have one too."

"She's stubborn sometimes, I've noticed."

"No, she's like that all the time, trust me." His eyes went wide with sincerity.

The kid was absolutely right. Jamie's stubbornness was legendary.

"But I found her weakness." I lowered my voice conspiratorially.

"No way. She doesn't have a weakness." He crossed his arms, expression skeptical. "My mom's the strongest lady I know. She's even stronger than some of my friends' dads."

"Yeah, she's tough, that's for sure. But I did find her soft spot. Want to know what it is?"

"Is that an actual question? It's redundant, right?" His sarcasm was perfect—obviously he'd inherited his mother's best traits.

"You got me." I laughed, finding it hard to stay serious. "But if I tell you, it stays between us. If she finds out we know, we're screwed."

Shit, language.

I wasn't sure what was appropriate for a nine-year-old. I'd been on my own when Caleb was this age. I'd have to watch my mouth.

"Okay, I can agree to that deal."

"Oh, shit. You already know the secret." Fuck, the language thing would be harder than I'd expected. I'd gotten too comfortable without responsibilities.

He looked at me like I'd lost my mind.

"Making a deal," I explained. "She can't resist. It's like setting up a dare or making a bet. She'll agree to what you want if you offer something she can't refuse. You just need to know what she wants."

"You said you met her six days ago?" He narrowed his eyes at me.

"Yeah." I laughed. "It's been a busy six days."

"She must really like you."

"Why would you say that? You haven't even heard of me until now. I bet she hasn't mentioned me once."

"Nope. You're right. Not once." The kid really knew how to make a guy feel good. "But you're here. My mom doesn't really have friends. Especially not ones hanging around our house at eight in the morning. She only sticks around people she really likes. You're here, and you seem to have her figured out, so that must mean she really likes you."

The wisdom of a nine-year-old made it all sound simple.

But maybe it was that simple. Jamie and I liked each other, we'd become great friends with incredible benefits, and I didn't want to be away from her. Didn't want to miss any of it.

"You're a lot like your mom. You're a pretty cool kid. And I really like her too."

"Yeah, don't get too comfortable, Eric. She's the best lady in the world, and she's the most important person to me. If you mess with her, I'll find a way to mess you up. My dad's a cop, you know."

"Hunter, I think you and I are going to get along great."

An hour with Hunter had exceeded every expectation. After the initial awkwardness, we'd fallen into comfortable, effortless conversation.

Jamie's child was as easy to fall in love with as she was.

He was smart. Raised with honesty, love, humility, and a healthy dose of humor. It showed in how he interacted, how he projected those qualities back. His awareness seemed light-years beyond his age. He considered the impact of his words and actions.

His take on what happened with his friend Jackson absolutely blew my mind. For nine years old, he was damn insightful. And it was almost a shame he was so aware, since it was obvious he was hurt by his friend's betrayal.

He was a good kid. Jamie's worries about her parenting skills were misplaced. Considering she'd done the job of two parents without support from her own, she'd done better than average.

Way better than Jackson's parents, that was for sure.

I'd been hoping Jamie would join our lazy morning before heading to the hospital, but my hopes shattered when she rushed into the kitchen, frantic.

She looked wild, ready to trample anyone in her way. Something was very wrong.

Hunter didn't seem to notice. "Mom, you should've told me you had a cool friend like Eric. Did you know his brother can skateboard? He's practically a pro. Eric said we could all go to the hospital together. I want to meet Caleb. Eric says if you agree, I can hang out with them sometime."

"Only if you agree." I added, watching Jamie's distracted movements.

We'd talked about Caleb nonstop. Once mentioned, he'd become Hunter's favorite topic.

But Jamie didn't acknowledge us. She bustled around, grabbing water and her purse from the counter.

Whatever was wrong, it was bad.

"I have to go to the hospital. Now. They called." Her voice was tight with barely controlled panic.

"Let me grab my stuff." I stood, taking charge. "Hunter, go change out of your pajamas. I'll drive you both over."

This I could handle. I'd been prepared for this moment since we'd left the hospital together.

It didn't reduce my worry, but it reassured me that her

behavior wasn't about me being here. She wasn't upset because I'd befriended her kid after spending the night in her bed.

"No." She shook her head. "I'll go alone. I'm okay."

"Mom, you shouldn't go by yourself." Hunter's concern was evident.

Smart kid. He was absolutely right.

"I love you, bud, but I can't wait. Everything will be okay."

She gave him a quick, tight hug before turning to me, her beautiful face void of emotion. "Can you take care of him? Please? Stay here, enjoy the morning, take him to the park or to meet Caleb—whatever you were talking about. I'll call when I'm there and know more about Dad's condition. I just need to get there now."

"No problem. You go. I'll handle everything. I'll bring Hunter to you as soon as possible."

"No." Her plea was desperate. "Don't bring him until I know it's okay. If things are too bad…"

"Of course, beautiful girl. Whatever you need." Just like every other time I'd said this, I meant it. I'd do anything to make things better for her.

On instinct, Jamie wrapped her arms around my neck and pulled me down for a solid, quick kiss.

My reaction was selfish, but it felt good that she'd turn to me this way. I couldn't resist holding her tightly for that brief moment. This was exactly where she belonged—in my arms, trusting me to take care of what mattered most to her.

Hunter's reaction was less enthusiastic. "I thought you said she was just your friend, Eric."

"Not now, dude." I shot him a warning look and pushed Jamie toward the door. "Call me soon."

The moment Jamie was gone, I ignored her instructions, turning to Hunter. "Go get dressed. We're following her to the hospital."

No way in hell would I let her carry this burden alone. Never again.

There wasn't much I could do, but I could be there. I could be ready when she needed someone to lean on. I could have her kid waiting when she needed him, too.

She still hadn't figured out she wasn't alone. Didn't matter how many times I'd told her—it wasn't sinking in.

So screw it.

I'd show her.

CHAPTER TWENTY-SEVEN

JAMIE

BOLD, BOISTEROUS LAUGHTER ROUSED ME FROM THE MOST explicit dream of my life.

God, I wanted to return to that blissful state, to finish what had begun—or let it finish me off. I wasn't picky. But as I lay half-awake, I couldn't recall the details. The harder I tried, the vaguer the memory became, until it was nothing more than an aching need.

Then that rich, deep baritone laugh hit me again. With each punch of Eric's exuberance, a zing of pleasure coursed through me, reminding me of what I'd been dreaming about.

Eric. His voice must've infiltrated my subconscious, bringing me to the brink of ecstasy with nothing but the sound of him and my imagination.

For a moment, I contemplated finishing what the dream had started. But then I heard Hunter's voice. My sexual frustration faded as my motherly instincts kicked in.

Hunter was here. How could I have forgotten?

I'd spent half the night pacing, waiting for his arrival, stressing over how to introduce him to the man who had me so tied in knots I momentarily forgot about my own child.

He was out there, laughing with Eric. It sounded like they were having a party for two, and I was suddenly curious about their interaction. Had Eric made the same kind of impression on my son that he had on me?

But before I could pull myself out of bed, my phone rang.

The chirpy ringtone sent a jolt of fear through me. I knew it wasn't anyone I wanted to hear from.

My gut told me it was bad news.

When I answered on the third ring, Nurse Judy's voice confirmed my fears. "Your dad has taken a turn for the worse. A prolonged decline is still possible, but the doctor's assessment is the most likely scenario."

And the prognosis was clear. He had a day, at most.

A day.

I'd been bracing for his passing all week but knowing it was imminent left me struggling to accept it. With an expiration date stamped on my father's life, I felt desperate for more time.

One day?

"I'll be right there." I promised, pulling on my pants and rummaging for a clean shirt.

I rushed into the kitchen, wearing yesterday's jeans and a faded radio station T-shirt from my teens, to find Eric and Hunter chatting over the remnants of breakfast. It was the exact scene I'd been trying to visualize only moments ago. Now, it barely registered.

Distraught and unsure what to do next, I made the awkward situation impossible. I kissed Eric. Arms around his neck. Hands in his hair. My mouth on his. And Hunter right there.

No introductions. Though, they'd clearly taken care of that themselves. No explanations. I didn't have any good ones, anyway. No acknowledgment of what I'd done.

Hours passed in my father's hospital room before it finally sank in.

I'd kissed Eric. In front of my son.

Heat crawled up my neck. I was an emotional decision-maker. Feel first, think later. It had led to impulsive choices and rushed resolutions before. But this?

My stomach twisted.

Leaving Hunter behind with Eric hadn't been my smartest decision. Still smarter than the kiss, but in the moment, it had felt like the only viable option. I didn't know what waited for me in my father's room, how bad it might be. I wasn't prepared to walk Hunter into something that dark.

But asking Eric to care for my child? That was different. Intimate in a way I hadn't examined. I worried I'd crossed a boundary I couldn't see. Worse, that I'd set my son up for confusion and hurt once we returned to Toronto.

What if I'd created a bond between Hunter and a man who, in a matter of days, would go back to being a stranger?

I'd told Eric I felt lost after my mom and sister died. I thought that was the deepest that grief had taken me. But sitting under the hum of hospital lights, everything felt disturbingly unbalanced. Tilted.

Nothing in my life looked the way it used to. Not my family. Not my future.

Not even me.

With fear overwhelming me, my instinct was to retreat to the bubble of security I knew best—the world where only Hunter and I mattered. Where, if I stayed locked in denial long enough, nothing could harm us.

Instead of calling Eric, I texted Hunter.

Grandpa seems okay. You should come to the hospital as soon as possible.

Between the lines, I was begging for my son to return to my side, praying he'd be safe when everything went to hell.

With a big, painful sigh, Dad roused from sleep. "Why'd you stay away so long, James? Missed you."

For so many years, I'd convinced myself he was heartless.

That alcohol had corroded his soul. But the truth was, he'd used it to hide from his emotions.

He'd run away, just like me.

Lost for words, I could only stare at him, my anxiety replaced by heartbreak and tears.

"I know I'm a bastard…I know I don't deserve…anything. Not from you. I'm your father. Still. Just wanted to hear from you…to know you're okay. Hoped I hadn't fucked you up too bad." His voice wavered, eyes closed, and my heart cracked at his raw, regretful words.

His honesty slashed a hole in my heart and fractured the dark perception I'd held for so long.

He may have been drifting in and out of awareness, but it was clear he'd been affected by our separation. Maybe even as much as me.

Had I been blind to it before?

Or were the guilt and resentment I felt simply lies I'd told myself? I'd promised Eric to stop pretending, but maybe I needed to make the same promise to myself. If I didn't face reality, I couldn't handle it when it hit me.

"Dad." My voice cracked with emotion.

"Just promise you'll give your boy a family. Real family. Love. Happiness."

"That's all I've ever wanted for him. Love and happiness."

"Family, James. Family." He finished on a wheeze.

I didn't want to make promises I couldn't keep. What did family even mean to him?

There wasn't a single relative left. My grandparents were gone, and my parents were only children. A great-aunt might exist, but even if I found her, what kind of family would that form for my son?

Did my father expect me to reunite with Dylan despite our differences? Would that make a family? It made no sense for him to ask me to sacrifice my happiness when it would hurt Hunter.

Did he really believe I could magically build a new family? He'd lived in a solitary confinement of his own making. Why did he think I could succeed when he'd so desperately failed?

But he was right.

Family was what had been missing from our tiny existence. Family was the bond my son needed for the happy life I'd always wanted for him.

Family was what I had to figure out.

But first, I needed to find out where my child was. My text to him had gone unanswered, as had my three follow-ups.

Worry gnawed at me as I imagined what that might mean.

Was he with Eric, having a good time? Were they down at the waterfront, where Eric and I had played just two days ago? Or maybe they were hiking my favorite trail.

I needed to push aside my doubts and call Eric. I'd left my child in his care. I trusted him more than Hunter's father, and almost more than I trusted myself.

But trust wasn't the issue.

It was fear.

A big, healthy dose of fear.

I was afraid of the situation I'd created, forming a relationship with a man who was far too earnest for a temporary fling. I was apprehensive about bringing this steadfast man into my son's life. Not because he didn't deserve it, but because I was terrified I'd screw it all up.

And I wouldn't be the only one hurt in the end.

CHAPTER TWENTY-EIGHT

ERIC

HUNTER AND CALEB WERE GETTING ALONG BETTER THAN I'D expected.

They sat side by side on the hospital bed, heads bent together over my phone, like old friends picking up where they'd left off instead of two people who'd just met.

When Caleb laughed—really laughed—something in my chest shifted. For that moment, he was himself again. High-spirited, on the verge of causing trouble, alive in a way that had nothing to do with machines or medicine.

The tight band around my ribs loosened a notch.

Even if it didn't last. Even if tomorrow swallowed this version of him whole. Right now, he looked strong. Like he could outrun the word cancer.

Just one more day.

As Day Zero crept closer, I could feel every possible disaster lurking in the shadows. I trusted Caleb to soldier on—he'd proven his strength time and again. It was all the variables I couldn't control that had my jaw clenched tight.

But Caleb was unfazed, talking about the transplant like the most exciting adventure of his life. I'd been calling it doomsday. For him, it was new hope.

My parents arrived first, Marc and Celeste right behind them. The room filled quickly, voices overlapping, chairs scraping.

Hunter fit right in.

Mom was smitten, fussing over him like a grandchild. Odd, considering he was only five years younger than her own son.

The hospital was still oppressive. Still fucking depressing. But being back with my family cut through some of that weight. Celeste was right. They needed me. Now more than ever.

I was grateful to be here for them. And Jamie.

This plan better not backfire.

Part of me knew the strategy—let Hunter and Caleb work their magic, show Jamie what we could be together. But using kids to trigger sympathy wasn't exactly the foundation for anything lasting.

And lasting was exactly what Jamie and I were going to have.

Whatever it took, whatever I had to tear down or build up, she was mine. The promise to her father had only solidified what my gut already knew. Not because a dying man had coerced me, but because claiming Jamie was what I fucking wanted more than my next breath.

Sure, my life was a mess. No job, no home to call my own. But for the first time in as long as I could remember, I had something that gave me purpose. Something on the other side of the darkness.

Jamie was that light. Every piece of her—the fun, sad, sexy, loving, beautiful, slightly crazy woman who'd gotten under my skin and rewired my entire world.

The urge to pull Hunter aside and explain everything burned in my chest. How much his mom meant to me. How we were meant for each other. How I planned to fight for her until she stopped running.

But that conversation belonged to Jamie, not me. He'd have questions that weren't mine to answer. Questions he might not even want me answering, if his reaction to the kiss this morning was any indication.

He'd been shooting me sideways glances ever since, eyes narrowed, lips pressed tight.

"So, after the transplant, you still have to stay here?" he asked, in awe of the process Caleb had just explained.

"Yeah, but it's not bad. I've got a couple nurses that are really sweet." Caleb smiled at Hunter, then looked at me with his usual mischievous smirk. Sweet was code for hot. My kid brother was always prowling.

"Caleb." I shot him a look of warning.

He ignored me, leaning toward Hunter. "But none of the nurses are as sweet as your mom. She took the best care of me. She's the sweetest."

Little troublemaker.

"It's true." Celeste nodded. "Hunter, your mom is fabulous. I don't say that lightly. She made Caleb feel better just by talking to him. So awesome she made me cry with her ridiculous perfection."

"I need to thank her for her generosity." Mom chimed in.

"Where is she anyway?" Marc asked innocently. "I haven't met her yet."

Every eye zeroed in on him. He was clueless. I hadn't discussed Jamie's dying father with her son present.

Though, he'd handled Caleb's illness and my family without losing his smile. Maybe Hunter was more resilient than I was giving him credit for.

"She's with my grandpa." Hunter sat taller, meeting Marc's question head-on. "He's here in the hospital, too. But he's not doing good. She's busy taking care of him now."

Marc looked between us, guilt creasing his brow. "I'm sorry. No one told me."

"It's okay," Hunter reassured. "I've never met him, so I'm not too sad. Except, it makes my mom sad. So I'm sad for her."

I'd always thought Caleb was the most amazing kid on earth, but Hunter was giving him a run for that title.

Jamie had raised a boy that was smart, funny, and compassionate. She was incredible, and her kid proved it. Just another reason I felt so strongly about her.

"Oh, *petite ange*." My mom's voice softened. "We are all so very sad for her. I hope she will let us help if we can."

I squeezed Hunter's shoulder. "You too. We're here if you need anything."

"Could you take me to see her now?" He turned his face up to meet my gaze, his eyes going watery.

"I don't think that's a good idea. She wanted us to wait for her call."

"But I left my phone. You rushed me and I forgot it. What if she's calling me now?" His anxiety peaked in a frustrated cry.

"Make you a deal," I said, hoping he didn't catch on to my tactic. "Stay here and chat skateboarding with Caleb. I'll go talk to your mom. I'll make sure you see her before your dad comes to get you."

Yes, I'd called Dylan.

It was the best solution I could think of. He should be there for his kid.

I knew how Frank Hartley looked yesterday, and it wasn't good. I could only imagine what worse meant. That was too traumatic for a kid.

Hell, it was traumatic for everyone.

Dylan might not be a major fixture in Hunter's life, but he was permanent. Right now, I couldn't say the same.

"Yeah, okay," Hunter replied. "Just please tell her I'm not a baby. I can handle it."

"Of course you can." I nodded at my mother, tears in her

eyes. "But she's your mom. It's her job to shield you from heartache."

"If it's hurting her, then it's hurting me," he whispered.

"Me too, bud. Me too."

Hunter launched himself at me, arms wrapping around my waist and squeezing tight, catching me off guard.

After only a moment's hesitation, I hugged him back. I held Jamie's kid like he was my own, pouring every ounce of love I had into the embrace.

CHAPTER TWENTY-NINE

ERIC

JAMIE WAS PACING THE LOUNGE ACROSS FROM HER FATHER'S room, phone pressed to her ear. When she turned and found me watching from the doorway, she startled.

"I was just calling you. What are you doing here?" Relief flooded her features even as anxiety tightened her voice.

"Came to find you. We hadn't heard from you, and I was worried."

"No, I mean what are you doing *here*? At the hospital? Where's Hunter?"

"We've been here all day, waiting for you. Hunter's with my family. He and Caleb are practically best friends now."

Her brows pinched together. "Oh wow. I hope that's okay with your family. I don't want to burden them."

Concern and bewilderment warred across her face as she pressed her lips into a thin line. She looked like hell—stressed, tortured, completely wrung out.

And still fucking gorgeous.

Even drowning in worry, she was thinking about everyone else first. Always putting others before herself, always giving more than she had.

"They're all fine. How are you holding up?"

Her eyes glazed with unshed tears. "I'm not sure. I keep thinking about Hunter, how I've abandoned him during another crisis. I hate the idea of him seeing me fall apart. I just didn't know what the right choice was."

"Hunter's fine. He's just worried about you."

She crossed her arms over her middle, holding herself together like she might break apart. "Can I confess something?"

Without waiting for an answer, she rushed on. "I was worried about Hunter, but I've been worrying more about you."

"What the fuck, Jamie?" The words burst from me before I could stop them.

She flinched, chin trembling.

Shit. I gentled my voice. "Why are you worrying about me? I should be the last person on your list right now."

"Really? Because you're practically all I can think about. My father's dying—he'll probably die tonight—but I'm focused on you, wondering if you're going to hate me when I leave."

There it was. The truth I'd been dreading, thrust into the open like a wound left to fester. It hurt worse acknowledged. So much fucking worse than I'd expected.

There really was no more pretending now.

This was Jamie being honest, dropping the walls just like we'd promised. And it was my heart getting crushed, my soul shattering as she told me this was the end.

"It's impossible for me to hate you, beautiful girl."

"Don't say that." She shook her head. "Nothing's impossible. You can't stop bad things from happening. Hating me is the only logical outcome. You don't even know me. Not really."

"I know enough."

Her hands balled into fists, one clutching her phone like she might crush it.

"Do we need to make another deal?" Mock irritation colored my voice.

She sighed in defeat. "What this time?"

"We've stepped into total honesty territory here. Let's stop pretending this doesn't matter. Stop acting like what's between us is some fake arrangement with the benefit of sex." I moved closer, claiming her space. "You agreed to let me into your club, but I want a ranking membership. I want the title to be real."

Too quiet. She was being too damn quiet, and doubt started clawing at my chest.

"You really want that?" Her whisper was barely audible, hands drifting toward her heart.

"Hell yes." The words came out rough, possessive. "Jamie, I know it's complicated—how we met, everything feeling so uncertain. I know you're not sure where you're headed or what comes next. You might be uncertain about me, but I have no doubts about you."

"I'm not uncertain about you, Eric. It's me I'm not sure of. I don't know if I can handle more than what we've been doing." Her voice cracked. "I'm not really a good person. I've done horrible things to get where I am. You don't know the half of it, and I don't think you'd like me if you did."

"Have you killed someone?"

Her face scrunched in confusion.

"Been an accomplice to murder?"

Again, that puzzled expression told me everything I needed to know.

"Jamie, I don't give a shit about your past. Especially since I know you did what you had to do. For yourself, and your kid. Those things don't define you."

I hooked a finger under her chin, urging her gaze up to meet mine. "Whatever you did before, you're a good person now. I've seen it. I know it. And I doubt anything you've done is half as bad as you think."

Tears tracked down her cheeks as conviction replaced confusion. "I stole things. Lots of things. More than just my dad's car. I've lied constantly—to get my job, to keep my job, to myself practically every day."

"Lying and stealing to put food on the table aren't the worst things I can imagine."

"What about blackmail?" The words came out like a challenge, daring me to find fault. "Dylan's mom was having an affair. I threatened to expose her unless she paid me. What do you think about that?"

"I think if she had anything to do with Dylan's initial reaction to your pregnancy, she probably deserved it."

"Are you kidding me?" Her voice pitched higher. "How can you brush that aside? Blackmailing someone is ruthless and vindictive. Good people don't do that, no matter how desperate."

"Would you do it again?"

"What?"

"If you could go back, change your decision, would you?"

She paused, breathing deep and even. "No. I wouldn't change a damn thing. I'd do it again without question. My son needed me, and I didn't have another choice."

"Then you're exactly who I thought you were all along."

She stared like she was still waiting for the other shoe to drop.

"Are you still feeling lost, beautiful girl? Don't you know who you are?"

"I used to. At least I thought I did." Her voice broke. "Now I'm not sure of anything."

"Let me tell you who you are to me." My hand slid to the back of her head, not giving her room to retreat. "You're a strong, independent woman who'd do anything for the people you love, even if it tears you apart inside. You're honest when it counts, with the people who matter. You're fun, mischievous, and sexy as hell."

I reached for her hand, bringing it to my chest, placing it over my pounding heart. "You're the most beautiful woman I've ever met, Jamie. Not just your face or your ass—though I happen to think both are fucking perfect—but *you*. Every piece of you. You're a goddamn beautiful person, and I can't imagine not having you in my life."

Someone cleared their throat behind me.

I didn't want to turn away from Jamie's astonished expression. Didn't care who was watching. Her reaction was too important to miss. Her cheeks flushed red, brow drawn tight, that sexy mouth hanging slightly open. Pure innocence wrapped in fire. No matter how corrupt she claimed to be, her heart was virtuous.

She was perfect, and I couldn't look away. Not with my heart exposed and my future hanging in the balance.

For a moment, she looked like she wanted to say yes. Like she wanted to try.

Say yes to me.

Instead, her misty blue eyes traveled over my shoulder. The uncertainty lifted from her features as her mouth curved into a soft, warm smile.

"You always have been pretty awesome," Dylan drawled.

My heart stopped. Pain rushed in to fill the empty space.

What the hell? Was she looking at him with love in her eyes?

"Maybe your awesomeness can forgive me? I somehow got coerced."

Domineering asshole. One more word and I'd either knock him out or crumple to the floor in devastation.

"It's okay." Jamie's eyes sparkled. "I was waiting."

I hung my head, closed my eyes in defeat, and let her go. It hurt too much to watch her dump my attempt at a future right back in my lap.

"Sorry, but I really did try to give you more time," he said.

More time? There could never be enough time with her.

"No, this is good. Well, nothing's good right now. But having all of you here helps."

All of you?

My eyes flew open. I spun around to face Dylan, shocked to see genuine guilt instead of the superiority I'd expected. Movement behind him drew my focus to the hallway, where Hunter stood beside Celeste as she pushed Caleb in a wheelchair.

Recognition hit like a freight train. The look on Jamie's face wasn't just love. It was devoted gratitude. Cherished appreciation directed at everyone who'd come to support her.

And I felt like a complete asshole.

My sick brother, demanding sister, Jamie's son, and her ex had all gathered to help her through this, all while I selfishly pushed her for a commitment.

Dylan stepped aside, allowing Jamie to pull Hunter into her arms. She kissed the top of his head. "Was this your idea?"

"Actually, it was all mine," Caleb boasted. "Hope it's not too overwhelming, but I figured you could use better company than Eric. He still hasn't picked up any of my cool. Sorry, I've tried, but some people just aren't capable of being smooth like me."

Jamie's laughter was real. And it was heart-stopping.

Caleb might be a shit-disturber, but I'd never been more grateful for it.

"I hope it's okay." Celeste sounded almost meek. It was out of character, but I was thankful for that too.

"Are you kidding?" Jamie smiled at her. "I'm thrilled. I can't tell you how much this means."

"We won't stay long," Dylan assured her. "Hunter wanted to see you before we leave. He'll stay the night with me if that's all right. I figured it would be best."

Interesting how Dylan had suddenly embraced this idea after I'd reminded him of his obligations. He'd been perfectly content to leave everything up to Jamie until I'd called.

Even more interesting was the strange look on Celeste's face as she watched Dylan and Jamie interact. When Jamie turned back to Hunter after nodding consent, Celeste kept watching Dylan with obvious interest.

Christ. My sister had fallen for the uniform and alpha charm. Thank God she was married. I didn't need to worry about her chasing after Dylan.

"Do you want to meet your grandpa?" Jamie asked Hunter.

"I don't know. I don't think so." Hunter's timid expression was highlighted by the death grip he had on his mother's hands.

Jamie looked uncertainly to Dylan, but when he only shrugged, her gaze shifted to me. Silently begging for guidance.

She could admit to doubts but asking for help was still outside her comfort zone.

"Your mom wants to do the right thing for you," I said. "But if seeing him feels too scary, that's okay. Nothing to be ashamed of."

"We all get scared sometimes," Caleb added.

Hunter looked from face to face, and after a moment of contemplation, he squared his shoulders. "Okay. I can face my fear. But can you go first, Mom? I want Eric to bring me in."

"Eric?" Jamie stepped back, looking at me with wary anticipation.

"Yeah. That's cool."

After an awkward silence, Jamie leaned down to hug Caleb, whispering something in his ear that made him laugh with pure joy. He'd always been the charmer, but I could see how thoroughly Jamie had charmed him right back.

Without another glance, Jamie headed toward her father's room.

"You know where to find us." Celeste turned to wheel Caleb back toward his room. "Don't rush back, big brother."

"Bye, Caleb. See you later," Hunter called.

Whatever Caleb replied was lost on me. I was too busy staring down Dylan. Present but unwilling to get involved. Maybe he was trying, but I still didn't like the guy.

"I'll wait here in the lounge." He yawned. "Let me know when you're done with my kid."

Ignoring Dylan's barely hidden contempt, I focused on Hunter. Just him and me and the ball of fear he'd been trying to control. His request to have me as backup was surprising, but it meant everything.

Having a purpose—a way to help—made me feel less like a bystander.

"You nervous?" I asked.

"A little."

"Need anything before we go in there?"

"No. I wanted to talk to you in private." His eyes sharpened, features intense. "About you and my mom."

I braced for uncomfortable questions. His hard glare suggested he had plenty.

But what he asked threw me. "She doesn't know what's happening with you, does she?"

Smart kid.

"No, she doesn't."

"Were you planning to tell her?" Without waiting for an answer, Hunter lowered his voice in clear warning. "Friends shouldn't keep big secrets from each other. Especially friends who kiss."

"Noted."

"Good. It's scary to tell the truth sometimes, but it's better. Trust me—I always feel better when I tell her the truth." He turned and walked toward his grandfather's room, leaving me stunned.

Fuck, he was right. "Hunter."

He paused in the doorway.

I caught up in four quick strides. "It's not fear holding me back. At least not the kind you're thinking. My fear isn't about your mom. It's about Caleb."

"I know. Just like I'm not afraid to meet my grandfather." His eyes went glassy, breath strained. "But I am afraid of what happens when he dies—how sad my mom's going to be. So, I'm still kinda scared to go in there. I don't think it matters why."

This kid's insight put me to shame. "You're right. Fear is fear. But you don't need to worry. I'm not leaving your mom alone. I promise I'll be with her. And I promise I'll tell her everything."

"Okay, good. But can you promise me one more thing? Give me warning next time you two decide to make out? Witnessing that was seriously disturbing."

"Hey, she kissed me. I can't be held responsible for my reaction to that."

"Stop. I don't want details. Save that talk for like three years from now, okay?"

"Deal."

Our laughter was genuine but brief. When Hunter looked back toward the open doorway, the mood turned somber.

Squaring his shoulders again, he declared, "Let's go meet my grandfather."

I didn't tell him I'd already met Frank Hartley. Didn't tell him how brave I thought he was. Didn't mention that despite my hope for the future, this could be the last time I ever saw him.

Instead, I wrapped my arm around his shoulders and squeezed. "Let's do this."

DAY MINUS 1

CHAPTER THIRTY

JAMIE

I'd always imagined my father's death would be tumultuous. He was such a demanding, volatile man, I figured his death would be equally loud and abrupt.

It wasn't.

He slipped away silently in the early morning hours as I sat by his bedside, holding his limp hand.

The timing matched almost exactly what the doctor had predicted, like they were counting down to his final breath. Or maybe they just knew how much morphine a failing body could tolerate before shutting down for good.

He never regained consciousness after forcing my promise to find a family. Never opened his eyes to meet Hunter. My son stared at his grandfather's sleeping form for what felt like an eternity.

God, I hoped this wouldn't mess my child up too badly.

But Hunter was stronger and more adaptable than I'd ever imagined. When he'd walked into that hospital room without hesitation, he wasn't my little boy anymore. Overnight, he'd become a young man.

While I worried about Hunter being exposed to illness and

death, he was busy worrying about me. I could feel it in the way he lingered longer each time we hugged.

At least he had that phone call to remember. That moment had impacted us all—like my father needed one last good deed to help balance all the bad he'd done.

I hoped he'd tipped his scale far enough.

I'd wanted Dad to be happy with me before he went. Secretly hoped to make amends for the shit we'd put each other through. To lay the ghosts of our past to rest.

Maybe in his mind, some of that was accomplished. Maybe talking to Hunter and seeing me was enough to give him peace.

Maybe I'd find peace with it too. Someday.

I'd been alone so long I'd forgotten it was by choice. But the world wasn't closed off. I didn't have to be alone anymore. There were good people out there. I just needed to be brave enough to let them in.

Without Caleb's mischievous ways, I would've been alone when my father passed. Eric wouldn't have been by my side, lending me strength. Without them, I'd have fallen into despair without a safety net to catch me.

"You look as exhausted as I feel." My voice came out raw with emotion.

I'd been pacing the lounge, waiting for reality to sink in and for the coroner to collect my father's body. I wasn't required to wait, yet I couldn't leave. I wanted to see him off properly, ensure he was still being cared for, even if just his body.

But time had stopped. I was anxious to move on, wipe this slate clean.

"I'm fine. You're the one ready to collapse." Eric shifted uncomfortably in the cheap hospital chair.

Why didn't they have decent furniture? Didn't they know people spent hours waiting while their lives fell apart?

"Come here, beautiful."

He was right. I was ready to fall over. Constant movement

was the only thing keeping me conscious. Maybe my pacing was an effort to hold grief at bay a little longer.

Eric's strong arms were inviting. I surrendered to the comfort he offered, not caring when I practically fell into his lap. His solid thighs became an island of reprieve as I sank against him, engulfed by his embrace.

"Thank you. I don't know if I could have done this on my own."

"You absolutely could have, but I'm glad you didn't have to. No need to be alone when I'm right here."

"You are. You have been since we met. Why?"

I should've had more faith, but I still didn't understand his motivation. What did he get from all this kindness?

"Because I want to be. Because I've never met someone more willing to give to others while expecting absolutely nothing in return."

"Sounds like you're describing yourself."

"No, beautiful girl. I have very solid expectations of getting something back." His dimpled smile was soft and sweet. "When I saw you with Caleb that first time, you gave him that gorgeous smile and I was gone. But when you cried in my arms?" His voice roughened. "I can't explain it, Jamie. I just wanted to be the one to make you smile again. Because it feels so fucking good to make you happy. Collecting those joyful moments with you—that makes me feel like the luckiest man alive."

Heat bloomed in my chest. "That was kind of poetic."

I kissed his cheek, breathing in his familiar scent. "Having you here means more than I can express. You've been so reliable, even though I've made you prove yourself over and over. I'm sorry if I seem ungrateful."

"Don't apologize. I'm happy to prove myself to you, for as long as it takes."

"I think it's my turn to prove myself to you." My lips sought his, inappropriate timing be damned.

He kissed me back, mouth soft and yielding. Comforting yet hot and enticing.

It would've been easy to let our kiss consume me. This man made me feel things I'd never experienced in ways I never imagined possible. There wasn't vocabulary to express the depth of what was happening between us.

But I didn't have time to try. Eric broke away, his eyes shifting behind me.

The coroner was there. It was time for me to move on.

The nurses hadn't rushed me. They'd suggested I spend as much time with the body as I needed. *The body.* I refused to think of my father as an empty vessel, but I couldn't stand sitting with his lifeless form, mocking me with stark proof of my denial.

Now he was being wheeled away under a white sheet, and I wasn't ready.

I needed more time.

My fists pressed against my aching chest as I held back the temptation to chase down the coroner. He probably felt nothing, carting a dead man away. This was just his job. He'd probably done it thousands of times.

But I wanted to scream at him. I couldn't stand his indifference. This wasn't just another corpse. Did he understand the gravity of this moment? Did he know that even though this was the end, I wasn't ready to let go?

A painful sob bubbled up, escaping before I could stop it.

I tried tamping it down with borrowed strength from the man behind me, his arms wrapped firmly around my middle. Without Eric's tight grip holding me back, I might've chased after that gurney.

But Eric held me until I stopped straining against him. Until my urge to run was gone. Until raw desperation deflated and left me sagging against him in defeated despair.

"That's it. I'm getting you out of here." His voice was low, commanding.

"I don't think I can leave." The words felt disconnected from me, my mind fogged with sorrow.

"You need peace and comfort at home, not strangers in a hospital." His arms tightened around me possessively. "Come on. I'll carry you if I have to."

"No." Survival instincts took over. Ten years ago, I'd chosen to leave my dad behind. Now I didn't have a choice, but the will I needed to carry on felt achingly similar. "I can walk."

Suddenly, leaving sounded like the most amazing idea. The only sensible option.

I could walk.

Better yet, I could run.

CHAPTER THIRTY-ONE

JAMIE

Sleep evaded me despite bone-deep exhaustion.

I rolled onto my side, then my back, the sheets tangling around my legs. My father's death was playing on a loop in my mind. Not because of how he'd died or my moment of weakness saying goodbye. Not even our week of heated, sorrowful words.

It was all the years before. All the time we'd wasted, and all the anger that felt so pointless now.

Eric had told me the past was the past, and no amount of dwelling would ever change it. He was right, of course. I couldn't move on if I stayed stuck worrying about things that were over. It was time to learn from my mistakes and move forward.

Figure out what the hell came next.

But it seemed impossible. I hadn't just lost my father—everything had changed. Even me.

I pressed my palms against my eyes, trying to stop the spiral of thoughts. One week. The best and worst of my life. Long enough to realize my protective bubble was fragile as tissue paper and I was suffocating inside it.

Now that bubble had popped.

But even with opportunity stretched before me, it all felt out of reach. Like standing at the edge of a canyon, my old patterns waiting to pull me back while possibilities called from the other side. Between safety and hope stood a chasm of doubt and fear.

Without a bridge it was inconceivable.

Eric had been building me one, but I needed to finish it myself.

I turned toward him, studying his peaceful face in the dim light filtering through the curtains. His hard jaw had lost its anxious edge. Even his untamed eyebrows looked calmer.

He'd crashed the minute we'd crawled into bed, pulling me against his solid warmth. I'd wanted to ask about last night's conversation, but exhaustion had claimed him first.

Did he mean what he'd said? Could we make this real?

I sat up, rubbing my temple where a headache was building. The questions were making me dizzy.

There were still so many variables. The biggest being distance. If I went back to Toronto, how would we build anything real? The next month would be filled with anxiety over Caleb. Eric wouldn't leave—I'd never expect that. But if I was back in the city, back at my job, back to my two-person bubble with Hunter, how could I give Eric what he needed?

More importantly, could I live with myself if I didn't try?

God, I need to stop. I was spiraling again, picking at the same wounds until they bled.

Eric had given me zero reasons to doubt him. Yet that twisted part of my brain—the part that conjured fake health problems and urged me to run—wouldn't shut up.

It wasn't him I didn't trust, it was our situation.

What if this connection was just comfort? What if our meeting was only meant to be a distraction—a momentary fling to help us both get through?

Eric stirred as I shifted restlessly beside him. I held my breath, waiting, but he settled back into sleep.

Enough. I needed to move before I woke him with my tossing and turning.

I slipped from bed, bare feet hitting the cold hardwood. Maybe physical action would quiet the chaos in my head.

I found myself at the closed door of my parents' bedroom, hand trembling as it hovered over the knob. It would be my first time breaching this threshold in over a decade.

As children, Trina and I were never allowed to enter this room unless invited. Even now, as an adult, opening the door felt like intruding on sacred space.

My palm slipped against the doorknob. The door cracked. My heart raced as I pushed it open with shaking fingers.

Air trapped in my lungs as shock hit me.

Nothing remained of what I remembered. Where Trina's room had stayed frozen in time, my father's was unrecognizable. He'd redone it.

Clean and clutter-free, it was masculine and bold. Dark woods, simple bedding, warm minimal lighting.

The only trace of my mother was a framed photo of her on the nightstand.

I moved further inside, running my fingers along the smooth surface of his dresser. Had he made these changes to rid himself of agony? Maybe it was part of his recovery from alcohol—a cathartic way to face loss and cleanse his mind and space of the haunting memories.

It was beautiful. Not just how it looked, but how it felt.

This must have helped him move forward. I sank onto the edge of his perfectly made bed, my chest aching with regret that he hadn't found this peace sooner. Sorry it took years of drinking and hiding before he finally turned things around.

God, how familiar that was.

I'd lost myself too. Hidden in a city of strangers. And it took losing my father to bring me back into the world.

Now I just needed to find the strength to stay.

CHAPTER THIRTY-TWO

ERIC

I STARTLED AWAKE IN THE DARK ROOM, ALONE. THE SPACE where Jamie should've been, cold and empty.

Fuck. I'd fallen asleep again, leaving her to cope on her own.

But where the hell was she?

I slipped out of bed, intent on dragging her back to it, forcing her to rest no matter what it took.

Soft light spilled from a doorway down the hall. Jamie sat on the floor of her father's room, surrounded by papers, clutching one document to her chest. Tears streamed down her face. Her hair was disheveled, eyes swollen, cheeks stained red.

Seeing her like that—broken and hurting—twisted something deep in my chest. I'd do anything to take away her pain, even if I could only ease it a little.

"Hey, beautiful girl. What're you doing?"

Her eyes met mine, drowning me in heartbreak. "I don't know." Her voice was thick with sorrow.

I moved into the room, sweeping papers aside to make space beside her. Close enough to touch, to shelter her with my presence.

"What've you got there?" I nodded at the document still clutched in her hands.

She looked at it like she was seeing it for the first time. "It's from my dad."

She handed it over without explanation.

It was a business license for Hartley Home Renovations, the registered owners, both Frank and Jamison Hartley.

"Looks like you're a business owner."

"I didn't even know he had his own company. He started it six years ago, and I had no idea." Fresh tears fell. "He named me in it from the beginning. He was thinking about me, even back then, and I was busy pretending he didn't exist."

"Stop beating yourself up. It won't help anything."

I shuffled through more papers, which were mostly legal documents, including a will.

"From the look of this, he's been organizing things for a long time."

My words only made her cry harder.

"Jamie." I gripped her chin, forcing her to look at me. "While he was doing this, you were raising your son. Your priorities were exactly where they should've been. Don't ever doubt that."

I traced my thumb down her cheek, following the trail of tears. One droplet clung to her lashes, threatening to fall. That single tear reminded me of her strength. Her ability to stand alone.

But she wasn't alone. I wouldn't let her be.

I cupped her jaw, and she leaned into my touch, seeking comfort.

"I'll never be allowed to doubt myself as long as you're around, will I?"

"Never." I kissed her forehead softly.

She sighed, meeting my eyes. "I guess I can live with that."

I didn't want to read too much into her words. There were

too many things left unsaid, any one of which could destroy the hope building inside me.

The hope that she'd stay.

After convincing her to leave the mess, I pulled Jamie back to the bed we'd been sharing.

It was too small for me, but I refused to complain when she draped herself over me, her head tucked under my chin. I'd sleep on concrete if it meant holding her like this.

Sleep tried to claim me, but I fought it. Jamie was still awake.

"What can I do to help you sleep, beautiful?"

"Nothing. I'll fall asleep soon, I promise. I just can't shut off my brain. Every time I start to drift, another thought hits."

"What are you thinking about?"

"I don't know. Life?"

A low laugh rumbled through my chest. "How specific."

She groaned. "This is going to sound so selfish…but it's been over twelve hours since I talked to Hunter. Last time I was away from him this long, I made myself sick with worry. This time feels different. Being away from him right now feels like a gift."

"Doesn't sound selfish at all." I smoothed a hand over her back, savoring her silken skin.

"No? I bet Vanessa and her crew would judge me for it."

"Maybe. But we've already established they're assholes. Who cares what they'd think?"

"You're right." The tension in her shoulders eased. "And I know Hunter's spending the time in a good way. Getting to know his father is important. Being around me when I'm this upset would be worse for him."

"Can I make a confession?"

"Of course." She lifted her head, and even in the darkness, her stare captivated me. "You've listened to enough of mine."

"I really enjoyed spending time with Hunter. He's great,

Jamie. Truly. And I'd like to hang out with him again…if I didn't mess up too badly with the foul language."

She smiled, resting her chin on her hand. "That's sweet."

"That wasn't my real confession." I smirked. "I wanted you to know you're not the only one enjoying private time. As happy as I was with your kid, I'm grateful for more time alone with you."

A smile quirked the corners of her lips, and her eyes filled with heat. Her hand drifted up my chest, nails scoring lightly before gripping my shoulder.

"I don't want to spend all our time sleeping." She dipped her head, trailing kisses where her hand had been.

"You sure?"

She answered with a slow, sensual kiss. Despite the exhaustion, my body came alive under hers.

Sex couldn't mend the pain, loss, or fear, but it could push them aside for a while. And if it's what she wanted, what she needed, I was more than willing.

She reached for the condoms in the bedside drawer, her breast brushing my chest, thighs gripping me, her silky hair trailing over my skin.

I watched with fascination as she tore the packet with her teeth, then sheathed me with careful precision.

I'd never thought of safe sex as anything more than an act of necessity, but watching her anticipation build as her delicate hands worked the rubber down my hardened shaft, seeing the need reflected in her eyes as she gripped me tightly, knowing her own excitement was escalating as she prepared to take me… suddenly safe sex was the most erotic thing I'd ever fucking witnessed.

We groaned in unison as our bodies joined, troubles falling away. Nothing had ever felt like being inside Jamie.

Nothing.

Fucking her was like a goddamn communion of our souls.

The ecstasy on her angelic face was more magnificent than any masterpiece. My name on her lips, more melodic than any symphony. When she came apart, pulling me right along with her, we found a place where only we existed. Where all we needed was each other to make things right.

This was it. The moment I was lost.

Fuck. Caleb was right.

Why had I ever tried to deny it?

I was head over heels, completely, ridiculously, fairy-tale style, stupidly in love with Jamie.

It was pure insanity, but I loved her. Without a single doubt.

But her sigh turned to a whimper, and suddenly she was crying again.

"Beautiful girl, I'm sorry. Was it too much?"

"No. God, no." She sobbed against my chest. "It was too perfect."

My heart slammed against my ribs. "Jamie, give me your mouth."

She raised her head, connecting her mouth to mine without hesitation. I kissed her with everything I had—lips, tongue, heart, soul.

"It was fucking perfect," I admitted when we parted.

Her sigh was content but tired. The tears had stopped, but tension remained.

"You need sleep." I bit back the urge to make more ill-timed confessions.

"Right. Sleep. You're tired too." She inhaled sharply, body going rigid, fingers digging into my side. "Oh…tomorrow is Caleb's transplant. You need to spend today with him. I'm so sorry—I almost forgot."

"It's fine. A few more hours sleep, and I'll be good. I'll head to the hospital this afternoon."

"I want to be there tomorrow. Day Zero. I want to hold your hand while you wait, like you held mine."

"Beautiful girl, nothing would make me happier. But that won't be possible."

Her face fell. "What? Why?"

"They don't allow anyone in the operating room, and I'll be too drugged to hold anyone's hand."

Confusion clouded her features. "I don't understand. Why will you be drugged?"

"Because I hear it hurts like a son of a bitch to donate bone marrow. I plan to be well medicated."

"What?" Disbelief replaced confusion. "You're Caleb's donor?"

"Yeah, beautiful girl, I am."

"Oh my God, Eric. This is huge. Why didn't you tell me?" The pain on her face hit me like a physical blow.

"That's exactly why I didn't say anything. It's not a big deal to me."

"Are you insane? How is this not a big deal?"

"Because it was just dumb luck that I was a match. A fantastic stroke of luck, but still just luck. There was no question about me being the donor. Just like there would have been no question if it were Marc or Celeste who matched."

I swallowed hard around the tightness in my throat. "Caleb needs this to live. I'm just lying on a table while doctors take some bone marrow. It's the right thing to do. The only thing to do."

I was aiming for sincerity, but the look in her eyes told me I'd fucked this up completely.

Hunter and Caleb were both right. I should've told her from the beginning. Should've trusted her with the truth instead of hiding behind my reluctance to make it seem bigger than it was.

Now I could see the hurt behind her glare, the suspicion I'd created with one omission.

Was it too late to tell her I loved her?

Would it matter now if I did?

CHAPTER THIRTY-THREE

JAMIE

THE SAFE IN DAD'S BEDROOM SHOULDN'T HAVE OPENED ON THE first try. But he'd always used Mom's birthday for passwords and combinations. Why would death change old habits?

I wasn't prepared for what I found inside.

His will left everything to me, with clear provisions for Hunter. I cried seeing notes about Hunter's education fund, monthly contributions made since his birth. *Monthly.* For nine years, while I'd convinced myself he didn't care, while I'd nursed my anger and righteousness, he'd been quietly saving for my son's future.

The betrayal was mine, not his.

My tears continued when I found my parents' marriage certificate. Its edges were yellowed, careful folds showing it had been handled often. Trina's birth record was there. Mine too, tucked beneath theirs like we were still his little girls.

When I understood the business license folded in his will, I dissolved.

So much crying. I'd spent half my time here in tears—more in the past few days than the past ten years. My face felt raw, eyes swollen nearly shut.

And I probably wasn't done.

Tucked in the back of that tiny safe was a sealed letter. My name scrawled across the envelope in Dad's messy handwriting. Opening it seemed impossible. Paralyzing. I set it aside, knowing I needed more strength to deal with whatever feelings his words would evoke.

That's when Eric walked in.

I hadn't heard his footsteps or seen his shadow, too lost in my flooding eyes and jagged breathing. But I *knew* he was there. The air itself changed, warm serenity sweeping over me like a physical blanket. His presence alone could shield me from pain and sorrow, some invisible force field that made the unbearable suddenly manageable.

We didn't need words. Never had.

Our connection felt otherworldly, like we'd been magnetized and drawn together by forces beyond understanding. I'd felt it from the beginning but hadn't recognized it until that moment.

Ever since Eric entered the hospital cafeteria, I'd been spellbound.

That was the moment my soul said, *You! Yes, you're the one!*

When he sat with me through my father's death, caring for me as I fell apart, my soul spoke again. When he continued comforting me, despite his own troubles, despite being sleep deprived and weary, my heart took notice. When he wiped my tears and looked at me with understanding no other man had ever possessed, that's when my heart and soul finally connected.

Yes. He's the one.

Lying with my head on his chest, listening to his steady heartbeat, I'd felt peace for the first time in years. Despite the whirlwind of emotions, despite life-altering events crashing around us, I could see possibility emerging from the wreckage. Even knowing the worst could still be ahead—Caleb's uncertain recovery, the chasm between our lives—I felt we could overcome it.

Together.

When I'd moved over him and he'd moved inside me, it felt like making those plans together. Our physical connection strengthened the emotional bond. No amount of grief could shadow my desire for him. He was comfort, a balm. The connection banished my remaining doubts.

Then, in our post-sex bliss, with me crying from the overwhelming beauty of it, he looked me in the eye and innocently shattered everything.

The connection, the wordless communication, the alignment of our souls. All broken.

Had I imagined it all? Maybe in my grief, I'd grasped on to something that never existed.

Eric was Caleb's donor. And it made no sense.

Not the medical procedure. That part was clear. It was his decision to hide it from me that I couldn't figure out. The careful omission. The deliberate withholding.

God, I was angry. It burned through me like wildfire. Unfathomable and un-fucking-stoppable.

"So you're having surgery tomorrow…doctors are going to stick needles in you and take your bone marrow?"

"It's not really surgery. It's an easy procedure on my end."

"Easy?"

Maybe he heard the anger threading through my tone or saw the doubt written across my face, because Eric pulled away—actually pulled away—swinging his legs over the bed's edge and turning his back to me.

The gesture felt like a slap. Cold, impersonal, and dismissive.

And it hurt like hell.

"Was it easy to keep it all to yourself?" The accusation spilled out before I could stop it. "Easier not to share details? Easy to put it out of your mind when you had me as distraction?"

"Christ, Jamie." He whipped around, fury blazing in his eyes. "This isn't about you. Don't you get that? This is about me. It was easier not to think about it because considering all the fucked-up, horrible ways things can go wrong, it's too fucking much to deal with."

His breath turned ragged, eyes wild. "I don't want to think about my little brother dying. And I sure as hell don't want to think about my donated cells being what might kill him."

My anger deflated like a punctured balloon, all that righteous indignation leaking out in one pathetic whoosh.

Once again, my emotional response had hijacked everything. I'd turned his heartfelt confession into something ugly. His omission hurt, but I'd been thoughtless.

"I'm sorry. That was selfish. I didn't mean it that way."

"Fuck, Jamie, I get it. I wasn't honest and it hurt you. I meant to tell you. It just never felt like the right time."

"It's okay. I understand why you didn't."

"No, you don't." His sigh left me breathless, like the room had no air. "All that shit about avoiding my thoughts—it's not the whole truth."

The burn in my chest intensified. "What's the whole truth?"

I gasped for air as I waited. The room felt smaller suddenly, walls pressing in. The silence stretched until I thought I might break from the tension.

"People have a way of romanticizing this kind of thing. They turn it into something it's not. Like an act of bravery." He cringed, his bold blue eyes watering. "I didn't want you to look at me that way. I'm not just the guy who's saving his brother's life. I didn't want you to fall for me because you thought I was some kind of hero. I wanted you to see me. Just me."

His gaze held mine, imploring.

"I did see you. I do. And I would have, no matter what. You promised me no more pretending. I trusted that. I told you everything. All my secrets. I trusted you."

"And now?"

Now? Now I felt like an idiot for believing in fairy tales and soul connections. Now I felt like that naïve girl who'd gotten pregnant at seventeen, thinking love could conquer everything.

"I still want to trust you, Eric. But I feel like you didn't give me a chance. You didn't give me your trust. That hurts, and I don't know what to do with it."

"Jamie, everything I said at the hospital—I meant it." His hand landed on my knee, his touch gentle but possessive. "I want you. I want us. More than just right now. Nothing's changed."

"But everything's changed. My whole world's upside down and I'm waiting for it to stop spinning. You say you know what you want, but how can you know, when nothing in our lives is normal? We've both been through so much shit—you're still going through it. How can you trust what you're feeling? How can I trust it too?"

"You want normal?" His voice turned hard, hand tightening on my knee. "I've had normal. Normal fucking sucked. That wasn't living."

His intensity didn't waver. "Things may be chaotic now. It may all feel messed up, but if I never experienced the bad shit, I'd have never gotten the opportunity to experience all the good I've had with you."

His voice broke with sincerity. "This is life, beautiful girl. Truly living and feeling. Sometimes it hurts. Sometimes it hurts a fuck of a lot. But that's only made me appreciate it more when it doesn't."

God, this man. He was poetic, romantic, and perfect in every way imaginable.

Even though he'd hidden this, I wanted to trust him. Wanted to believe he had some mystical way of knowing everything would be all right. I wanted confidence in myself to get this right. Faith in the future.

But faith couldn't be manufactured or willed into existence. I had to find it organically, authentically.

And I needed to do that on my own.

My aching chest squeezed tighter as I made excuses to end our conversation, leaving it unresolved. Too tired to think, too worried about Caleb, too upset over my father to make decisions.

Were any of them true? Sure. But they were also convenient shields against having to make any hard choices right now.

Eric didn't question my deflection. He simply accepted what I offered and wrapped me in his arms, pulling me back down to the mattress like he could hold me together through sheer force of will.

As we lay in that ridiculously small bed, my mind refused to quiet. I didn't want to lie to him, but sleep remained elusive. Eyes closed, breathing controlled, Eric's solid warmth engulfing me, I contemplated the last eight days. Our confessions and omissions. The promises made and broken.

But the past wasn't what haunted me. It was the future—all those unknown variables stretching ahead like an endless maze.

How could something unknown already hurt so fucking bad?

DAY ZERO

CHAPTER THIRTY-FOUR

JAMIE

TODAY WAS THE DAY.

Day Zero.

The day Eric had been dreading. The one he'd tried to push from his mind with desperate intensity. So terrifying he'd hidden it from me like a shameful secret.

The day that could make or break it all.

The last time I stood in these sterile halls, grief had taken its time to overwhelm me, shock holding it at bay like a dam about to burst. This time, hope hung thick in the air around me.

Still, I wasn't comforted. Hope could be the cruelest thing of all, lifting you to dizzying heights before dropping you into free fall.

In the hallway, Eric stood close. Close enough that I could feel the heat of him at my side. But he was quiet, his attention fixed on his family in the waiting room only a few feet away. They filled the space with low voices and forced optimism, clinging to each other.

He didn't join them.

He stayed planted in front of me.

When he finally moved, it was deliberate. A step in. A hand

at my waist, firm and steady, anchoring me where I stood. His lips brushed my forehead. The kiss was restrained, almost reverent. It felt less like affection and more like absolution.

"Thank you," he murmured.

A few moments later, a nurse appeared in the doorway and called his name.

He didn't look at me again. He just turned and walked away.

That was all I got.

I had no idea what he was thanking me for. For coming? For not running when he told me his secret? For pretending everything was fine when we both knew it wasn't?

The doors swung closed behind him, and he was gone.

The rejection lodged somewhere deep. What was the point of those few seconds of privacy if he wouldn't even look at me?

They took Caleb back not long after. We crowded into his room before they wheeled him out. One by one, we said our goodbyes. When it was my turn, I wrapped my arms around him and held tight.

"You're going to kick cancer's ass," I whispered.

He grinned like this was a challenge he'd already accepted.

Then he was gone too, swallowed by the same doors.

The waiting room filled with the quiet chaos of people trying to sit still. Coffee cups. Half sentences. Forced optimism.

My mind kept drifting backward.

After our fight, Eric and I had fallen asleep tangled together. He'd held me so tightly it bordered on desperate, like he was afraid I'd slip away if he loosened his grip.

Yesterday, when I woke, he was already dressed. Composed in a way that made everything harder. He'd handed me coffee, pressed a careful kiss to my mouth, and told me he was spending the day with his family.

No invitation.

Last night, he'd called to say he was staying with his family.

The words had cut sharper than I'd expected. Of course he should be with them. I would have done the same.

It still felt like being edged out.

Today, though, he'd asked me to come. To be here before they took him in. To wish them luck.

I'd promised that much. But nothing beyond it.

The decision to leave had settled quietly inside me before I even arrived.

Once everyone had returned to the waiting room and the adrenaline of the sendoff began to fade, I stood.

"I'm going to head out," I said.

The silence that followed was immediate. Shock flickered across their faces.

I forced my voice steady. "Can someone call and let me know how it goes?"

Sylvie reached for me first. I stepped into her space and kissed her once on each cheek, the familiar Quebecois greeting suddenly heavy with finality. She broke down, gripping my hands like I was taking something with me when I walked away.

Even Celeste—intimidating, domineering Celeste—had tears in her eyes. Marc and Glenn each hesitated before pulling me into firm, wordless hugs. Embraces that felt like forgiveness I didn't deserve.

From the doorway, I turned back for one last look.

They'd drawn together without thinking, closing ranks in the center of the waiting room. Arms looped around waists. Hands settled on shoulders. Bodies angled inward, forming a tight circle that shut out the rest of the world. They held each other while they waited for the two missing pieces who would make them whole again.

This was what family looked like.

The sight pressed hard against my chest, tightening my throat.

They had exactly what I'd promised to give Hunter. Not just relatives. True belonging.

Family wasn't about blood or obligation. It was acceptance and alliance, people who chose to love you despite your flaws and stand by you when everything fell apart.

I'd made that promise for my son, but standing there watching the Alexanders, I realized how desperately I wanted it for myself too.

A new kind of hope bloomed in my chest, terrifying in its intensity.

Maybe I could have this. Maybe I could build something real and lasting.

I just had to put myself out in the world and try.

CHAPTER THIRTY-FIVE

JAMIE

It wasn't just the Alexanders I left behind when I pointed my car east. Hunter stayed too. Dylan had promised to take good care of him, with his mom and stepdad on standby, ready to help if needed.

They were getting to know each other now, feeling their way through something that should have existed years ago. Testing boundaries. Learning how to stand in the same room as father and son without dragging the past in between them. It was long overdue, and the truth of that pressed hard against my ribs as the highway unspooled ahead of me.

For years, I'd blamed Dylan for not showing up. Accused him of indifference. But I'd been the one reinforcing the distance. I built the walls. I justified every barrier as protection, telling myself I was shielding my child from instability when I was also shielding myself.

But God, he wasn't just my child. He was *ours*.

The difference mattered more than I'd ever admitted. What I'd called protection had also been control. And it had cost them time they could never get back.

Dylan and his family, no matter how ugly our history, were

trying now. Late. Imperfect. But trying. The past wasn't going to rewrite itself, and dragging it forward only kept us trapped there.

If I didn't interfere, Hunter had a chance at something resembling family. Maybe not big or traditional, but real. A father willing to try. Grandparents who loved him, even if their feelings toward me were complicated. Even if everything else in my life collapsed, he would still have them. And he would still have me.

That was more than nothing.

The drive back to Toronto was miserable. Patrol cars dotted the highway, forcing me to crawl at the speed limit when all I wanted was to press harder on the gas. Halfway there, the two coffees I'd swallowed out of habit forced me off at a service station that smelled like exhaust and overheated pavement.

With just over an hour left, apprehension crept in. Quiet at first. Then insistent. Every kilometer felt like a countdown.

Was I doing the right thing?

Sitting on a picnic table at a highway rest stop wasn't relaxing or private, but I loitered there anyway. I carelessly sprawled out on top of the table, soaking in the warmth of the early summer sun. Or was it still late spring? It was too hot for May, it felt like early July weather.

God, what was I doing? Contemplating the seasons?

No, I was stalling.

Trouble was being pregnant and alone at seventeen. Trouble was being broke with nowhere to go. Those were storms I understood. This was different. This time the choice was mine, and it didn't just affect me. It touched everyone.

Choosing shouldn't have felt like this.

Only two hours since I'd left and my conscience was already eating me alive. But that was the problem with running. No matter where you went, how long you stayed gone, trouble always caught up.

A hot breeze whipped my hair into my mouth, and I forced

myself to breathe evenly. I refused to unravel alone at a highway rest stop. For a moment, I closed my eyes and pretended the sun's warmth was Eric's arms around me, steady and solid, the way he'd anchored me all week.

The illusion didn't hold. The sun was a cheap replica, and thinking about him only reopened the ache in my chest.

Enough.

I was a survivor. A battle-scarred warrior. One week didn't get to undo me. I'd managed on my own before, I could do it again.

But before I could move forward, something from the past had to be faced.

My father's letter was in my bag, waiting for me. It was now or never.

His note was a single page. Not the novel I would've written. Just handwritten words that would either destroy me or set me free.

James,

Time is a fickle bitch. We live thinking we'll have more of it. Until tragedy hits and we realize time isn't infinite.

My tragedy wasn't losing your mother and sister. It was losing you. That was the thing I could have prevented, or at the very least tried to reverse. But like I said, time is a fickle bitch, and I always thought I would find the strength and courage to fix things with you. I just ran out of time. And I never had strength or courage.

Don't ever run out of time. Don't end up a regretful old asshole like me. Don't waste a single moment held back by fear.

I let fear rule me.

I'm dying knowing I wasted years because of it.

You should always be bold. Take life by the fucking horns, or whatever cheesy motto you want to adopt. Just go out and do it, no matter how hard it seems. Trust me when I say, the most intimidating parts of life are the most worthwhile. You should always be fearless.

I think maybe you already are.

Your mom would have been proud of you. I was wrong when I said you'd disappoint her. I'm the only one who let her down. She'd have been so happy to see the smart and brave woman you've become. She would have been the proudest grandmother. And she would have bragged to all her friends about what a wonderful mother you are.

I would like to say that I'm proud of you too, but I know you made yourself despite me, not because of me. I'm amazed by you, all the same.

I love you, Jamie. I'm just sorry it took me this long to say it.

Be brave, fuck fear.

Love always,

Dad

Truth rang from every line.

There was nothing to fact-check, no hidden motive to untangle. I didn't need to analyze his tone or second-guess his intent. Somewhere deep inside me, I recognized it. This was what I had been searching for all along. The clarity. The guidance. The steady hand I'd pretended I didn't need.

It wasn't just my father's truth. It reached further than that. Universal in a way that startled me, especially coming from him. The timing felt almost uncanny, like the words had waited for the exact moment I was ready to hear them.

It was so perfectly aligned with the chaos in my head that my vision blurred.

Not from sadness. Not from regret. There was no sharp edge of grief cutting through me.

It was joy—pure and startling, almost violent in its force.

It surged through my chest, crashing into every dark corner I'd been nursing. The doubts. The fear. The ache that had been living under my ribs and crushing my heart for days. None of it stood a chance.

The pain loosened. The apprehension dissolved. I could do this.

Be brave.

Fuck fear.

DAY PLUS 1

CHAPTER THIRTY-SIX

JAMIE

I DANCED THROUGH MY DOWNTOWN TORONTO APARTMENT, singing off-key and not caring who might hear.

Anyone watching would never guess my father had died two days ago. That I'd left my son behind. That somewhere in a hospital, an extraordinary man and his family were waiting for a miracle I'd walked away from.

No one would know and, in that moment, I didn't feel it either.

The darkness that had been stalking me for over a week had simply…lifted. In its place was something bright and steady. I was filled with confidence, momentum, and a sharp, electric optimism that made it impossible to stand still.

I moved because I could. Shimmying through the kitchen. Spinning past the couch. I'd spent too much of my life sheltering in place. Not enough time dancing.

Even without my voice echoing off the walls, the apartment hummed with life. Street noise rose through the open windows. Car horns. Snatches of conversation. A siren somewhere in the distance. Neighbors moved above and below me, footsteps and plumbing and the faint thud of bass through drywall.

That was what I'd always loved about this city. It swallowed you whole and somehow made room at the same time. You could disappear into it without ever feeling erased. There was comfort in the anonymity. In being one of millions. In knowing no one was watching too closely.

But it was lonely, too.

I lived surrounded by people who didn't know my name. Neighbors were door numbers. The couple in 810 fought like it was a nightly ritual, their arguments bleeding into the hallway, and no one intervened. It was just part of the collective noise.

Copper Ridge was the opposite. There, everyone knew you. Not just your name, but your business. People took care of each other. If something looked off—like a daughter breaking into her father's home after a ten-year absence—someone called the police. Concern, community, maybe a bit of gossip, were all part of the charm.

Ten days there. One day back here. The contrast felt sharper than it should have. Strange how quickly I'd adjusted to trees and water and open sky instead of glass towers and concrete.

It was hotter here, too. Thick, city heat clung to skin. Maybe it was the density, all of us packed together, generating warmth. Or maybe it was my manic dancing.

I'd stripped down to a tank top and sleep shorts, refusing to turn on the air conditioning before June. Stubbornness had always been one of my more consistent traits. Sweat slid down my spine, and I ignored it.

I was halfway across the living room, still moving to a song only I could hear, when a sharp knock cracked through the noise and froze me in place.

The building's front lock had been broken since I moved in, but I wasn't expecting anyone for hours. I checked my tank top wasn't too revealing and opened the door, prepared to be diplomatic.

My stomach dropped.

Eric stood with his arm braced against the wall, paler than usual, his forehead dotted with sweat. His hard stare couldn't hide exhaustion so deep I worried he might collapse.

"Eric, what are you doing here?" I gasped. "Come in, you need to sit down."

His eyes flashed with something close to anger. He stalked past me into my apartment without a word. I closed the door and turned to find him right there. In my space.

His stormy expression made me feel like I'd done something terrible. My actions probably warranted his wrath, but it still felt intense.

"Let me get you water, then you can tell me why you look ready to murder me."

"No." His glare was unwavering.

"Okay, well, at least—"

"No, Jamie. Don't move from this spot. I came here to tell you something, and you're going to stand here and fucking listen."

The command in his voice stopped me more effectively than his body blocking the door ever could. I'd seen Eric angry, protective, and controlled. I'd watched him carry fear and remain steady.

This was different.

Not out of control. Not explosive. This was focus—hard and unyielding.

He'd never been cruel, never careless with me, so there shouldn't have been anything to fear. And yet the force of him, the way he occupied the space, pressed the air thinner in my lungs. Anxiety flickered under my skin.

So did something else.

New heat sparked to life within me as desire pulled my body tight.

"You can't run away from me, Jamie. I won't let you. You can't just disappear without a word and think I won't chase you down." He was breathing hard, chest rising and falling sharply. "You left me unconscious on an operating table for fuck's sake."

The accusation landed heavy, but he didn't shout it. He didn't need to. The restraint in his voice made it worse. "My mother was in tears when she told me you'd come back here, and I was too drug-hazed to understand why."

Any weakness from the procedure was buried under something stronger. He looked steady on his feet, jaw tight, shoulders squared like he'd forced his body to cooperate through sheer will.

"Worst of all, they wouldn't let me out of the hospital. Wouldn't let me drive to chase you down." His eyes burned into mine. "What the hell were you thinking?"

"Eric." My voice was soft, apologetic.

"I'm not done." His savage growl had my mouth snapping shut. "I mean that, Jamie. I'm not done with you. And I'm not letting you be done with me either. I know you're scared. You've dealt with more than most, and you probably think this thing between us was temporary. Or fake. Or just a distraction."

His brow pulled tight as he dragged a hand through his hair, frustration bleeding through the movement. The sight of it, the tension in his forearm, the way his chest rose and fell, made my pulse kick hard.

"But it's not" he continued, voice thick but steady. "It's none of those things. Hell, I don't think it ever was."

For a second, the edge slipped. He looked at me fully, not guarded, not composed. "Jamie, beautiful girl, I'm in fucking love with you. I don't want to lose you. I refuse to let you go."

God, this man. He had no idea what he did to me.

"Are you done?" I asked finally, because if I didn't say something, I was going to break.

His expression darkened. "Really? That's your reaction? After everything I just told you, that's how you're going to play it?" He was seething. And fuck…it was sexy as hell.

"Eric." I raised my voice, not wanting to poke the beast but needing his attention. "Did you not notice you're standing beside a stack of boxes?"

That slowed him. Confusion flickered across his face as he finally glanced around the apartment.

The wall was lined with boxes—everything prepped for movers. If he'd stepped further in, he'd see only furniture and appliances remained. Everything else was packed and ready.

"What?" He looked genuinely thrown.

"Did you really think I'd just run away? Without even saying goodbye?"

"Yes. I thought you were scared."

"I am. I'm really, hugely scared." My stomach took flight. "I've never been more afraid in my entire life. Not even pregnant and alone.

"For the first time in years, I've let someone in." The words tumbled out now that they'd started. "I'm putting my heart, my future, in someone else's hands. Do you understand how terrifying that is for me?"

My fingers curled together under my chin, not dramatic, just desperate for him to see it. To see me. "But there's something that scares me more. Running again. Shutting myself down. Locking everything up because it's easier than risking it. I couldn't do that this time. I wouldn't survive it. Not now that I know what I'd be walking away from."

His eyes searched mine, sharp and relentless, like he was testing every word for weakness.

I closed the space between us before I lost my nerve. My hands came up to his face, thumbs brushing the rough line of his jaw. He went still under my touch, but I could feel the tension humming in him.

I kissed him lightly, just once.

"I'm really fucking in love with you too," I whispered.

Honest words. The truest I'd given him. Without pretense or prelude.

His jaw flexed. His brow pulled tight. The look on his face shifted into something rawer, something almost pained.

Then his hands were on me.

He trapped my waist in his sublimely strong grip and pulled me flush against him, right where I belonged.

And he kissed me.

Not tentative. Not careful. It was deep and consuming, layered with frustration and relief and something possessive that made my knees weaken. Every time his mouth found mine, it felt inevitable.

When he pulled back, his forehead rested briefly against mine. "You're not running away from me."

"No. I'm running toward you. Looking to the future might be scary, but I know I want you in it. That's practically all I know, but at least that part's solid."

"Christ, I'm an asshole."

"No, you're not." I shook my head. "I should've told you what I was planning. Leaving like that was a jerk move. I didn't even decide until yesterday morning. And I thought maybe I'd already screwed this up. I didn't want to add to the stress of Day Zero or make it about me. It was supposed to be about Caleb."

He held my gaze, still intense, still not letting me look away. "Couldn't you have waited?"

"I should have. I'm sorry. I just couldn't stand waiting and worrying in that hospital another day. You showed me my path, Eric. I didn't want to wait to take it."

"Shit." His expression softened as he dragged a hand over the back of his neck. "I'm sorry I yelled at you. Should've given you the benefit of the doubt. I feel like a prick."

"Can I make a confession?" A nervous heat crept up my cheeks, but I didn't look away. "I kind of like it when you're demanding. Even when you're a bit of a jerk. It turns me on."

A slow, dangerous smile curved his mouth. “You turned on now, beautiful girl?”

“Maybe.”

One second there was space between us. The next, my back hit the door with a solid thud, his big body crowding mine as he took my mouth before I could take another breath.

Electric current ran up my spine, eagerness fueling desire. But this wasn’t just chemistry snapping into place. This time felt like he was fully mine. Like his heart and soul belonged to me.

His hand tangled in my hair, not rough but firm enough to tilt my head back, exposing my throat. My breath caught as his mouth traced from my jaw down to the curve of my neck, slow and possessive.

A shiver tore through me, need pulsing between my thighs. I fisted my hands in the hem of his shirt, tugging it up and over his head with impatient fingers, breaking the kiss only long enough to strip the fabric away and toss it aside.

With impatience of his own, Eric pushed my sleep shorts down past my hips, forcing them down my thighs. They dropped to the ground, and he smiled.

Desire coiled tighter inside me. I wanted to wrap my legs around him, grind against him, chase the release already building. But he held himself steady, and that kept me in place. He wasn’t rushing. He was choosing the pace.

He broke the kiss and looked at me, really looked at me, as his hand slid between us. His touch was deliberate, unhurried, tracing through my slick heat before brushing over my clit. The contact made my breath catch, my hips instinctively pressing forward.

The way he watched me wasn’t just hunger. It was focused intent. And it was almost reverent.

Even pinned between his body and the door, I didn’t feel overpowered. I felt chosen. Like he was responding to me, not overtaking me.

"Tell me again," I demanded.

"What do you want to hear, beautiful?" His thumb circled slowly. "That your body drives me crazy?"

I shook my head.

"That I'm still pissed you left without telling me why?"

I shook my head again.

"What then?" His voice softened, lips tipping into a playful smile as his hand moved with confident precision. "You want to hear how much I love you? How I've been in love with you from the start? How I'm never letting you go?"

"Yes." I hissed as he plunged a finger deep inside my core. "Yes, I want you to tell me that. Show me that. Tell me you love me over and over. I'm never going to get tired of hearing it."

"Jamie, I love you. You'll never have to ask again. I'm going to show you every fucking day. Every fucking night," he growled, adding another finger. "Three times on Sundays. Gonna love you so much you won't be able to walk straight."

His mouth found mine again, slower this time but no less consuming, his hands guiding, building, bringing me right to the edge.

When the orgasm finally hit, it was hard and bright, my fingers digging into his shoulders as I broke against him.

He stayed with me through it, murmuring words of love against my skin. When he sank himself inside me, it was with love on his lips. As he pumped desperately into me, I moaned his name, and he answered with love. When he came deep inside me moments after my second release, he breathed a contented, *I fucking love you.*

We stayed there afterward, pressed together against the door, his forehead resting on mine.

I was the most satisfied and well-loved woman in the world.

"Eric?"

"Yeah, beautiful?"

"I love you."

He laughed softly, looking down at me like I'd just handed him something priceless. The sound vibrated through his chest and into mine, and I felt it everywhere we were still joined.

Then reality snapped back in.

"Shit. We didn't use a condom."

"I know. And it was awesome." His smile stretched wider.

"Aren't you worried?"

"Hell no. I'm relieved." He brushed my hair back from my face, calm where I was spiraling. "I'm not giving up more bone marrow anytime soon. Nothing to worry about, beautiful."

"Pregnancy?"

"I'm not worried. You said you're covered—I trust you, Jamie." His gaze held mine. "And even if something happened, I'd handle it. I take care of what's mine. And you…are mine."

To prove his point, he kissed me again while his still twitching erection ground into me.

I was his. He trusted me. And I trusted him.

"Maybe you should sit down now. You probably need to get off your feet before you fall over." I wasn't even sure he was supposed to be out of the hospital yet.

"You questioning my stamina?" His brows lifted, amused.

Before I could answer, he pulled free and scooped me up with easy strength. "Never mind sitting. It's hot as hell in here. We need a shower. Point me in the right direction."

A shower sounded perfect, but when Eric took a step with me in his arms, he staggered.

"Eric, put me down right now."

"Fuck." He exhaled sharply, lowering me to my feet. "Sorry, beautiful. You might have to walk. I'm in a bit of pain. Think the meds wore off."

"There's ibuprofen in the bag in the bathroom. Go take some and get the shower started. I'll find towels."

The apartment was almost entirely boxed up, but everything was labeled. I found the linens quickly and carried them down the hall. By the time I returned, steam was already curling out of the bathroom.

He was standing in front of the mirror when I stepped in.

"Holy shit, Eric, your back..."

His entire left hip and lower back were bruised deep purple and blue, swollen in places, the skin stretched tight and angry. It looked brutal.

He glanced at the mirror, then back at me with a shrug that didn't quite hide the stiffness in his posture. "Not as bad as I thought it might be."

"Looks like you've been in a fight…with a car."

"I'll be fine." He rolled his shoulders like he could shrug off the bruising and stepped into the shower. "Just a little pain." His eyes darkened as he moved under the spray. "But if you really want to take care of me, get in here."

Water ran down his chest, over muscle and ink and healing skin. He wrapped a hand around his cock with a crooked grin. "You take care of me. Then I'll take care of you. Then maybe we see how generous we're both feeling."

A laugh caught in my throat. We had four hours before the movers showed up. Four uninterrupted hours.

Something told me we weren't wasting a single minute of it.

He looked determined, not just to prove his stamina, but to prove something deeper. That he was here. That he wasn't fragile. That loving me hadn't cracked him open beyond repair.

I felt the same pull, fierce and certain.

But this time, there would be condoms. Passion didn't cancel out common sense. Eric might be fearless when it came to consequences, but I knew better than to treat something as life-altering as a child like a casual byproduct of an impulsive moment.

"Get over here, beautiful," he called over the rush of water. "Just keep me off my back, okay?"

He winked, and for a split second the world tilted the way it had the first day we met. That same magnetic pull. That same dizzy certainty.

My man.

The thought settled into me with surprising ease.

I stepped into the shower, and when his hands found my waist and his mouth found mine, everything aligned again. The noise in my head quieted. The doubts thinned.

I didn't know exactly what the future held. I'd probably lose my footing again. That was who I was. But the idea of getting lost didn't terrify me anymore.

If I wandered, he'd come looking.

We had each other.

For the first time in a long time, that felt like enough.

DAY PLUS 847

ERIC

Maybe life wasn't about chasing one perfect moment. Maybe it was about recognizing the ones worth claiming when they stood in front of you. Those rare intersections where everything aligned into something solid. The kind you grabbed with both hands and didn't let go of.

Nervous energy moved through me in sharp, restless waves.

I inhaled slowly. Held it. Let it out through clenched teeth.

My hands weren't steady. My stomach refused to settle, no matter how measured my breathing was. I'd walked into an operating room without blinking. I'd faced fear head-on and held my ground.

But this?

This had me exposed in a way nothing else ever had.

Everyone around me looked calm. Smiling and relaxed. Like this was just another beautiful day. Meanwhile, I was one breath away from being sick.

Not because I wasn't ready.

Because I'd waited so fucking long for this. And some ruthless part of my brain kept whispering that something could still go wrong. That she could change her mind. That old habits would take over, and she'd run.

Christ. *Get it together.*

The doors opened. Light poured in first, blinding and absolute.

And then she was there.

Jamie stepped forward, sunlight catching in her hair, her white dress falling clean and simple around her. The noise around me faded. The crowd disappeared.

Mine.

She was mine by choice. In commitment. In the promise I was about to make and uphold with everything I had.

After two years, she still had the power to knock the air from my lungs. Still had the ability to unbalance me with one look. And standing there now, walking toward me, she didn't look fragile. She looked certain.

More beautiful than ever.

When she reached me, I took her hands without hesitation. Held them firmly, grounding both of us. The minister spoke, words floating somewhere beyond the edges of my focus, but those details weren't important.

Her blue eyes locked onto mine, and everything else fell away. That look was the only thing that mattered. Her love was my entire world.

We weren't chasing a perfect moment. We were building something permanent.

For better or worse. Here and now.

She wasn't slipping away again.

And I wasn't letting go.

JAMIE

When I first met Eric, I thought he'd found me. Rescued me from a life I'd already decided would be small and contained. I'd convinced myself I was destined for quiet sacrifice, raising Hunter alone, preparing for the day he'd outgrow me.

But truth was, we found each other.

We'd both been wandering. Both terrified of who we were, and what we were doing. Fear had been our compass, pointing us toward safety instead of happiness.

Even now, dancing in his arms at our wedding reception, doubt still whispered. Did we really know where we were headed? Would old instincts resurface when things got difficult?

Maybe they would. Life had a way of humbling even the best plans. Eric had always said that. Control was never guaranteed.

The difference now was that we weren't drifting. We were choosing.

Dad's business had been my lifeline, even if some clients still looked twice when they realized their contractor had breasts. Ridiculous, but I was building something, piece by piece.

Eric never treated my ambition like an inconvenience or a threat. He stood behind it fully, offering support without making it about himself. There was strength in that, in the quiet way he made space for me to grow.

And he'd grown too.

Watching him step into his role at Copper Ridge Resort changed the way I saw him. The resort carried his family's name, but the marketing position hadn't been handed over out of obligation. They'd recognized what I'd always known. He had creative vision, and discipline. The ability to lead without overpowering.

He earned it the way he earned everything else, with focus and follow-through.

Hunter's preteen sarcasm could cut glass now, but he was thriving here in Copper Ridge. He lived for architecture how-to videos, skateboard tricks, and the ridiculous dog we'd caved and bought him.

Best of all, he had two father figures who actually showed up. Even Dylan was trying, though Eric still had to nudge him sometimes.

And Caleb. Sweet, fierce Caleb, who'd stared down cancer and taught us what it meant to truly live. Without him, without Dad, Eric and I might never have collided at all.

Two lost souls, finding home in each other.

As Eric spun me slowly, I closed my eyes and let gratitude flood through me. We'd found love in our darkest moment, when everything was falling apart. That love had become our map, showing us not just tomorrow, but how to treasure today.

We still took life one day at a time, only now it was to savor each precious moment.

Together.

CALEB

Jamie looked incredible in her wedding dress. More stunning than the day I'd met her two years ago, if that was even possible.

Eric stood beside her beaming like the happiest guy on the planet. *Lucky bastard.*

Together, they were enough to make even the coldest heart melt. The love and devotion radiating between them was almost disgusting. But only because what they had was so damn perfect it could make nearly anyone jealous.

And I had been jealous. Of Eric, mostly.

I'd convinced myself I was in love with Jamie. Watching them together had eaten away at my heart as diligently as cancer had eaten away at my body.

It hadn't taken long to realize that as perfect as Jamie was, she was perfect for my brother, not me. Those feelings I'd clung to so desperately? They'd had everything to do with my near-death experience and nothing to do with her.

Being fourteen and thinking I was dying had made me desperate to experience everything possible. Since my body couldn't handle daring adventures, my mind and heart had done all the exploring instead. I'd been grasping for feelings that weren't really there.

Two years later, any lingering jealousy came from wanting what they had—that type of love—not from wanting her specifically.

Being cancer-free still felt surreal. Sometimes I forgot my lifespan had been miraculously expanded, thanks to Eric and those doctors.

The transplant had saved my life, but watching my brother find his happy ever after had saved my hope for the future.

So instead of jealousy, I chose gratitude. I was alive. Eric had remembered to credit me in his wedding speech. And I could still appreciate how incredible Jamie looked in that dress.

Most of all, I was grateful for the type of love that existed in storybooks. I was glad it was real. And I was happy as hell that my brother had managed to find it—even if he didn't believe in fairy tales.

I did.

DYLAN

Eric Alexander could go fuck himself.

Thank You for reading Wild Surrender!
I hope you enjoyed it and will consider leaving a review. Reviews mean the world to little indie authors like me. I read and appreciate every single one!

If you want even more Eric and Jamie, sign up for my newsletter, Letters from the Edge, to get a Bonus Scene.
https://kimberlyquinn.myflodesk.com/wsbonus

Are you ready for your next wild adventure?

Some hearts can't be tamed.

Welcome to Copper Ridge, Ontario—a resort town on the edge of Georgian Bay where the winters are fierce, the summers are stunning, and the romance is anything but tame. The Wild Savage Hearts series follows four unforgettable love stories set against the backdrop of Copper Ridge Resort and the untamed beauty surrounding it. These books are about taking chances, finding yourself, and falling hard in a place that feels like home.

<u>Wild Savage Hearts</u>
WILD SURRENDER
WILD OBSESSION
WILD DEVOTION
WILD PROMISE

Keep reading for a preview of Wild Obsession, the next book in the Wild Savage Heart series.

WILD OBSESSION

Everyone in Copper Ridge knows my name.
Sergeant Dylan McCoy. Protector. Reformed bad boy still paying for old mistakes.
I finally have my act together. Keeping it that way has one rule: No more scandals.
Then Chantel walks in like temptation incarnate. Sean follows, all daring charm and sin. Separately, they bring me to my knees. Together, we're a fuse already lit.
With them, I'm not the cautionary tale or the uniform. I'm finally honest in my own skin.
And that might be the most dangerous thing of all.
Because in a town that thrives on gossip, a man like me doesn't survive another explosion.
Wanting them both could turn redemption into ruin.
Risking my badge. My reputation. My heart.

***Wild Obsession** is the second standalone in the gritty, untamed **Wild Savage Hearts** series.*

In this book you'll find a polyamorous, blue collar, alpha-hole single dad who's obsessed with both a hockey player and a smart, sassy heroine. Can their relationship survive this small town and all its secrets, lies, and judgment?

Chapter One

Dylan

Backyard barbecues would never be the same, and it was a

goddamn shame. Meat, beer, and good friends were always a winning combination.

But this?

This had no business being called a barbecue. This should have just been labeled what it was—an experiment in torture.

The burgers smelled good, but there was no beer, and other than my kid, Hunter, there wasn't a friendly face in sight.

And the Alexanders had a big backyard, filled with a lot of people.

Hunter spotted me from across the yard and came running, crashing into me with enough energy to slosh the lemonade someone had forced into my hand.

"Dad, you're here! Did you see? Caleb has a trampoline!" And just like that he was gone again, already halfway back across the grass.

But considering he was busy turning eleven today, I was happy he'd noticed me at all. Fuck, I was shocked as hell to have been invited in the first place.

I didn't really know the Alexanders, except for Eric. But he was dating Hunter's mother, so we weren't exactly friends.

This party had been a choice between two kinds of losing.

Skip it, and I'd confirm every bad thing they already thought about me. I'd be the asshole who didn't want to spend time with his kid. The guy still carrying a torch for his ex. The deadbeat who couldn't get his shit together.

Show up, and I'd be the guy nobody knew what to do with. The outcast who forgot everyone's names. The one they'd all hoped wouldn't accept the invitation.

Either way, I was the loser.

So I forced myself through the door. For Hunter. Because no matter what it cost me, I wanted to be part of his life. To prove myself worthy of my son.

I watched him jump on the trampoline, his laugh ringing out

across the yard, while I shrugged off the stares of judgmental strangers.

Fuck 'em.

"It's Dylan, right?" Eric's brother-in-law ambled up to me, a look of curiosity on his face.

"Yeah, hi…" What the hell was his name?

Instead of filling in the blank for me, he rocked back on his heels with the bored restlessness of a man who'd run out of people to talk to. "How's life in law enforcement treating you?"

Great. Small talk. Annoying as fuck, especially from a guy just as out of place here as I was.

He'd been hanging around the edges of the party, neglected and forlorn. Even his own wife, Celeste, had studiously ignored him. He was a loser.

We were now a loser party of two.

"Work's fine," I said, aiming for congenial, but sounding more like a bitter fucking ass. "I've been thinking about moving from the local force to Provincial."

"You're applying to the O.P.P.?" a sweet, lilting voice asked from behind me.

Jamie.

Her presence made me both excited and sick at the same time. The fact that she'd managed to sneak up on me, when every one of my senses was wired to track her, proved just how far out of my element I really was.

Eric was right beside her, of course. He still didn't trust me alone with her. Not that I blamed him.

Honestly, I wouldn't trust me either.

I'd save his life in an emergency or help him change a flat. Hell, I'd even consider lending him money. But when it came to Jamie, no fucking way was I doing the honorable thing.

"Isn't the Provincial force a lot more demanding, and more dangerous too?" the brother-in-law, with the name I couldn't remember, asked.

"Sure. But I'm not the kind of guy who's easily scared off." A smirk pulled at the corner of my mouth and my gaze shifted to Eric.

I couldn't help myself. I enjoyed antagonizing the guy.

Our feud was low-key but consistent. An underhanded jab from me, followed by a poorly veiled threat from him. Childish, maybe. But it was the one place in this whole goddamn yard where I felt like I had any control.

"Dylan's always been a risk taker," Jamie cut in, flashing me a harsh glare. "Why don't you tell John about some of the other things you do? Like the volunteer stuff at the mission?"

John. That was the loser's name. No wonder I couldn't remember it. It was as average and unremarkable as the man himself.

Jamie's warning was clear, though. Hunter's birthday party wasn't the place to be rude or start a verbal war with her boyfriend.

But damn, when she gave me that saucy look, I couldn't help but want to bend her over the picnic table and slap her ass right in front of him.

The memories came easy. Her body, the sounds she made, the way she used to beg so sweet. Unsuitable thoughts for the company I was in. And I didn't give one single fuck.

"Of course, Jamie." I stressed her name, so she'd catch that I'd used it. No more calling her princess, just like she'd asked.

Her eyes narrowed. She knew exactly what I was doing, even if she'd never admit it. That was the thing about her—she'd been playing this cat-and-mouse game with me since we were fifteen. She kept me on my toes, kept me guessing, kept me chasing, without even trying.

I'd loved her for it.

Hell, I still did. And maybe I always would.

"The volunteer work's just part of the job," I said with a

shrug, turning back to John. "Community outreach is an important part of police service."

"And we're all so grateful for the service you provide." Eric all but rolled his eyes.

"Yeah, well, I love my community. When I decided on the job, I knew it would have challenges. But I like a good challenge. Keeps things interesting."

Eric's snarl might have frightened away another guy. In fact, he scared poor loser John, who mumbled incoherently under his breath as he scurried off toward his wife. Not me, though.

I widened my stance and smiled brighter.

"Oh, for goodness' sake, Dylan. Will you please cut it out?" Jamie's voice dropped, letting me know I'd pushed far enough. "I was going to thank you for showing up, but sometimes I seriously question your motives."

"Sorry." I wasn't. Not for pissing off Eric, anyway. "Old habit, I guess."

She studied me for a moment, something shifting in her gaze. "Listen, we're about to make an announcement. I wanted to give you fair warning in case you need to make an excuse to leave. No hard feelings."

"No hard feelings?" I scoffed. "The three of us are nothing but hard feelings, don't you think?"

Read the rest of Dylan's book in Wild Obsession:
https://books2read.com/wildobsessionwsh

WILD DEVOTION

Lush lips, dark eyes, hips for days—one look and I know. Zadie is every damn thing I want.
Except I'm a twenty-one-year-old virgin.
She's seven years older, pregnant with another man's baby…
And she just put me in the friend zone.
Fine. I'll be her friend. The best she's ever had. The one right across the hall.
Because the only future I've ever wanted is the one she's about to have.
Let her ex come back if he dares. He'll find out exactly how far I'll go to keep what's mine.
For her. For that baby. For us.

Wild Devotion *is the third standalone in the gritty, untamed* ***Wild Savage Hearts series****.*

In this book you'll find a forced proximity, friends to lovers relationship between a twenty-one-year-old virgin hero, and his cousin's best friend (who happens to be pregnant with another man's baby). Perfect timing for him to fall first...and so much harder.

WILD PROMISE

Being the fun guy with a killer smile has gotten me everything I've ever wanted.

Except Melina Marshall.

The only woman I want is the one person who gives a damn that I'm the owner's son.

She's ambitious, disciplined, ice-cold. Completely untouchable.

Too bad for her, the maddeningly sexy way she follows every rule I've ever broken puts her directly in my sights.

I want her. She wants a promotion. And the no fraternization policy at my family's five-star resort means we can't have both.

But I kiss her anyway.

And we get caught.

Now the promotion she's bled for is on the line, and so is my chance at keeping her. No amount of money or charm is going to fix this — unless I do the unthinkable.

Wild Promise *is the fourth standalone in the gritty, untamed* ***Wild Savage Hearts series****.*

In this book you'll find a forbidden workplace romance between a billionaire bad boy and the good girl who refuses to want him. He falls first in this story about secret pining, backstabbing coworkers, meddling friends, and proving that charm isn't everything, but love might be.

ACKNOWLEDGMENTS

When this book was first published, I had zero expectations. As a first-time author, I wasn't sure anyone would read it beyond a few friends.

Over the years, this story has received so much love from readers, reviewers, friends, and family. To this day, I'm still humbled and amazed.

Now, in its third edition, many hands have touched this book. And I hope it's touched a few hearts in return.

Suzanne, without you, this book wouldn't exist. From the moment I admitted I was writing it, you've been in my corner. You'll never know how grateful I am for your love and support.

Sybil, without your encouragement, this book wouldn't have its beautiful new facelift. I appreciate your advice, your honesty, and your heart. Your friendship means the world to me.

Mackie, you probably guessed that parts of this story were inspired by you. You're still the best surprise I've ever had. Always will be. I love you, forever and always.

Thank you, all of you.

And remember…

Be brave. Fuck fear.

ACKNOWLEDGMENTS

[illegible]

ABOUT THE AUTHOR

Kimberly Quinn is a *USA Today* bestselling romance author, born storyteller, and lover of morally gray heroes. She earned her bestseller status contributing to a hit multi-author anthology under her former pen name, Kim Bailey.

Today, Kimberly writes romance with rough edges. Her gritty stories feature beautifully flawed characters pursuing love at all costs. She enjoys lively conversations—usually with imaginary people—and can often be found daydreaming at work.

When she's not busy writing, you can find her with a coffee in hand, a dog at her side, exploring the wilds of her hometown in Ontario, Canada.

www.kimberlyquinnbooks.com

instagram.com/kimberlyquinn.books
facebook.com/kimberlyquinnbooks
bookbub.com/profile/kimberly-quinn
amazon.com/stores/Kimberly-Quinn/author/B0BV18S35M

www.ingramcontent.com/pod-product-compliance
Lightning Source LLC
LaVergne TN
LVHW030916080826
845145LV00013B/2920

* 9 7 8 1 9 8 9 1 1 2 4 5 8 *